USA TODAY BESTSELLING AUTHOR

KRISTEN PAINTER

A MIDLIFE
FAIRY TALE

THE
ACCIDENTAL
QUEEN

THE ACCIDENTAL QUEEN:
A Paranormal Women's Fiction Novel
The Accidental Queen, Book One

Copyright © 2022 Kristen Painter

Published in the United States of America

Sparrow "Ro" Meadowcroft is about to get the promotion she's always dreamed of – curator of the museum where she works. She loves old things and the history that surrounds them, so when a patron leaves some items to the museum, Ro is eager to dig in.

The sword in the stone that comes with those items is clearly a joke. A well-made but obvious replica meant to be a conversation starter. Why anyone would think that belonged in the museum is beyond her, but she can't resist taking a crack at it and finding out if she's the chosen one.

And as it turns out...she is.

To everyone who's ever found a gray hair and wondered what came next.

CHAPTER ONE

Once upon a time, there was probably a woman who grew older without getting gray hair.

That woman, Sparrow Meadowcroft thought, was not her.

Nope, today Ro had spotted *more* gray hairs. Not just one or two this time, but enough that the whole lot of them could be considered the beginnings of a streak.

A gray *streak*. At fifty-two. She didn't know whether to laugh or cry. She leaned away from the mirror. Maybe she'd go with practiced indifference and just pretend like it didn't bother her so people would think she was that well-adjusted.

After all, that attitude had gotten her through a lot of the tough spots in her life so far. Besides that, she didn't have the time or money to do anything about her hair. Okay, she *could* afford it. Living in the city wasn't cheap, but if she really wanted to, she could find the funds. There were things she could give up.

But would she really trade her morning doughnut and mocha latte for flawless hair?

Nah.

But maybe after she got her promotion.

Although giving up doughnuts and fancy coffee might help her shed the extra pounds she'd started picking up in the last few years. That was one of the signs of midlife, wasn't it? Extra pounds. Weird aches. Joints that made strange clicking noises. Hot flashes. Night sweats.

And gray hair.

It was more of a surprise that she hadn't turned gray sooner, honestly. She had no complaints about her life, not many anyway, but it hadn't been the easiest. Especially the single mom part. Still, she had her beloved son, James Thoreau aka JT, and a job she loved almost as much, despite the fact that she hadn't had a raise in three years. But it would be coming, along with the promotion.

She got to work in an amazing space around amazing things. And after years of putting in extra hours and doing all the little things no one else wanted to do and working her way up, she was finally going to be put in charge of the place. She couldn't imagine working anywhere other than the Museum of Historical Arts.

She stopped looking at her hair and went out to the kitchen. Mrs. Edna Wigglesworth meowed up at her. Benny, Ro's other cat, a sleek little house panther, was lounging in the cat condo, looking out the window.

"Okay, Wiggy, I hear you. Breakfast is coming." Ro reached down and gave her cranky, senior tortie cat a scratch on the head. Wiggy pushed against Ro's caresses, a sure sign she wanted more. Regardless of her many demands and her often terrible behavior, Mrs. Wigglesworth was good company and great entertainment. Benny was a love bug and much better behaved, which always surprised Ro, since he was still practically a kitten.

She'd never intended to have pets in this small apartment, but when her next-door neighbor, Mr. Louis, had passed, the people who'd come to clean out his apartment had crated his two cats up with the end goal of dumping them at the pound.

Mr. Louis had not only been a good neighbor but a truly wonderful old gentleman. Ro wasn't about to let his cats be disposed of so heartlessly. She'd watched them a few times when Mr. Louis had traveled to see his brother in Minnesota. She knew they were sweet animals.

She'd immediately taken them in. She hadn't needed to think about it. There was simply no other acceptable option.

Benny had taken to Ro right away, but Wiggy's true love was JT. Whenever he came to visit, she was all over him. She'd even sit on his lap if he'd let her. Which he did.

Wiggy treated Ro more like staff.

Ro fixed two dishes of wet food by splitting one can in half. Wiggy's current favorite was tuna, so Benny didn't get much say in the matter. Ro put the dishes on their mat. Benny hopped down to investigate breakfast, but Mrs. Wigglesworth commenced eating immediately with a great deal of enthusiasm, expressed in occasional grunts and a low growl if Ro got too close.

"I promise, Edna, I'm not about to take your breakfast. Have a good day." Benny rubbed against Ro's leg. She gave him a scratch on the head, too. "Love you both. Don't shred the toilet paper, Edna. Again. Please."

Ro put on her suit jacket, grabbed her tote bag, double-checking that she'd put her lunch in it, and headed for the stairs. Thankfully, she was only on the second floor of her building, even if taking the stairs was good exercise.

The museum was fifteen blocks away. During the shoulder seasons of late spring and early fall, when the weather was temperate, she liked to walk. Well, she didn't *like* to walk, but she knew it was good for her and just the sort of thing that would catapult her into a more active lifestyle, which would in turn cause her to lose those fifteen pounds or so that were really keeping her from being her best self.

The walking never did any of that, but hope sprang eternal. And by now, it was more like twenty-five pounds.

Maybe she'd get the sugar-free mocha latte and a muffin at City Donuts this morning. She wouldn't. She already knew that, but it was something to think about.

She went one block and turned right, which put her directly in front of the subway entrance and City Donuts.

She went inside, got in line, and ordered a Boston cream, a raspberry-filled, and a mocha latte. Full sugar, full fat, full joy. The raspberry filled, to go as always, went into her tote bag.

The latte and the Boston cream she carried with her as she went down the subway station stairs and ate her doughnut while she waited on the platform for her train. A few minutes later, a rush of wind and a low rumble announced its arrival.

The ride was thankfully uneventful. Some mornings, you just never knew what you might encounter. Like the

4

homeless man who wore his pet ferret around his neck like a scarf. Ro was always sure to give him a dollar.

As she exited the subway station, she tossed her empty coffee cup and finished her walk to work. She entered the building through the employee entrance around the block, a side door capped with a marble arch and coronets.

Kwame, the morning shift security guard, gave her a bright smile as she walked through the metal detector and showed him her badge. "Good morning, Dr. Meadowcroft."

"Good morning, Kwame. How are you?" She dug into her bag and pulled out the second doughnut she'd bought and handed it to him.

"Very good." His smile somehow got bigger and brighter. "Thank you."

"You're welcome." She smiled back and went on her way.

Her office was on the fourth floor. It never failed to give her a little trill of pride to see her name and title on the door: *Dr. Sparrow Meadowcroft, Assistant Curator.*

But it would be even better when the Assistant was removed.

She unlocked the door and went in, flipping the lights on. Her desk was stacked with work, the surrounding shelves neat but tightly packed with an ever-growing collection of reference books.

Today would be a busy day. There were new acquisitions coming in, and they'd need her attention. She wasn't sure everything would work in the museum, but such was often the case with bequeathed items.

Whatever didn't work, she might be able to find homes for in some of the sister museums around the city. It was within her purview to do that, and she much preferred that to simply storing the unusable pieces in the museum's vast two-level basement.

Things stored there rarely saw the light of day. Oh, there were occasions when a new exhibit was displayed and a few pieces would be brought up, but for the most part, the basement was a secret treasure trove of random antiquities. In fact, sorting through that basement was one of her many ongoing projects. It would probably never be completed, but at least she was making an attempt.

Responding to emails took up a good part of her morning until Sutherford, the exhibit designer, knocked on her door and stuck his head in. "That Clipston bequeathment is here. The guys just unloaded it."

Ro looked at her watch. It was later than she thought, but her answer was already on her tongue. "So soon?"

He nodded. "Yep."

"Okay. Thank you." She picked up her tablet to do her cataloging on and went down to Basement One, where all new acquisitions were inventoried and checked in. She took the central stairs, her way of making up for the sugar bomb breakfast she'd had, even though she had it every morning and even though she knew the stairs wouldn't burn a quarter of those delicious calories.

She also liked to take the central stairs because they allowed her to walk through the museum proper. She liked to observe the museum's visitors. Catch snippets of their conversations. See the looks on their faces as they took in the exhibits.

She had her favorites, of course.

The Egyptian pieces—the faience figures, especially—were one. Anything Roman glass another. Pre-Columbian masks. European Bronze-Age jewelry. Mosaics of any kind. She was fascinated by textiles, too. Clothing, tapestries, rugs. Weapons of any age, region, or material were always worth a good study, too.

Honestly, there wasn't much she didn't enjoy. There was very little that didn't spark her curiosity or tease her imagination into drifting back to the time and place and person who'd last seen an object in use.

How could you hold a three-thousand-year-old axe head and not wonder about the laborer who'd used it? How could you admire the beauty of an ancient bracelet and not imagine the person who'd worn it?

She smiled. That curiosity, that sense of wonderment that remained with her, was probably why she was so good at her job. She was, too. She knew that, because she'd seen the attendance numbers. Since she'd become assistant curator, attendance had risen, as had the museum's panache.

In fact, the MHA was hosting more private parties lately than it had in years. Even the garden was booked. For a spring wedding, of all things.

She walked into Basement One. Beyond the unloading area, which was serviced by a freight elevator and a large ramp that led up to a big garage door, rows and rows of metal shelving filled the space.

The shelves reached to the ceiling and could be accessed by a tall set of rolling steps. Basement Two had the same shelves and rolling steps.

But her eyes were focused on the crates before her. The Clipston bequeathment. Maybelle Brightwater Clipston was one of the city's oldest remaining bluebloods. Or had been until her passing at one hundred and two a few months ago.

Ro had met with her numerous times, finding the woman to be remarkably spry for her age. She was sharp-witted, too. Ro hoped she aged half as well.

In the last few years, Maybelle had become increasingly reclusive. Ro hadn't seen her for nearly eleven months, and on their last visit, Maybelle had wanted Ro's reassurance that she would deal personally with the things Maybelle intended to leave to the museum.

Ro had given her that reassurance, even though Maybelle had been cagey about what those things were. The house, one of the few remaining old mansions in the city that hadn't been chopped up into smaller apartments, was chock full of antiques.

Ro had spotted several items that were museum-worthy, but no amount of hinting or questioning had confirmed they were among the pieces Maybelle planned to bequeath.

Now Ro would get to open the crates and see exactly what treasures Maybelle had left the museum. There were three crates in total. A tall one, about three feet by three feet square and five feet high, a squat one the size of a hope chest, and another the size of a washing machine.

Well, a standard washing machine. Ro had a compact stack unit, because that's all that would fit into her apartment. She'd had to give up some of her kitchen space to make it work, but it was worth it not to have to haul her clothes to the laundromat.

She stared at the tall one. There was every possibility that contained a statue. A long-lost Rodin, perhaps? Or something older and more Roman? It could even be Egyptian. Or Syrian. Rubbing her hands together, Ro went to the worktable against the wall and found a pry bar. She was eager to see what was in all of these crates, but that tall one made her the most curious. Which was probably why she'd save it for last.

She'd get the lids off of them all first, then dig into the contents.

Removing the lids took a good twenty minutes of serious prying. About five minutes in, she'd taken her jacket off. Now she was a little sweaty.

Estevan and Salifya, the two main warehouse guys, usually handled all of the uncrating. But she'd promised Maybelle to do this personally, and Ro wasn't one to go back on her word. She'd told them yesterday she'd be taking care of this and asked them to work in Basement Two, getting some of the shelves inventoried.

With the lids off, tufts of shredded packing material poked out of the crates, but nothing had been revealed yet. She'd have to get a good deal of packing material out of the way before she could see the contents. She hauled over one of the recycling containers and carefully removed handfuls of shreds, starting with the hope chest-size crate.

After another twenty minutes or so of work, she'd uncovered what looked like a Yuan Dynasty celadon jar, except the glaze color, which should have been green, had a hint of blue in it, and the ornamentation didn't look quite right. Research would be required to accurately date the piece.

There was also a rolled tapestry wrapped in paper. She moved that to an examination table. The next crate held a large, carved wooden chest inlaid with stones, a collection of some interesting jewelry pieces rolled in a length of ivory suede, and a pair of lady's silk slippers with gently curled toes and embellished with beautifully embroidered dragonflies and beetles accented with faceted beads.

At long last, she dug into the tall crate. Ro had pulled out the packing material to reveal what was probably one of the most disappointing items ever donated to the museum.

It was, in simple terms, a collector's item. A fancy souvenir, basically. She was looking at a sword in a stone. Nothing more than an expensive conversation starter, because no doubt it *had* been expensive. A beautiful sword that was clearly well-made, even if it was essentially a sight gag to make the viewer instantly think about *Excalibur.*

Had Maybelle commissioned this piece for her home? She'd been a big fan of literature. Ro had seen the woman's library, which had been wall-to-wall books, but so had much of the rest of the house. Books had been everywhere.

Ro sighed as she surveyed the items. She'd been hoping

for better. Perhaps that was unkind, but it was true. Maybe there was more to the collection than there appeared to be, however. But the sword in the stone would be the last item on her inspection list.

She pulled on some white cotton gloves and began with the tapestry. She adjusted its position on the big examination tables and gently unrolled it until it was flat, removing the paper that had protected it. The fabric was in excellent shape with no damaged areas that she could see. A little fading, maybe, but that was to be expected. She'd retrieved her tablet and now used it to take photographs to document the tapestry's condition.

Next, she brought over a stepstool and climbed up to get a better picture of the tapestry as a whole. Often, up close, the images became less discernable, so viewing them from a distance helped her understand the intended picture. She put the tablet aside and studied the image.

It was a coronation scene. A young man kneeled before a throne, surrounded by others who were presumably royals and nobles, in a room with pale golden stone floors and pillars. Gothic-arched stained-glass windows shed prisms of light over the space.

The throne was built of the same pale golden stone but inlaid with expanses of precious and semi-precious stone. Blues, purples, and deep greens. The top was carved to represent the phases of the moon.

The scene was intricate and detailed and really beautiful. But much like the vase, it was nothing Ro could immediately place. Possibly medieval? She came down off the stepstool to examine it more closely, because at a distance, the people seemed to have slightly pointed ears.

Up close, under her magnifying glass, that detail appeared to vanish. A quirk of the design? It would take more studying.

She rolled the tapestry back up, then spent some time with each of the items she'd found in the crates, except for the jewelry, which she'd carry upstairs with her for closer inspection. For each item, she took photos, checked them over for maker's marks, and documented any damage or imperfections or blemishes.

All of them gave a similar result. They were familiar, each one echoing a time and place, but nothing that Ro felt comfortable pinning down.

What a curious collection Maybelle had passed on.

Ro pulled her cotton gloves off and went to log her findings into her tablet with more detail. On her way to the worktable, she passed the sword in the stone again.

She stopped, smirking at the object. She put her gloves and tablet onto the worktable and went to have a closer look.

The sword was really magnificent. It was possible that whoever had forged it had done so with no idea it was going to be used as a prop in this amusing display.

She put her reading glasses on and had a better look at the hilt. The stones embedded in it seemed to be amethyst, something like blue sapphire, and emerald. They weren't, of course, but that's what they looked like. Probably just glass. The pommel held a large disc of mother-of-pearl that gleamed like a full moon.

Then a thought struck her. Hadn't the throne portrayed in the tapestry had the same stones? She glanced over at the examination table, even though the tapestry was no longer on display there.

Curious. Come to think of it, the jewelry had been in those colors, too. As had the slippers. She went to have a look at the jewelry again. It was a suite, containing a necklace, earrings, a bracelet, a ring, and what seemed to be finger caps—two pointed, enameled items that almost appeared to replicate fingernails. Although not quite. They were a little too narrow to fit over fingers. Still, they reminded Ro of Chinese nail guards, worn by nobility to signal wealth and power.

All of the jewelry was either enameled or carved from whole stones. The necklace and earrings were strung beads, each bead a gem that had been carefully shaped to look like a flower bud. The flower was an amethyst, the leaves of emerald.

The suite was beautifully done and had a definite art deco influence. And yet ... not exactly.

With a shake of her head, she went back to the sword. She'd seen a lot of weapons in her years. Weapons that spanned many centuries and ages, made from all sorts of materials.

Despite the fact that she knew this sword shouldn't be of any real value, all of her instincts said it was.

Had Maybelle done this on purpose? The very wealthy could sometimes be odd, that much was true. They could afford to be.

Ro turned her attention to the stone the sword was

sunk into. It, too, looked real. Not like a hunk of poured concrete painted to look like a stone.

She removed the remaining bits of packing material as best she could. The piece was still inside the box. It was too heavy for her to move, which definitely added to the feeling of authenticity.

Where had Maybelle kept this in her house? Obviously, in a room Ro had never been privy to.

Ro went to the intercom and pressed the button to speak to Basement Two. "Estevan? Salifya? Are you able to come to Basement One? I need help moving something."

A few moments later, the intercom crackled to life. "On our way, Dr. Meadowcroft."

She nodded at Estevan's reply and put her hands on her hips to wait. She was going to figure out this sword and stone business once and for all.

There was no way Maybelle would have gifted a practical joke to the museum. Would she?

CHAPTER TWO

Using brute strength and the padded dolly, Estevan and Salifya got the stone moved out of the box.

Ro nodded. "Thank you."

Estevan smiled at the sword. "I saw that movie when I was kid. I always wanted to try it."

"Go ahead," Ro said. "I don't know what will end up happening with that piece, but there's not much chance it'll end up on display in the museum. It's more of a curiosity than anything."

"Yeah?" Estevan looked at her.

"Yeah," she confirmed.

He tipped his head at Salifya. "You know about the sword in the stone?"

Salifya snorted softly. "Even in Africa we know about *Excalibur*, my friend."

Estevan took his leather work gloves off, went over, grabbed hold of the sword and pulled. Nothing. As expected.

Salifya rubbed his hands together. "Maybe I am the king." He took his turn, with the same result.

"Well, you tried," Ro said. "Unfortunately, it looks like

neither of you are the once and future king, so it's a good thing you didn't quit."

They laughed.

Salifya leaned on the dolly. "You want us to break these crates down? Take the pieces to recycling?"

"Not yet. These items might need to go back into those crates for a little while." She glanced at her watch. "You guys should go have your lunch."

Estevan picked up his gloves off the table and tucked them into his back pocket. "Fine by me. You going to be working here all afternoon, Doc?"

Ro shook her head. "No. I'm going to finish cataloging these pieces, then I'll probably have you guys store them until I know where they'll be going. But it might take a day or two before I'm ready for them to be moved." They might not be going anywhere if she couldn't put a time, place, or value on them.

"All right. See you later." Estevan and Salifya left, most likely headed to the employee break room.

The MHA had a small employee cafeteria. It was served by the same kitchen that handled the museum's café, but the menus were very different. The employee cafeteria reminded her of high school, serving three selections every day, plus a salad bar.

She ate there occasionally, but more often, like Estevan and Salifya, she brought her own lunch. It was cheaper. And usually tasted better.

With the two men gone, she walked back to the sword and the stone. She really wanted to figure out what

Maybelle had intended with this donation. A joke? Or was there really something to it?

As she stared at it, the air kicked back on. She'd been sweaty but now felt a chill. These basements were temperature- and humidity-controlled to help preserve the items in them. She put her jacket back on, took a moment to check her phone for messages, then tucked it into her pocket and returned to the object before her.

She walked around it. She crouched down and looked at it from a different perspective. She pulled the stepstool over and got a bird's-eye view.

Nothing popped out at her. There were no maker's marks anywhere she could see. If they were under the stone, she'd need help to lift it. No blemishes or telltale indications that the stone was manmade, either.

So how had the sword gotten in there?

She sat on the first step of the stepstool, put her elbows on her knees and her head in her hands and just stared, hoping something would come to her. She wished she could ask Maybelle about it, but obviously, that wasn't going to happen.

Ro was thinking about heading back upstairs when her phone vibrated with an incoming message. She checked the screen. It was from JT. *Still on for dinner Saturday?*

She smiled. *Yes.*

Frankie's House of Beans?

She laughed. *No! Malones. My treat.* She shook her head. She loved that boy more than life itself.

Hard to imagine her life without him now. Also hard to

imagine that he was the result of bad judgment and a youthful indiscretion.

She'd been working on her Master's. Nearly done, too. But a misguided affair with a visiting professor had ended with him returning to England, and a few weeks later, she'd found out she was pregnant.

Rhys Saunders Shaw was a handsome, erudite, sophisticated Brit who'd charmed the pants off of her.

Literally.

She'd struggled with what to do. Especially because Rhys had taken off for England without even saying goodbye.

She quickly realized she'd been nothing more to him than a couple of weeks of fun. A way to pass the time.

She'd tried to find him, but he hadn't given her any way to contact him, and none of the schools she contacted in England knew anything about him. It was like he'd vanished into thin air. There'd been no way to tell him about the baby. Although she wasn't sure he would have cared.

She'd finished her Master's, barely, and a month later had given birth.

It was history repeating itself, in a way. Her mother hadn't been married, either. But unlike her mother, Ro hadn't dumped her child off on a relative to raise.

Single motherhood had been hard. Harder than all of her years of schooling. She was thankful for Aunt Violet's help. But Aunt Violet had already raised Ro. It seemed unfair to ask much more of her, so Ro had done as much as she could on her own.

Aunt Violet, of course, had helped without being asked, stepping in to pick up the slack and making it possible for Ro to get her doctorate.

She sighed. Not a day went by that she didn't miss Aunt Violet. Even though she'd lived to be ninety-six, it still felt like she'd left them too soon. Hard to believe she'd been gone ten years already.

JT had loved that woman madly. As for Ro's mother ... Ro wasn't entirely sure where she was. Last she'd heard, Starlynn, a name her mother had given herself in the Sixties, was living on a yoga ranch out west. Whatever a yoga ranch was.

Ro went back to examining the sword, but the meaning and purpose of the object continued to elude her. And as it was unlikely she was going to figure it out today, she really ought to go back to her office and get started on the rest of her work.

She stood up, unable to take her eyes off the sword. Shame such a beautiful piece of craftsmanship was stuck like that.

How had no one ever managed to remove it from the stone?

She smiled. She really *should* give it a try. Wasn't that the point of this piece? To remind mankind that they were not the chosen one of legend? That fairy tales and fantasies were a realm of the mind and not reality? Maybe it was.

She walked over to the sword, wrapped her hands around the hilt, and pulled.

The sword came free.

Everything around her went dark with a great, whooshing sound.

The darkness only lasted a second or two. When it disappeared, she was no longer in Basement One. She was in an enormous room with stone floors, stone walls, and an intricate stone roof that reminded her of an English cathedral.

She faced tall, arched stained-glass windows that let light into the space, coloring the supporting pillars. The sword was still in her hands.

Under her feet lay a thick purple rug. She turned and realized she was standing in front of a dais that held an ornate stone throne.

What on Earth was going on? What kind of trick was this?

The throne, inlaid with flat panels of gemstones, was crested by more carvings that represented the phases of the moon.

Just like in the tapestry.

In fact, the whole room looked like the one in the tapestry. The stone even had the same golden hue.

An angry voice shouted behind her. "You! Who goes there?"

She spun around, still gripping the sword, to see two very large men in uniform approaching with swords of their own. Which were currently pointed at her.

She swallowed and shook her head. "I ..." She really didn't know what to say.

All at once, the men focused on the sword in her hand.

Their eyes widened, and they went to their knees, bowing before her, heads down.

Their ears were pointed.

A breath passed as she took them in. "Listen, I don't know where I am or what I'm doing here. I'm sorry for intruding. I promise you, that wasn't my intention."

When neither man moved, she tried a different tack. "You can get up."

The first man lifted his head to answer her but remained on his knees. "You bear *Merediem*. The royal sword. Where did you come by it?"

She looked at the sword in her hand. There was nothing about it that looked royal to her. It was a great sword, no doubt about that, but royal? "I took it out of a rock. A big one."

He bowed his head again. "A queen. After so many years." He seemed to be speaking to himself. Or maybe the man next to him. He looked at Ro again. "Permission to rise?"

"Yes, again. Please get up. Both of you."

The men got to their feet.

She took a step toward them. They backed up. She frowned. "Are you afraid of me?"

"Not afraid, your ladyship." The man shook his head. "But there are protocols ..."

That answer really didn't help her. "Can you tell me where I am?"

"The throne room."

She nodded. "I had that part figured out. I'm talking bigger picture. Where in the city am I?"

"The city?" He glanced at the man beside him as if needing help to understand her.

She decided to start over. "What's your name?"

"Gerrard."

"And you're a soldier of some sort?"

He nodded. "I'm an Interior Royal Guard, First Class."

"And what building are we in?"

He was starting to look at her like she wasn't right in the head. "The royal keep."

"Can you be more specific?"

"Castle Clarion, Stronghold of the Radiant Fae, Home of The Empty Throne, in the Land of The Ungoverned."

So very *Game of Thrones*. But what were the Radiant Fae? Maybe she was having a hallucination. Sure, this felt real, but wasn't that what made hallucinations so terrifying? She looked around, hoping something might suddenly make sense. "A castle, huh?"

"Yes, your ladyship. Castle Clarion."

"It's beautiful." She smiled. "You can call me Ro."

He shook his head, frowning. "I cannot. Royal protocol forbids it."

"Royal protocol."

"Yes, your ladyship."

She looked at the sword. That she'd pulled from a stone. Could it really be that simple? "Are you saying you believe I'm someone important because I hold this sword?"

"You told me you pulled it from a rock, and I believe you. There's no other way you could be holding it now.

Unless you took the sword from someone else who pulled it free."

"I didn't. I swear. So it's common knowledge that the sword was in a stone?"

He nodded. "It was embedded in that rock over a century ago. One of our prophecies told us a day would come when the throne of Castle Clarion would once again be filled by whoever removed *Merediem* from that stone." He cleared his throat softly. "Unless you lie, that person would be you."

"And where exactly was that stone?"

He glanced at his companion once again before answering. She couldn't help but notice his pointed ears again. "We only knew that it resided somewhere in the mortal world."

"The mortal world." Ro exhaled. This was a pretty elaborate setup to be a prank. But if she went with the supposition that this was all really happening, that she had pulled a magical sword from a stone and somehow been transported to a fae realm, then okay, she'd go along with that until proven otherwise. But another question remained: What was Maybelle doing with the sword? And all the other items she'd bequeathed, which now seemed very much like they also belonged here?

CHAPTER THREE

R o sat on the steps that led to the dais. "I hope you'll forgive me, but this is a lot to take in. You understand that, right?"

The guard beside Gerrard raised his hand. "Your ladyship, if I may?"

She nodded. "Go ahead. But please, tell me your name."

"Leo, your ladyship."

"Thank you, Leo. What is it you want to say?"

"A question, please?"

"Sure."

"You're from the mortal world, then?"

She nodded. "Apparently, I am."

He went on. "You've never been to the fae realm before?"

"Never even knew it existed." If these two were actors, they were really good. She rubbed the bridge of her nose. If only she could call Maybelle. At that thought, Ro dug into her pocket and pulled out her phone. No signal. Well, that just sealed it, then, didn't it?

Gerrard spoke again. "Your ladyship, I should alert the high council." He smiled. "Your arrival has been long awaited by this entire kingdom. Today is a glorious day."

"Um ... sure." How was she going to explain to them that she couldn't stay? That she had a life in the city and a job that she loved there. Not to mention her son and her cats.

Gerrard and Leo bowed, then backed out of the room through a set of impressive double doors of carved wood, and bolted down the hall beyond.

She supposed she should just stay here and wait. Surely someone on the high council would understand her situation and know how to get her home. Because there had to be a way home. And soon. There was every possibility that someone at the museum had noticed she was gone. Maybe even that the sword was missing. Would they think she'd stolen it? That could be a real problem. Especially with the promotion coming up.

She did her best not to freak out as she rested the sword across her knees. She studied the disc of mother of pearl set in the pommel, then glanced at the throne behind her. The visible phases of the moon were all done in mother of pearl. Was the disc in the pommel meant to represent the moon?

The doors burst open, and Gerrard and Leo returned with a man who looked to be in his eighties. *Late* eighties. He was tall and thin, something his voluminous robes did nothing to hide. He wore a baggy cap over his long silver hair, but it was tilted, exposing one pointed ear. Despite his undaunting appearance, he still carried an air of authority about him.

She stood, picking up the sword. "This is the high council?"

"No, your ladyship," Gerrard answered. "This is Uldamar Darkstone, the First Professor of Magic."

She wasn't sure how he was supposed to help, but she smiled all the same. "Nice to meet you, Professor Darkstone."

He came forward and bowed with surprising suppleness, then rose to his full height. His eyes narrowed. "Uldamar will do. The guards informed me you pulled the royal sword, *Merediem*, from the stone."

It wasn't a question, but she answered it anyway. "I did, yes. And then I ended up here."

"Where did you come from?"

"The Museum of Historical Arts. Basement One."

He nodded as though he were thinking. "I've been to that museum before. Many years ago. That is where you happened upon the stone and sword?"

"Yes. But I didn't really happen upon it. It was bequeathed to the museum by a patron."

"I see." He lifted his chin slightly. "And you are a worker at the museum?"

"You could say that. I'm the assistant curator. Soon to be *the* curator. Basically, the person in charge of the museum."

"Ah, very good." He nodded some more. "Perhaps you'd be willing to take me back there? Show me personally that you're able to remove the sword?"

"Sure, except I have no idea how to get back."

"No, of course you don't." He smiled. "I can arrange that. So you'd be willing then?"

Did he not believe her? Or was it royal protocol to have proof? Either way, she didn't care. "As I said, yes."

A commotion in the hall caused them all to look at the doors. Five people jostled through them to stand behind Uldamar.

He held his arm out toward them. "Some members of the high council."

A stout woman with short red curls spoke to him. "Are we sure?"

"No, Professor Featherlight, we are not," Uldamar replied. "But we will soon know."

The burly man next to her crossed his arms. "Good. We need proof. It's been too long."

"Too long," agreed the balding man at his side. He pushed his wire-rimmed glasses higher up the bridge of his nose. "But she looks suitable."

Ro put the point of the sword into the rug and leaned on it slightly. "I'm right here, you know. Talking about me like I can't hear you is rather rude."

The second woman lifted her chin and looked down her long nose at the rest of the council. "Let us not begin with impolite actions." She strode forward and bowed. "My ladyship, I am Prilla Bowsinger. I am the First Professor of Manners."

"Nice to meet you, Professor Bowsinger."

She smiled. "May I ask your name, your ladyship?"

"Of course." Ro went formal, since that seemed to be the style. "I'm Dr. Sparrow Meadowcroft, Assistant Curator of the Museum of Historical Arts."

The faces in front of her went blank. Mouths opened.

Eyes blinked. There seemed to be a general sense of shock and disbelief.

Professor Bowsinger regained her composure. "Are you by any chance Violet Meadowcroft's kin?"

Ro nodded. "I am. She was my aunt. My great aunt actually."

"Was?" Uldamar asked.

"Yes," Ro said. "She passed away almost ten years ago."

With his thick, scraggly brows arched, Uldamar looked at Professor Bowsinger. "She doesn't know."

Professor Bowsinger shook her head. "I think not."

Ro sighed. "You're talking about me like I'm not here again."

Professor Bowsinger smiled. "Yes, I suppose we are." She clasped her hands before her. "Forgive us. This is quite a momentous day. Your arrival has been foretold, but to be honest, some of us were beginning to think it might never happen."

"My arrival?"

Professor Bowsinger gestured to the sword. "The one who could free *Merediem* from the stone. Of course, you'll have to demonstrate that to us, just as a matter of record. You understand."

"I'm not entirely sure I do." Ro shifted, taking her weight off the sword. "I'd love some clarification. I understand the basics. I think. I pulled the sword out of the stone, and now you believe I'm the next ruler, correct?"

Professor Featherlight stepped forward. "Correct. But there will be no coronation until we see it for ourselves."

Ro didn't think now was a good time to tell her that

there would *never* be a coronation. That news could wait until she was back in her own world.

What a strange thought that was to have.

"I understand," Ro said. "But won't the current ruler be a little upset that someone else is going to take their place?"

Uldamar shook his head. "We have no current ruler. We haven't had one since the sword was put in the stone."

"Remind me. How long ago was that?"

"One hundred and thirteen years ago."

"Oh." That was a long time to be rulerless. She took another look around. Things seemed well maintained. But maybe outside these doors the kingdom was in chaos. Hard to say. "I guess you're really looking forward to having one then."

He nodded. "We are."

"How did the sword get in the stone?"

Everyone in the high council looked at Uldamar.

He sighed. "I put it there."

She stared at him. How old *was* he? "You did?"

"Yes. At the time, there was no other option, I'm afraid."

Professor Featherlight shook her head, making her curls quiver. "There really wasn't."

The big, burly councilman spoke. "All agreed it was the best possible solution."

"To what?" Ro asked.

The balding man with glasses immediately answered. "That's a story for another time and place."

Ro wondered why. "And you are?"

"Spencer Cloudtree. First Professor of History."

Ro smiled. "I love history. It's kind of my thing."

He smiled back. "That is very nice to hear."

"Are you all professors? Where do you teach?"

They looked to Uldamar again.

He explained. "First Professor is a title held by someone on one of the councils. In the mortal world, a professor is someone who teaches. In the fae realm, a professor is someone who professes the guidelines and knowledge about a particular area with greater expertise than anyone else."

She studied him. "Then a First Professor must be the person who knows the most about that subject."

"Correct. Or they are at least *deemed* to know the most. Or be the most proficient in it. You understand."

"I do. Then you know more about magic than anyone else in this realm?"

He shook his head. "Just in this kingdom. The Grym Fae have their own court."

"The Grym Fae?"

He nodded. "You'll learn about them soon enough. First, we must ascertain that you are, indeed, the one the sword has chosen."

"Right. Can I ask just one more question?"

They looked at each other and quickly nodded as a group.

"How did you know who my aunt was?"

CHAPTER FOUR

Professor Bowsinger answered. "Because she lives here."

Ro frowned. "You must have the wrong woman. Or there's another Violet Meadowcroft. My Aunt Violet passed away. I was at her bedside. Trust me. I organized her funeral." Ro exhaled as memories of that dark day swept through her. "You can't mean the same Violet who raised me."

Uldamar took a step toward her. "Your ladyship, there are many fae who inhabit the mortal realm. You're a prime example of one. But after a certain number of years, they must return home or their age would give them away."

Ro lifted her empty hand, palm out. "Hold up. You think *I'm* fae?"

Professor Featherlight snickered. "Of course you are. How do you think you got here?"

Ro shook her head. "Sorry, but I'm as human as any of … okay, presumably none of you are human. But I am."

"No," Uldamar said. "You're not. Neither is your aunt."

Ro sat down. She had to before her knees gave out for reasons that had nothing to do with her age. This was a lot to take in. "I need to see her." There was no other way to be sure the woman they were speaking of really was her aunt.

Uldamar pressed his lips together in a firm, hard line. "We must first be sure that—"

"I get it. You want to see me pull the sword out of the stone again. And I will. But I'm not moving until I see my Aunt Violet. You want your proof? Well, I want mine, too." She was on the verge of angry tears.

This whole situation seemed like a crazy dream, but if Aunt Vi was really here, Ro would know the truth. Aunt Violet would tell her what was going on. And if these people were just trying to manipulate her in some way, well then, she'd know that, too.

Uldamar nodded to Leo and Gerrard. "Bring Violet here."

The two guards nodded and left.

Uldamar came over to Ro, his brows bent in understanding. "I realize this must all be a big shock to you."

She snorted. "You can say that again. Ending up in a different world? Finding out my aunt is still alive? Finding out I'm fae? Supposedly. It's a shock, all right."

He passed one palm over the other in a circular fashion, and suddenly he was holding a mirror in his hand. "Look for yourself if you don't believe me."

Neat trick. But magic was explainable. She took the mirror and gazed into it.

Her mouth came open. She was still herself, but she looked different. Almost...beautiful. Like she'd put an Instagram filter over her image. Her eyes were brighter, the hazel much greener than she'd ever seen it, her skin clearer. The gray in her hair gleamed silver while the rest of it had gone from dull brown to dark caramel. She turned her head. And her ears were pointed.

She frowned. More magic. "That's not me. That's another trick of yours."

"I promise you, it is not." He gestured to a place on the step next to her. "May I?"

She nodded.

He sat. "You've always looked that way, but the mortal realm distorts the fae's natural beauty. It's a good thing, too, or we'd stand out terribly when we're there."

"You've been to my world?"

"I have. Enough to know that I prefer this realm."

"Did my aunt know she was fae?"

"I don't believe so. There are so many who don't."

"So when she died …"

"She actually came here."

"But I saw her body. I held her hand as she slipped away. You can't tell me that wasn't real."

"I won't, because it was. But mortal death is a singular event, I promise you. Something each fae can only do once."

"And then what?"

"And then they are transported here. But they may never return to the mortal world. Not without very special permission and under the guise of magic to shield their true identity. Although there are some who attempt it, it's not something looked upon lightly."

His eyes were remarkably blue. Like cornflowers.

She handed him back his mirror. "This really is a *lot*."

"I understand." The mirror vanished with a pass of his hands.

She jerked her chin at the movement. "Can all fae do that?"

"Magic?"

She nodded.

"All fae *have* magic. Their skill depends on many things."

She thought about that a moment. "Do I have magic?"

"You pulled that sword out of the stone, didn't you?"

She nodded. "I did."

The throne room doors opened. Leo came through, then Gerrard. At his side stood a petite, round woman with sparkling brown eyes, her head crowned with a silver braid of hair. Her smile was as big and warm as Ro remembered. She wore a flowered apron over her robes.

Tears spilled down Ro's cheeks as she got up. "Aunt Violet?"

"Hello, my darling girl." Violet spread her arms wide. "What a happy surprise this is."

Ro rushed into Aunt Vi's arms, too overcome by emotion to speak. All she could do was hug her aunt tight. She smelled like the same lavender soap that Ro remembered.

Aunt Vi patted her back, sniffling as her own tears flowed.

After a few moments, they pulled back to look at each other.

Aunt Violet cupped Ro's cheek. "You're just as beautiful as I remember you. It's so good to see you. Are you here because you're ... dead?"

Ro laughed suddenly. "No. I'm here because I pulled *Merediem* out of the stone."

Aunt Violet gasped. "You did?"

Ro nodded. "It showed up at the museum, stuck in its stone, and I pulled it free. There's a lot more than that, I assure you, but for the moment, that's the important bit."

Aunt Violet hugged her again. "I can't believe you're here. If I could have contacted you, I would have, but ..."

Ro nodded. "I get that it's not allowed." She glanced at her aunt's apron. There seemed to be smudges of flour on it. "Were you baking?"

Violet nodded. "Yes. I own a bakery now."

"That doesn't surprise me at all. You always did make the most amazing cookies, cakes, and pies."

Her aunt shrugged like it was nothing. "I had to find a way to earn a living. And it keeps me busy."

"It's so good to see you." It hadn't quite sunk in that Aunt Violet was really here, but it made Ro think about someone else. She turned suddenly to look at the members of the high council. "Do you know Maybelle Brightwater Clipston? Is she here, too?"

They all looked at each other. Finally, Professor Bowsinger answered. "It appears none of us know her. We'll have to consult the record keeper."

Ro looked at her aunt again. "I have to go back. I wish I didn't, but I do."

Aunt Violet nodded. "I understand. You have JT to think of. How is our boy? I miss him so much."

"He's good. I think he's struggling a bit with his job."

"Oh? What is he doing?"

"Working at an architectural firm, which he always wanted to do, but I don't think it's turning out the way he thought." Ro was pulling that all from her mother's intuition. JT hadn't said any of that. Yet. "We're having dinner on Saturday. I'm hoping we can talk about it then."

"You …" Aunt Violet shook her head and took hold of Ro's hands. "I was about to say you let me know, but I was assuming you were coming back. You're not, are you?"

Ro couldn't lie to Aunt Violet. "I don't see how I can."

Uldamar strode toward them from the steps. "What do you mean you aren't coming back?"

Ro held onto one of Aunt Vi's hands as she turned to face the man. "I understand that you people think I'm your prophesied ruler, but I have a life in the city. A home, a son, a job, cats. I can't just walk away from all of that."

Uldamar looked like he was either going to yell at her or cry. He took a breath and did neither. "You must at least give us the opportunity to show you our world and what kind of life could be yours if you stayed. You can certainly bring your son and your cats, too."

She shook her head. "JT would never leave." Would he? Benny wouldn't care. And Wiggy wouldn't notice if she was living here or in Timbuktu.

"But you will at least give us the chance?"

She glanced at her aunt. "I will give you that chance but only if it means I can spend more time with my aunt."

"That's fine. Twenty-four of your mortal hours then."

Ro frowned and let out a breath. "I'll have to put in

notice that I'm taking a personal day." She hadn't taken one in years, so it shouldn't be a problem, but she had the Clipston bequeathment to finish up. Although now that she got to thinking about those pieces, maybe she didn't. If those things all belonged to this world, there was no way she could exhibit them at the museum.

That all assumed that her absence hadn't been noticed yet. Maybe she'd get lucky and Estevan and Salifya would take a longer lunch than usual.

But the Clipston pieces stayed on her mind. Maybe they should be returned to this realm. But how would she explain that the entire bequeathment had been unusable? Better to claim they needed restoration, then put them in storage and let them fade from memory. Easy enough to do in those basement depths.

"We should go," Uldamar said. "So you can show me your proof. Then we can come back, and I can show you our proof about why you should stay."

Ro nodded. "All right." She hugged Violet one more time. "I want to see you when I get back."

"Me, too. I want to see you. I'll bring you some goodies, as well."

Ro smiled. Aunt Vi hadn't changed a bit. "See you soon." She looked at Uldamar. "How do we do this?"

"Through a portal. I'll show you."

She glanced at the high council. "Are they coming, too? Because that's a lot of people." Not that Basement One couldn't fit them all, but if anyone were to come down there, or if Estevan and Salifya came back from lunch while the council was there, it would be a lot to explain.

Uldamar spoke to the group. "I assume you'll take my word for it? As First Professor of Magic, I feel that ought to be sufficient."

Professor Bowsinger answered first. "I'm fine with that."

Cloudtree spoke up next. "Agreed. Your determination is enough."

The rest of them nodded.

"All right then," Uldamar said. "Off to the portal we go."

CHAPTER FIVE

The portal was a small stone gazebo in an anteroom just a few feet down the hall. From what Ro could see, the entire castle was built from the same pale golden stone as the throne room. Tapestries hung along the walls, intermixed with paintings. The tapestries bore the same style as the one currently in Basement One, confirming Ro's thoughts that those things belonged here and not in the MHA.

There were no windows in the section of hall they traversed, but farther on she could see a few arrow slits, long, narrow windows designed to allow arrows to be shot through them while keeping the archer safe. Those windows were dark. But there had been light coming through the stained glass in the throne room.

She stopped and stood at the entrance to the anteroom, sword still gripped firmly in her hand. "What time is it here?"

Uldamar, who'd already gone inside, came back out and looked in the same direction she was. "The same time it is in your world."

So the fae realm was on Eastern Standard Time? "Then why is it dark outside?"

"It's not. Those arrow slits are covered by banners that hang on the outside of the castle."

She looked at him. "What kind of banners?"

"Heralding the arrival of summer and all the joys that season brings." He gestured toward the stone gazebo. "May we go through?"

She took one more look, then followed him in.

The anteroom was round, following the shape of the gazebo and allowing for about a three-foot boundary around it.

Uldamar stepped into the gazebo and stood slightly off center. He gestured for her to join him. "Stand here. Beside me."

She did as he asked. "How does this work?"

"Fae magic." He smiled and slid a ring off his finger. "I could take us, but perhaps it would be better for you to do it. You'll need to put this on."

She tucked the sword under her arm to free both hands. The ring was a wide silver band with seven or eight slender movable bands around it. Rings on top of a ring. Each slim inner band held a tiny round gemstone set in gold. Small vees were designed into the top and bottom of the main band, perfectly aligned with one another.

She put it on her pointer finger, holding her hand out. "Now what?"

"Since you don't know the coordinates yet for where you need to go, simply line all of the stones up with the notches, then think very precisely about where you'd like to return to. The portal will take us to the closest possible location."

She cut her eyes at him.

"I promise," he said. "It will. There are portals all over your city."

"Can you go to different cities? Different countries?"

He nodded. "With the right ring, you can go anywhere you need to. Provided there's a portal there to receive you. From outside the fae realm, you can return to a portal from any location. No portal needed."

"Interesting. So I just line these up …"

He took hold of her arm lightly. "That's right. Then visualize where you want to go."

She lined up the gemstones. They seemed to hold in place as if held by a magnet. When they were in a row, she closed her eyes and thought about Basement One.

A moment later, she felt the same sensation as being in an elevator. She opened her eyes to look at Uldamar and realized they were already in Basement One.

His blue robes were now an outdated blue suit under which he wore a blue sweater. His hair was still gray, but the silver gleam was gone. He looked about the same age but didn't seem as spritely.

"That was fast," she whispered as a little bout of nausea struck her.

His eyes narrowed as if he sensed her queasiness. "That'll pass. After a few trips, you'll get used to it." He looked around. "Interesting. This is not a portal." He looked at her. "What was here before this building?"

"An old subway station, but it was demolished when the museum was built to make way for the basements." She exhaled, then swallowed down the saliva that reminded her of her bouts of morning sickness. "How did you know I felt nauseous?"

"Happens to everyone the first time." He nodded. "An old subway station. That explains a great deal." He looked around, smiling. "So many treasures. Reminds me of the royal storehouses."

She still had the sword under her arm. She left it there so she could pull the ring off. "Here."

He took it and put it back on his finger. "Feeling better yet?"

"It's passing. I'll live." The morning sickness she'd had with JT had been a lot worse. She took the sword by the hilt again. "Should I just put this back into the stone?"

He held his hand out. "Allow me."

She gave it to him carefully, so he could take it by the hilt. She looked around after he took it but didn't see signs of anyone else. The space was quiet. Good. She did not want to have to explain who he was or what he was doing here. Or where she'd been. Or why the sword had disappeared from the stone.

He walked over to the stone, lofted the sword with both hands, spoke a few soft words she didn't quite catch, then slid the blade back into the rock. He stepped back. It looked exactly as it had the first time she'd seen it.

He stepped away. "All yours."

Maybe she'd get lucky and the sword wouldn't come free this time. Except ... she really wanted to see Aunt Violet again. How amazing would it be to have that dear woman back in her life? Back in JT's life, too?

Was there a way she could make that happen? She had no answer for that just yet, but sometimes a solution didn't come until she'd had a good night's sleep. That's all she needed. A good night's sleep. Maybe she'd wake up and find out this was all just a dream.

But she didn't really think this was a dream anymore. Not while standing in Basement One. She walked over to the stone, put her hands on the hilt, and pulled.

The sword sang as the metal slipped free of the stone.

Uldamar bowed low, holding the courtesy for a moment longer than he had the first time. "You truly are the prophesied one. Our queen."

She shook her head, but he couldn't see her. "I really can't be that. I'm sorry."

He wasn't frowning, but he wasn't smiling, either. "You said you'd give me twenty-four hours to show you the fae world and what your life would be like there."

She nodded. "I did. Does that mean we're going back immediately? Because I need to let people know I won't be in tomorrow." It was a Friday. They'd just assume that her personal day was so she could have a long weekend. "And I have to be back on Saturday. I'm having dinner with my son, and I am not going to cancel that."

"You will be back by then."

"Okay. I also don't want to leave my cats. Benny might be all right, but Edna is old and particular and prone to mischief. There's no telling what she'll do if I leave her alone overnight."

"You can bring them."

"Will there be a safe place for them to stay? A place they can run around?"

"Yes. Plenty of room and very safe."

"All right. We'll have to go back to my apartment to get them."

"That's not a problem."

He wasn't giving her an out. But one day was no big deal. She hadn't taken time off in ages. It might be nice, actually. Like a weird little vacation before the job of curator began, because that's what was happening on Monday. Her promotion would be made official.

"I need to run up to my office, send the email about not being in tomorrow, then we can go." She handed him the sword. "You'd better hold on to this. I can't really walk through the museum holding something that's supposed to be a valuable, ancient artifact without raising some questions."

He took the sword. "But *Merediem* is exactly that."

"Right. But it's not a *human* artifact."

"No, it is not."

"I'll be back as quickly as I can."

He slid the sword carefully through his belt so that it hung at his side. It was a curious sight, an old man in a vintage suit armed with a sword. He looked around and nodded. "I'll be here."

"Great." She hesitated, wondering if she should tell him not to touch anything. With a shake of her head, she pushed the elevator's call button. This was not the time to take the stairs and possibly run into someone. She wanted to get Uldamar out of here as soon as she could.

She stepped onto the elevator, then turned around and pressed the button for the fourth floor. As the doors began to close, Uldamar stared toward the examination table where the tapestry and the rest of Maybelle's items were still sitting out.

"Don't—" But the doors closed.

She rolled her eyes and exhaled. This was one of the weirdest things that had ever happened to her. And that included the time she'd discovered an unopened package on one of the shelves that had turned out to be a rare Egyptian funeral shroud over two thousand years old.

It had been mailed to the museum in the Forties and somehow stored and ignored. She'd built an entire exhibit around that piece, which had been extraordinarily successful.

The doors opened onto the fourth floor. She went to her office as quietly and unobtrusively as she could.

She typed out an email, making numerous typos because she was hurrying. She took her hands off the keyboard, made herself breathe, then proofread and made corrections. Looked good. She added the proper recipients, then hit Send.

She grabbed her purse and went back downstairs, again via the elevator.

Uldamar was standing by the examination table. He looked up as she returned. "These are valuable items."

"I assumed as much."

"They belong in their home."

She couldn't argue that. "I understand, but the museum also knows they've been donated. They need to

45

disappear into the system before they can be returned. If they go missing now, that'll raise a lot more alarms than if that happened in a year or so. With enough time, they won't ever be missed."

He frowned.

"Look, I know it's not ideal, but that's how things work."

He waved his hand over the table. "You're just going to leave them here while you're gone?"

"I wasn't going to, no, but you haven't really given me a chance to do anything with them." They needed to be crated back up and stored on a shelf where they would, hopefully, soon be forgotten. She would write up a report saying the objects were strictly decorative in nature and of no historical value to the museum. That would be the end of it.

He seemed to consider her words. "I can help you. It was not my intention to make you feel … rushed. As the First Professor of Magic, it is my job to serve the queen in whatever capacity she requires."

She bristled at that word. Queen. He was assuming a lot. But they could discuss that later. "Well, then, I'll take the help. Those things need to go back into the—"

"We're back," Salifya called out as he and Estevan came down the loading ramp.

She went over and put a hand on Uldamar's arm to keep him from doing anything. "Warehouse men. They work here."

He nodded but said nothing.

"Great timing," she said with a smile. "I hope you had a good lunch, because I need you to pack these things back up into their crates. Just leave them here on the floor for now, though, and I'll deal with them as soon as I can. Will you guys take care of that for me?"

They were both eyeing Uldamar. Estevan nodded. "You got it, Doc."

Ro felt she needed to explain. "This is Professor Uldamar. He wanted my opinion on a Peruvian flask. We were just leaving."

That seemed to do the trick.

"See you later, Doc," Estevan said.

"I won't be back until Monday. I'm taking a personal day tomorrow. Have a good weekend." She moved Uldamar toward the loading ramp. It would be the easiest way to get out of the museum unseen.

"You, too," Salifya said.

She tried to position herself in such a way that she stayed slightly behind Uldamar, effectively blocking the men's view of the sword in his belt.

As soon as they were outside, she pulled him around to the side of the building. "You can't just walk through the streets of the city with a sword on your hip. I know strange things go on here, but that might be a bridge too far."

"Perhaps you're right." He removed the sword from his belt and held it by the hilt, then put his palm flat against the point and pushed.

She gasped, expecting the blade to go through his hand. Instead, the sword shrank down to the size of a pen.

He tucked it into the inside pocket of his suit jacket. "Better?"

She nodded, unable to figure out how he'd done that. "Yes. But how—"

He smiled. "Fae magic."

CHAPTER SIX

The walk to her apartment didn't take long, although her stomach grumbled on the way past City Donuts. The smell of yeasty, sugary goodness made her slow down and inhale.

Uldamar looked into the shop. "They sell sweets?"

Ro nodded. "Some of the best doughnuts you'll ever eat." She stopped suddenly. "You want one? My treat."

He hesitated.

"Come on," she said. "Have you ever had a doughnut?"

"No."

"Then you really should. They're delicious. And I haven't had lunch, so why not?" Plus, it wouldn't hurt to get on the old guy's good side. She opened the door, releasing more of the tantalizing aroma onto the street.

He nodded as the fragrance washed over him. "All right."

There was no line, so she went straight up to the counter, deciding instantly that a half dozen was the way to go. She wanted Uldamar to have the full experience. "I'd like a six-pack, please. One rainbow sprinkle to start."

Uldamar was staring at the wall of doughnuts behind the counter.

"Go on," she said. "Pick out five you'd like to try."

"Five? I have no idea."

"Just pick the ones that look the best to you."

The counter girl stood ready to fill the rest of their box.

Uldamar seemed to be giving this serious consideration. "Blueberry cake." He looked at Ro. "What is s'mores?"

"Chocolate, marshmallow, and graham cracker. Classic combination."

"All right." He nodded to the girl. "One s'mores. And a jelly filled. And an apple cinnamon." He stared at the flavors and began shaking his head. "I don't know what else. You pick."

That was easy. "We'll take a Boston cream for the last one." She smiled at Uldamar. "Another classic. And my personal favorite."

"But you didn't get that flavor."

"Because I already had one for breakfast this morning."

He smiled. "You like sweets."

"Who doesn't?" She paid, then took the box, and they left. "You can eat these while I pack an overnight bag. I can make a pot of coffee if you like. Do you drink coffee? *Is* there coffee in your realm? Because if there's not, that might be a deal-breaker. Coffee is pretty important. I like tea, too, but coffee is number one."

He smiled. "We have coffee. And tea. And tisanes."

"Which are ... like herbal tea, right?" She pointed so he'd know to go left.

"Yes. Very good."

She gestured toward her building with the box of doughnuts. "I'm just right up here."

They went up the steps to the entrance, where she dug out her keys to let them into the building, then held them in her hand for the flight up so she could let them into her apartment.

She flipped a light on after opening the door. If she'd known she was going to have company she would have straightened up a bit. She set the box of doughnuts on the kitchen counter. "Sorry about the lack of organization."

He walked in and looked around with a slightly bewildered expression. "This is your entire dwelling?"

"Well, the bedroom's back there." She nodded toward it. "Although it's not exactly what you'd call spacious. And then there's the bathroom." She went over to it, opened the door all the way, and flipped on the light.

Wiggy came charging out, leaving a trail of toilet paper fluttering behind her.

Ro sighed. "Wiggy, we talked about this." Little white scraps of TP covered the bathroom floor, and what remained on the holder looked like it had exploded.

Uldamar craned his neck to see in. "Your cat did that?"

"Yes, she did. She hates toilet paper. Not sure why." Ro shot Wiggy a look, but she was now sitting on the radiator in front of the window, cleaning her foot like it had suddenly become the most important job in the world. Benny was nowhere in sight, which meant he was probably sleeping in a hidden spot somewhere. Possibly under the bed or in her closet.

Uldamar smiled. "She is a creature of mischief."

"You can say that again."

"She is a creature of mischief."

Ro snorted as she bent to pick up all the scraps of toilet paper. "Look, help yourself to the doughnuts. I can make coffee if you like. It'll take me a few minutes to pack a bag for myself and get the cats' stuff together."

"I don't need coffee, but it's kind of you to offer. I must ask, however … aren't you going to introduce me?"

Ro straightened, making her knees pop. "To who?"

"Your cat."

"Sure." Was that a fae thing? "First Professor Uldamar Darkstone, meet Mrs. Edna Wigglesworth. Not sure where Benny is. I'll introduce you to him when he shows up."

Uldamar bowed to Wiggy. "A pleasure to meet you, madam."

Wiggy, who'd stopped chewing on her toes to look at him, meowed loudly.

Uldamar nodded.

Ro just shook her head and went back to her bedroom. Benny was curled up in the laundry basket. She kissed him on the head. "Hiya, Benny boy. Those were clean clothes, you know. I guess that should be my motivation to actually fold things when they come out of the dryer."

He curled up a little tighter, making her smile. She got out her weekender bag. She had no idea what to pack for an overnight stay in the fae realm, but stretch jeans and comfortable shoes were always a good idea.

She added pajamas, the kind with pants and a button-up top, to her bag, along with the matching robe. Those had been a gift from JT last Christmas, along with a beautiful pair of gold hoops that had become her go-to earrings.

In fact, she had them on now. They needed to go with

her. On impulse, she grabbed the small, framed photo of JT from her nightstand and stuck that in her bag as well.

She stared at it, lying on top of her things. Was it possible this was a trick? That letting her come back had only been a way of placating her? They weren't going to kidnap her or anything, were they? They'd seemed nice enough.

But the thought remained that maybe going back wasn't such a great idea. Then again, when in her lifetime would she ever get a chance like this again? Plus, there was Aunt Violet.

With an unsettled sigh, she went back to packing.

Toiletries were next. Not an easy task. She used about five different things on her skin, another two on her eyes, and a neck cream. None of which seemed to be performing as advertised, but she wasn't a quitter.

She didn't wear a lot of makeup, but she did wear some. A little foundation with SPF in it, some mascara, a touch of liner and lip color, which she usually dotted on her cheeks like cream blush, too. Plus an eyebrow pencil. Hers had started disappearing around the age of forty-three and showed no signs of returning.

Once in a while, if she had a meeting, she added a little eyeshadow. She didn't imagine she'd have any meetings in the fae realm.

She added a pinstriped blue button-up shirt and her favorite long cardigan in a deeper blue. It had bands of red at the wrist and near the bottom hem, which added a little color. Next was a pair of leggings and a long, lightweight tunic top.

Beyond the bedroom, she could hear singing.

She peeked out the door and saw Uldamar sitting on the floor in front of Wiggy, who was still on the radiator. He had the box of doughnuts in his lap, and although he was holding one with a bite taken out of it, he was now singing softly to her.

Ro couldn't make out the words, but he had a lovely voice.

Wiggy's eyes were shut, and she almost looked like she was smiling. Ro's brows bent at the sight of the two of them.

Apparently, Uldamar was a cat whisperer.

Ro went back to packing, throwing in a few last-minute items that she probably wouldn't need but better safe than sorry. She did her best to put the thought that she might not return out of her head.

She zipped her bag, brought it out and set it by the door. "You two seem to be enjoying yourselves."

Uldamar looked over his shoulder, smiling. There was a little chocolate glaze in the corner of his mouth. "These doughnuts are very good."

"I'm glad you like them." She came over and looked in the box. There were three left, one of which was the rainbow sprinkle she'd wanted. She snagged that one and stood back, taking a bite. The sugary goodness calmed her nerves a little. "I just have to pack up the cats' stuff, then put them in their carriers and we can go."

He nodded. "Take your time."

"Um, about the cats. Are you guys going to be able to

provide me with a litter box for them? Otherwise, I'll have to bring one." That would be a pain to travel with.

He nodded, his mouth full of s'mores doughnut, and mumbled, "Mm-hmm."

"Great." She finished the doughnut and went back to packing. Into a tote bag, she put a few cans of Wiggy's favorite tuna food and a can of Benny's chicken, which Wiggy might decide at any time was her new favorite; the already opened bag of treats; their brush; and one of Benny's favorite toys, a catnip-filled piece of felt sushi. She hesitated, then added the crinkle ball that Wiggy had been in love with last week. Hard to tell what might catch her fancy.

Also, that was probably a lot to pack for an overnight stay, but neither of the cats was going to complain.

Ro got the carriers out of the closet.

There were already fleece blankets in both of them from the last time Ro had taken the pair into the vet. Just yearly shots for Benny and a senior wellness exam and yearly shots for Wiggy. The vet had been happy to report that Mrs. Edna Wigglesworth, although nearly fourteen years old, was in fine shape. Benny, as always, had been loved on and treated as if he were the best thing since sliced bread, purring the entire time. Edna had bitten the vet tech right before she'd peed on the exam table.

"I'm all ready to go," Ro announced. "Just need to put the cats in their carriers and we can head back. Or do we need to find a portal?"

Uldamar pushed to his feet with the now empty doughnut box in hand. He popped the last piece of blueberry cake into his mouth and chewed, swallowing before he answered her. "We can leave from here. We'll be back in the fae realm before you know it."

"Leaving from here is good. These carriers roll, and I can stack one on top of the other, but they still aren't the easiest to maneuver." Ro put the carriers on the kitchen counter, opened the doors, then went to get Benny from the laundry basket.

He snuggled up against her when she picked him up. "Come on, baby. We're going on a little adventure."

He went into his carrier without a fuss.

Wiggy would be another story. She was already looking at Ro with squinty, skeptical eyes.

Ro picked her up gently but firmly, scruffing her neck so there was no chance of escape. "Deep breaths, Mrs. Wigglesworth. This is just a quick trip, I promise. And it's not to the vet."

Wiggy had already started her heavy breathing, a sure sign she was bothered. Ro rushed her into the carrier before Wiggy could get traction on the carrier's opening with her back legs. If she did that, it was game over. "Come on, Wiggy. We're not going to the vet, I swear."

Edna meowed plaintively.

"She's unhappy," Uldamar said. "And a little scared."

Easy enough to see, Ro thought. But that made two of them.

CHAPTER SEVEN

"Hold tight to the carriers and hold tight to me," Uldamar advised, sticking his elbow out toward her. He had the strap of Ro's weekend bag slung over his shoulder.

Ro had a good grip on the telescoping handle of the carrier Wiggy was in. Benny was in the one on top of that, since he weighed less. The bag of food and toys rested on top of his carrier. The two carriers were secured together by Velcro loops on both ends. The whole kit hadn't been cheap, but it definitely made taking them to the vet a lot simpler. She nodded at the cats. "It's okay, guys."

She looped her arm through Uldamar's and nodded. "Ready when you are."

He looked at her. "No, you're not. You're worried."

She exhaled. "I am. You're right."

"About?"

"Being able to return. I will be allowed to, right?"

"Of course. We would never hold someone against their will. Especially not someone we were counting on to be our next ruler." He frowned, then laughed. "We aren't the Grym Fae, you know."

"I'll take your word for it." She didn't know anything

about the Grym Fae, but his assurances were about as comforting as they could be under the circumstances.

Uldamar aligned the gemstones on his ring. "Here we go."

The world shifted and wavered, and in a split second, they were back in the stone gazebo. Her stomach roiled, and she took a deep breath, but the nausea wasn't nearly as bad this time.

A loud crack blocked out all other sound, and the carrier handle jerked in her hand. Ro glanced down to see the bottom one had shattered in pieces, but there was no sign of Wiggy.

There was, however, an older woman sprawled on the stone floor. Her hair was a shaggy mix of brown, ginger and white, as was the oversized cardigan she now wore. She had piercing green eyes that turned up at the corners. She sat up, looked at Ro and wrinkled her nose. "I hate that carrier. But this definitely doesn't look like the vet's office."

Ro stared at the woman, her mind trying to make sense of what she understood to have happened. "Wiggy?"

"Who else?" The woman sprang to her feet with surprising agility. Her nose wrinkled again as she stared toward the hall. "I smell rodents." She looked back. "Benny, do you smell that? Rodents!" Her eyes were wild, and she was smiling from ear to ear. "This place is all right. Is JT here? I love JT."

Ro's mouth was open even as she looked at Uldamar. "Is that my cat? What happened?"

His smile was tight but apologetic. "That does sometimes happen, although to be honest, it's rare. I suppose it might be rare because not many animals travel through the portals."

Ro checked on Benny. He seemed curious but otherwise his usual self.

Wiggy took off like a shot, careening out of the room and into the hall.

"Wiggy!" Ro dropped the bag of food and toys and went after her. "Please don't run away." She grabbed hold of Wiggy's big fuzzy cardigan. "Please. We're just visiting. We'll be home tomorrow."

Wiggy swatted at her. "I'll be back. As soon as I've done a little hunting." She took off down the hall with surprising speed.

Ro took a few steps after her, then hesitated. What was she going to do? Wrestle an old woman to the ground?

Uldamar came out to the hall. "She'll be back. I'll put the word out that she's on the loose. She'll be fine."

Ro didn't know what to think. She exhaled. Mrs. Edna Wigglesworth as a cat was nearly impossible to control. Ro couldn't imagine how much worse she'd be as a person.

Uldamar patted her arm. "I promise she'll be okay."

"I hope so." Ro nodded, not entirely convinced. Although maybe being human, or rather fae, since Ro wasn't completely sure what Wiggy had turned into, would be a good thing for Mrs. Wigglesworth to experience.

Ro went back into the portal to collect Benny. She detached the top carrier, which only had a carrying handle, and stared at the remains of the main carrier. That was seventy bucks down the drain.

"I'll take care of that," Uldamar said.

"I can do it," Ro said. "I just need a trash can."

"Nonsense," Uldamar said. He waved his hands over the bits and pieces, and with a swirl of gentle sparkles, the carrier was made whole. "Good as new."

Ro glanced at him, her brows raised. "Thank you. That was impressive." She reconnected Benny's carrier to the rolling one and grabbed the handle.

"You're welcome. Now, if you'll come with me, I'll show you to your quarters."

She went with him. They turned right, the opposite direction from where Wiggy had gone. Ro glanced down that side of the hall, but there was no sign of her.

They passed the darkened arrow-slit windows, but then there were some larger windows that weren't covered by anything.

Ro stopped in front of them and stared out, her first glimpse of the fae realm before her. "Oh, it's beautiful."

Uldamar smiled. "Our home is graced with a tremendous amount of natural beauty."

Ro stood and just looked. Rolling green and purple hills made up the horizon line, a faint haze blurring their edges. Small dots of white were visible in a few spots. Sheep, maybe? Some of the fields were striped with crops.

Directly below her were the castle grounds. Manicured lawns unfurled before her. On the edges there were intricate gardens, some walled by neatly trimmed hedges. Topiaries in the shape of dragonflies marked the opening of a hedge maze.

Trees lined the drive off to one side and seemed to

delineate the castle's borders as well. Beyond those borders was more farmland. Then spreading out from there and gently sloping into the valley was the town or village or whatever they called it.

Stone buildings and cottages, many with thatched roofs, some with slate, all with colorful shutters, sat on both sides of the cobblestone streets. Every home and business had window boxes filled with vivid flowers and more potted outside their doors. Along the streets, trees stood tall and lush, casting shade on the sidewalks.

Smoke drifted up from a few chimneys. People walked along, carrying baskets of goods, stopping to chat with each other. A few had dogs on leashes. A cat slept in the sun on someone's stoop. Horses and mules pulled carts through the streets. She could just make out an open square that had a fountain in it.

The village went down into the valley and then up again on the other side, split by a crystalline blue river that led out to the edge of a large lake. No, that was too big to be a lake. A sea.

Back to the river, bridges crossed it in three places to connect it to the village on the other side. Each bridge was decorated with bright flags waving in the breeze. The whole scene was awash in sun, the azure sky above dotted with only a few fluffy white clouds.

It was like a glimpse into a forgotten time, if the people of that time had all had pointed ears.

She shook her head, not quite believing what she was seeing. "It's like something out of a fairy tale."

He smiled. "Welcome to Summerton."

"Is that the name of the village?"

"That's the name of our kingdom. The one you'd rule over. The village you see is Rivervale."

"Are there other villages?"

"Yes, quite a few."

She looked at him. "Are you from here?"

He shook his head. "I was born in Greenhaven."

She tucked that information away as she took one more glance outside. She turned the carrier so Benny could see out. "Look at that, Benny. Isn't it pretty?"

His little face was pressed to the carrier's grated door. Probably looking for birds.

She nodded at Uldamar that she was ready to go.

He started walking again, turning down another hall and arriving at a set of wide steps that curved to the right. Guards stood on either side. They had swords in their belts but also held long pikes.

"It's my honor to introduce Lady Sparrow Meadowcroft," Uldamar said to them. "She pulled *Merediem* from its stone."

The guards' eyes went wide, and they each went down to one knee, heads bowed.

Uldamar cleared his throat. "She has not yet accepted the crown. You may rise." As they got up, he went on. "She is visiting briefly with us, so please allow her passage as needed."

The guard on the right answered him. "We will, Professor Darkstone."

"Thank you." Uldamar gestured toward the stairs. "Almost there."

Ro started up alongside him. At the top of the stairs was a foyer area that was nearly the size of her apartment. There was a bench nearby, along with a pretty woven rug in blue, turquoise, and purple that covered most of the stone floor. Tapestries covered the walls, and sconces flickered, brightening the space.

Ahead of her were two big metal doors covered in gold filagree and panels of semi-precious stones. The handles were also gold, about a foot in length, and capped at each end with what looked to be enormous black pearls.

Ro's brows went up. "Based on the guards downstairs and the look of this door, this isn't the guest room, is it?"

Uldamar smiled. "It's the royal chambers."

"I'm not sure I should be staying here. It might give people the wrong impression." Like she was accepting the job.

"I promised to show you what your life would be like. Staying in the guest quarters would not accomplish that."

She supposed he had a point there. It still made her feel a bit like an interloper. And slightly bad that she might be giving some of the citizens false hope.

He took hold of a handle and pulled, standing out of the way so she could go ahead of him.

She went through, rolling the carrier behind her. She'd stayed in a beautiful hotel suite once, in Cairo, when she'd been there to speak at a conference about the importance of antiquities and how they reconnected people with the past. She'd thought those rooms could never be topped.

She'd been wrong.

CHAPTER EIGHT

The first room was another foyer, smaller and much more foyer-like, with a side table over which a large mirror hung. More tapestries covered the walls, but ahead of her, an arched entrance led into a sitting room. The floors were tiled with large slabs of translucent ivory stone shot through with veins of coffee brown and gold. Tiny squares of mother of pearl were inlaid at the corners. The effect was such that the floor almost seemed to glow, especially with the natural light pouring in from the banks of windows on the right side.

The two seating areas were both made up of three big overstuffed couches in ivory suede and a pair of large, gilded chairs with tapestry upholstery. In the center was a low, gilded table topped with mother-of-pearl tiles. An enormous fireplace sat against the wall nearby, its hearth in the same stone as the floor, but the mantelpiece was painted a shimmering pearl.

Over the mantel was a portrait of a young man in purple robes and a thick, bejeweled chain, ears as pointed as everyone else she'd seen.

"The late king," Uldamar offered. "May his eternal rest be peaceful."

Ro wanted to know more about him, but that time

would come. She turned to take in the rest of the room and have a look at the view.

Tall, potted palms flanked the windows, which were trimmed with long, white sheers held back by loops of gold satin. The windows were open, letting the breeze drift in.

Ro had never smelled anything so good. It was sweet and floral, and the closest she could recall smelling anything like it before had been in Hawaii, where the plumeria outside her room had made the air as sweet as candy.

"This is beautiful."

Uldamar smiled. "And you've only seen a portion of it."

Chapter Nine

He took her through another set of double doors and down a wide, short hall that angled left. It had a single door on each side and more sconces to light the way. He gestured first to the door on the left. "The royal office, complete with letter-writing desk."

Ro instantly wanted to see that. Desks, especially antique ones, were fascinating and said so much about the people who used them.

Then he pointed to the door on the right. "The royal reading room."

She loved the idea of a reading room. What was the purpose of being royalty if you couldn't have a dedicated reading room? To Ro, that sounded like the ultimate indulgence. One she was completely on board with. She wondered if there was a library to go with it.

Then she wondered something else. Would she be able to borrow some books from it? Reading about this world would no doubt be enthralling. She hesitated. "Is there a library?"

He blinked at her as if the question caught him off guard. "I assure you, the royal library exists and is quite well populated."

She smiled. "I can't wait to see it."

Straight ahead of them was yet another set of double doors. These were dark wood with a simple mother-of-pearl inlay, but their simplicity only added to their beauty. He opened them, flinging them wide. "The private sitting room, beyond which are the royal bedchambers, dressing area, bath, and lounge."

The private sitting room was half the size of the first and decorated in slightly darker shades—warm cream, dusty plum, and soft teal. The fabrics were plush velvets, smooth satins, and silky chenilles. A curved-back lounge near the fireplace looked like a great place to nap. The long couch had ample pillows and a fuzzy, knitted throw over the back of it.

The room was cozy and inviting, but the bedroom beyond had already caught Ro's attention.

She went through, rolling the carrier along. "Look at that bed, Benny."

The bedroom was huge, and so was the bed. It had to be bigger than a standard king. It looked wide enough for four or five people to sleep in. The silk coverlet and pillows were done in the same cream, plum, and teal shades trimmed in velvet ribbons and tassels. The bed had pillars at each corner and silk draperies drawn back to give the sleeper, or sleepers, a full view through the windows across from it.

Those windows were actually doors, she realized. And there was a balcony beyond. A large one, fully furnished with seating areas and more potted plants. She left the carrier and went to the doors, eager to step outside and have a better look.

"Your ladyship," Uldamar said quickly. "If I might show you the rest of the quarters first?"

She hesitated, her hand not quite on the door handle. "Sure." She didn't want to be rude. There would be time to check out the balcony when the tour was done.

It occurred to her that while she might not have a phone signal, her camera still worked. Would they let her take pictures? Or would that be forbidden? She had a feeling she knew the answer.

He smiled. "Very good. The dressing chamber, bath, and dining lounge are right this way."

She left Benny in the carrier and followed Uldamar through a wide arched doorway. There were more potted palms and a dining area with a large table and cushioned chairs in the center of the room, and a chaise lounge against one wall. More windows, too.

On the back wall was a wide, arched opening. There was a small space beyond, then two open doors. On one side was the dressing area, easy to tell by all of the clothes hung on racks along the walls, the big mirror with a platform in front of it, and the island of shelves and drawers.

More shelves lined one wall. Those shelves were filled with hats, shoes, and other accessories. A mix of men and women's things, so there must have been a queen, too.

On the other side was the bath, which seemed to be appointed in the same translucent stone as the first sitting room. Ro squinted. Steam rose off a large body of water visible a few yards in. "Is that a swimming pool?"

"The royal bath, your ladyship." Uldamar led her into the room. "It's fed by our natural hot springs."

"It's the biggest bath I've ever seen." Stone stairs led down into the clear, blue-green water. It reminded her of some of the Roman baths she'd seen. On the edges were three low, wooden benches, one to a side. A stack of fluffy white towels sat at the ready on top of the closest bench, making it seem as if someone was about to arrive for a swim.

He nodded. "Many of our rulers have used it for swimming as well. The fae are very fond of water, and bathing is quite often a shared activity."

There was no smell of chlorine. Her brows went up, imagining the previous king and queen and what kind of shared activities might have gone on here.

Uldamar chuckled. "I can assure you, the nature of this pool and the springs that feed it mean the entire system is thoroughly flushed every eight hours or so. Not to mention, no one has been in this bath in over a century."

She nodded. "That's good to know." Maybe she'd take a dip after all. There was no tub in her tiny apartment, only a stand-up shower. She looked around. There were a few more closed doors along the back wall.

He pointed to the first one. "The royal water closet."

She hoped that meant toilet. There was nothing primitive about this place, but if they were still using animal-drawn carts, outhouses wouldn't be that much of a leap.

Then he pointed to the next. "The royal massage room."

She smiled. "I get it. It's good to be the queen."

Uldamar laughed. "We believe our rulers should be well treated." He pointed to the third door. "The salon."

"You mean beauty parlor type of salon?"

He nodded. "In the king's case, it functioned as the barbershop. The queen tended to use the vanity area."

"These are definitely very royal accommodations." Ro looked around. In the far corner, a good-size litter box had been set up. That made her smile. How had they known? Or had the king and queen had cats? It also made her realize she'd have to explain to Wiggy that things needed to be a little different in that area. "I'm honored to be allowed to stay here."

He bowed. "You're very welcome. If I could show you one more thing …"

He walked over to the countertop where the sink was and touched a thick cord hanging next to it. "You'll see these in all the rooms. One pull and you'll summon a member of the household staff, so if you need anything, that's all you need to do."

"Good to know." She had no intention of using that.

"In the case of residency, the ruler would have a dedicated royal staff and guards that are on constant duty."

Together, they walked back out to the bedroom.

She nodded. Wouldn't that be something? "So the guards in front of the stairs aren't there all the time?"

"No, they are. But when we have a ruler, they often have a personal guard as well. One who's with them all the time."

"Oh. Like a bodyguard?"

"You might say that."

She frowned. "Does the ruler of Summerton really need a personal bodyguard?" She glanced toward the doors and the balcony. "It seems so idyllic here."

He smiled as if trying to reassure her. "It is, very much so, but our ruler's safety isn't something to be shirked or taken for granted. I doubt your president goes anywhere without similar precautions."

"True. That makes sense. But I don't think the Secret Service hang out in his personal quarters."

"The guards stay at the door unless otherwise requested."

Benny meowed.

She looked at Uldamar. "Would it be okay for me to let him out of his carrier? The doors are closed, right?"

"It would be fine, and yes, I closed the doors behind us. He may roam freely."

She unhooked the top carrier, put it on the ground, then crouched next to it to open the door. "All right, Benny boy, go explore. Don't fall into the pool, please."

Cautiously, he took a few steps out, glancing around, nose busy sniffing all the new scents. He came out a little farther and rubbed against her knee.

"Hi, baby. We're just visiting, okay? But I'm sure you'll find lots of interesting things to check out." Ro lowered her voice to a whisper. "Please don't throw up on any of them. Also, that man is Uldamar."

Benny's tail lifted a little higher into the air, and he trotted off toward the dining lounge. She stood up, hoping he didn't decide to poop in any of the potted plants.

He was generally a very well-behaved cat, but in a new environment like this, it was hard to say what he'd do.

"Thank you for the tour. Will my aunt be able to come visit me?"

Uldamar didn't answer right away as if choosing his words. "In the castle? Yes. I am sure that would be fine."

"But it's not standard protocol, is it? I mean, I'm not really your queen, so it would be a little off-book to have someone else visit me here. In the royal chambers."

His expression became slightly tense. "That would not be ... an incorrect reading of the situation. I'm sorry."

"No, it's fine. As long as there's a place we can visit, I'm fine with that."

He exhaled. "Of course."

Soft, pleasant chimes sounded from the other room. She turned. "What's that?"

"Someone at the door. I'll see to it."

"A doorbell. Cool. Thanks." She wasn't sure what she was thanking him for. She wasn't expecting anyone. As he left, she felt the balcony calling her name.

She went over and opened the nearest door. Sun washed the balcony in bright, warm light. She stepped out, inhaling more of the sweet-scented air and taking a good look around. What a gorgeous place to spend time in.

She walked to the railing, also made of stone like the carved balusters holding it up. She put her hands on the sun-warmed stone and closed her eyes for a moment. Bird-song and the distant hum of insects filled the air. Then, faintly, music.

She opened her eyes and looked toward the village. It must be coming from there.

She took her phone out of her pocket and snapped a few quick pictures, then tucked it away again. Her gaze returned to the village. She followed the central river toward the body of water it emptied into. Definitely large enough to be considered a sea. It opened up like a wide vee in the distance, and quite a ways out, there was a good-size island with substantial elevation.

She turned to see where the other side of the sea went.

And saw something she wasn't expecting.

At about the midpoint of the water, the sky turned dark, as did the water beneath it. Fog rose like a wall from that spot, dividing the realm like a curtain.

Through the veil of mist, Ro could make out another castle with a village surrounding it, much like what she imagined this side must look like.

But the entire landscape was bathed in gloom. The castle was built of dark stone, and the structure itself had hard angles, steep peaks, and deliberately crooked lines.

Something about the place sent a chill through her. Maybe because the haunted house-decrepit ruins vibe was instantaneous. Although the castle didn't look dilapidated or decayed. Just creepy.

Uldamar walked out onto the balcony. "Just a house-maid to say tea is ready."

Ro tipped her head toward the land across the sea. "What is that on the other side of the water? Is that part of Summerton?"

He stared toward the dark, misty castle and its

surrounding grounds. He took a deep breath and sighed. "No. Half of the sea is, but that is the home of the Grym Fae."

"What's it called?"

"The water is known as the Whistling Sea." The muscles in his jaw tightened, and his eyes took on a steely glare that held no warmth. "The palace is Castle Hayze, the village surrounding it is Dearth, and the kingdom is known as Malveaux."

Chapter Ten

Queen Anyka Blackbryar stared through the windows of her royal chambers in Castle Hayze and across the Whistling Sea to the disgustingly sunny Kingdom of Summerton and sighed.

Beside her, Zephynia, the Royal Seer, was giving her the same warning she gave Anyka nearly every fortnight. "Mark my words, Your Highness. They are a simmering pot, ready to boil. And when they do, the first goose they will cook is Malveaux."

Anyka reminded herself that patience was sometimes the only way to deal with the well-meaning. "Thank you for your words of advice, Seer."

Behind Anyka, her personal guard, Trog, shifted slightly at his post by the door. He was usually as still as a rock, but he did that sometimes to remind others of his presence. As if a six-and-a-half-foot troll with flaming red hair in a braid down his back could be missed.

Zephynia snorted. "Did you even hear me?"

Anyka nodded. No other member of the royal cabinet would dare speak to her that way. She'd once had the Minister of Goods set adrift on the Boiling Lake for such a thing. But Zephynia was a distant cousin and took liberties. Too many, perhaps. Anyka cut her eyes at the old woman. "I did. I promise."

"But you don't believe me."

Anyka ground her teeth together. She could only take so much. With a single word, she could have Trog remove this old woman from her sight. Or she could summon Nazyr, her Minister of Magic, to turn the crone into a newt.

But Anyka was queen. There was no real need for her to hold her tongue any longer. "You must admit that you've been giving me this same advice for ages. And Summerton has been rulerless for over a century. It's hard to worry much about an enemy that has yet to arrive."

Zephynia frowned. "The day will come when that will no longer be true. Then what? Then we fall because we were not prepared?"

"We are prepared, Seer. I promise you that." Her armies were large and well-practiced, although for certain they were as weary of their exercises as she was of Zephynia's dire predictions. Anyka lifted her head, trying to remember what it felt like to feel the sun on her skin. She pulled her robes closer. Castle Hayze never lost its chill. "Your diligence will not go unrewarded."

"The only reward I seek is the safety of our kingdom."

Anyka made herself smile. The expression didn't always come off as comforting or pleasant, but she tried. "I wish you a good day."

Zephynia, knowing she'd been dismissed, let out a,

"Hmph," and waddled off to wherever it was she roosted when not sharing her insight into the future.

Anyka rested her hands on the windowsill. Frost bloomed in the corners of the glass. She closed her eyes. For all of Zephynia's predicting and foretelling, there was one thing the old woman had never seen.

Just how bone-deep tired Anyka was of being queen.

She'd been raised from birth with one goal in mind—her ascendance to the Malveauxian throne. She'd just never imagined it would be hers the same day she turned sixteen.

A party had been given in her honor, a party the entire kingdom had been invited to celebrate. Work had been halted, stores closed, parades marched. All in honor of Princess Anyka.

What a black day that had been. In the midst of the celebration, her father, King Lyonus, and mother, Queen Arylias, had been murdered with deadly fire lily tincture, a well-known Summerton poison.

Anyka had survived only because her parents had drunk first of the wine meant to toast Anyka's birthday. The captain of the Royal Guard, Sebastyan, had knocked the cup from her hand as she'd lifted it to her lips.

She smiled. She'd married that brave young man. Her smile faded. And now he was seventeen years gone as well.

She still saw him in the eyes of their only child, Princess Beatryce. And it was for Beatryce's sake that Anyka remained on the throne. If Anyka abdicated, Beatryce would either have to take her place or fight off any contender who wished it for themselves. Either way, it was not a life Anyka wished for her daughter.

Beatryce had yet to be hardened by the world they lived in. And Anyka liked it that way. Better she stay soft and sweet and kind than be forever tarnished by her birthright.

And so Anyka ruled with the iron fist and steel spine and sharp blade that had given her the reputation of being Malveaux's Evil Queen.

She didn't mind. Much. It didn't keep her from being pursued by suitors, but she had no trust in any man who thought he could tame her. Her gut, something she'd come to rely on over the decades, always felt that any man who came after her wanted one thing and one thing only.

Her throne.

And as tired as she might be of it, that seat was still her power. She'd not give it up for any man. Not when it was the one thing that kept her and Beatryce alive.

Because the moment she was deposed, she had no doubt death would come for her, and possibly Beatryce, in some form.

Her enemies were spread far and wide.

But she was so very bored of ruling. Some days she thought the dull routine might drive her mad. She stared across the water at Summerton again. Maybe someday their prophesied ruler would come, and then, as the Malveaux prophecies claimed, the Grym throne would be overtaken.

She laughed. They could try. And she might actually

welcome such an event. It would give her a means of venting the lingering anger over her parents' deaths.

And then, when Summerton's ruler had done his best, Anyka would strike and steal the royal sword and crown herself queen of both kingdoms. The Radiant Fae would rue what they'd done to her parents. She'd see to that.

Someday.

Wings fluttered behind her. Anyka brushed her braids back and tipped her head to the side as Galwyn, her raven, alighted on her shoulder.

Today was not that day.

Of course, there was always the chance another of the prophesies would come true and the sister kingdoms of the Radiant and Grym Fae would be brought back together as one, the great rift between them healed.

Sure. That would happen. She couldn't imagine a ruler who would be able to do that.

She drew her hand through the air, casting her magic toward the sea. The mist darkened, blocking the sight of Summerton. Enough of that.

Farther below, in the village of Dearth, lights flickered on. Lanterns being lit. Magic being sparked to illuminate what was left of the day.

She exhaled in relief as she reached up to pet Galwyn's silken feathers. "How are you, my pet?"

He bent his head and leaned into her. She smiled. "I missed you, too. Should we go back to work?"

Galwyn cawed softly, a throaty sound that made her smile widen.

She returned to her desk. There were missives to

answer. Requests from citizens of the realm. Occasionally, some from the farthest lands, where the trolls and goblins and gnomes lived.

She sat and studied the stack of scrolls and letters awaiting her reply. With a weary sigh, she plucked one from the top and opened it.

The trolls wished to send a delegation the following month to be certain their peace treaty remained strong. Had it been a year already? She guessed it had been. "Scribe!"

Trog was only part troll, something no one could mistake by looking at his thick neck, broad build, and height. He would never be a scholar, but as a guard, he excelled.

Her scribe, Chyles, came in a few moments later. "At your service, Your Highness."

"Letters to answer."

He nodded and took his place at the small desk adjacent to hers, dipping his quill in ink and positioning it over a length of parchment.

First, she looked at Trog. She trusted him about as much as she trusted anyone, but no one was privy to the crafting of her correspondence. "Wait in the hall."

He grunted and left his post to guard the door from the other side.

She reread the letter from the trolls' Minister of Peace, then dictated to Chyles, "To Frugel Strongmouth. Dearest Minister, your request to meet next month is agreeable. I look forward to being reminded of why our peace accord remains in my best interest. Regards."

Chyles nodded, his quill flying over the paper as she spoke. He was smiling.

She knew he enjoyed his job, although she wasn't entirely sure why. Perhaps he liked being so close to the seat of power? Or perhaps it was because he'd only recently been elevated to this position. In a few more months, the smile could be gone.

He rolled a blotter over the parchment, then stood and presented it to her for her signature.

She took her quill and scrawled her name across the bottom. "Why do you smile when you work?"

He blinked, and the smile vanished. Perhaps he'd been unaware of his own expression?

"My work is pleasant."

She sat back and narrowed her eyes. "Is that it? Pleasant work?"

He chewed at his bottom lip.

"You're in no trouble, Chyles. You do good work. I have no complaints. I am merely curious." There were downsides to being so fearfully respected.

"I would never speak a word of what goes on here, your grace, but in truth ..." He looked at her like he was trying to be sure that's what she wanted. Truth.

She did. "Go on."

"I am well aware that this position is likely the highest I will ever rise in my career, but I am grateful for it every day. I am front and center to your rule, and it is"—he licked his lips—"exciting."

She smiled. "I'm glad you take such delight in your

work." She studied him a moment longer. "Are you afraid of me?"

He hesitated. "I do not fear you, because I have no reason to, but I respect you greatly and understand the power you wield is absolute. I serve at your pleasure, therefore, I am always mindful that what is best for you is best for me."

What a cunning answer. Her appreciation for him increased. "You may go further than you think."

CHAPTER ELEVEN

Ro nodded, understanding the Grym Fae were not the best friends of the Radiant Fae, even if she didn't know why. "I see. That's Malveaux. Are the Grym Fae enemies then?"

Uldamar tore his gaze from the increasing darkness across the water. It was nearly impossible to see the kingdom now. "Yes. But things didn't start that way. We were once sister kingdoms. Citizens came and went between the two without a thought. We traded goods, built ships together, worked in tandem."

"Interesting."

He shook his head. "That was centuries ago, though."

She leaned against the railing. "What happened?"

He shrugged. "What always happens when there is power in the mix. Accusations, broken promises, hurt feelings, betrayal, pride, greed ..."

His gaze seemed far away. Lost in the history of that time, maybe?

Ro could respect that. History often made her lose her place in reality.

He smiled as he came back to her. "My apologies." He waved his hand near his head. "My mind wanders at times."

"No apology needed. I get it."

"Once upon a time, Summerton was ruled by a queen, Malveaux by a king. Neither were married, but they became acquainted because of their positions. They fell in love. Their marriage was considered the ultimate joining of the two kingdoms."

He gestured toward the wide stone bridge that crossed the sea. "They each walked across that bridge and met in the middle, where their vows were said. The shores on both sides were crowded with citizens. At the time, their wedding day was spoken of as the most important day in the history of our realm."

He laughed bitterly. "Now, it is referred to as the beginning of the end."

"Why?"

"The queen gave birth to twin boys, but the midwife lost track of which had been born first. There was no way to know. A decision was made that when the day came, the kingdoms would be ruled separately. So a coin was flipped and an eldest chosen. He went on to rule his father's kingdom, and the second son ruled Summerton."

Ro let out a little sound of understanding as the picture took shape. "But one who'd been chosen as the eldest thought he should have had both."

Uldamar nodded. "Sibling rivalry reared its ugly head."

She stared out at Malveaux, what little of it she could see. "And things have never been the same again."

"No. They've grown worse, actually."

"Why is that side so dark?"

"Legend says the brother that took Malveaux's throne

traded his soul for power in an ancient black magic ritual in an attempt to overthrow his brother. He failed, but what you see is the result of his sinister exchange."

That gave her a little shiver. And another thought. She had a feeling the sword in the stone was part of this. "Where does *Merediem* fit in?"

"That is a story unto itself. Another time, perhaps? Tea is ready, and your aunt is waiting."

"Oh! I had no idea. Yes, another time." Maybe she'd find some books in the library that would give her a history lesson. "Lead the way, then."

"My pleasure."

As they went back inside, Ro started to laugh. Benny was in the middle of the enormous bed, one foot stretched overhead as he groomed the fur on his belly. "Benny, I'm not sure the royal bed is the best place for your bath."

Uldamar chuckled. "He's fine. It's nice to see life in these old chambers again."

Ro shook her head all the same. But at least he wasn't running the halls of the castle like Wiggy probably was. Ro left the apartment and went down the steps with Uldamar. "Any news on Mrs. Wigglesworth?"

"Nothing yet, but I'll check after I see you to the conservatory."

"Thank you."

The conservatory was a large sunroom at the back of the castle. Beyond it were the private gardens, which looked spectacular. Ro would have loved to go out and explore them, but nothing really mattered except seeing her aunt.

Violet smiled as Ro walked in. "Hello again, my beautiful girl."

"Aunt Vi!" Ro hugged her again, still in disbelief that her aunt was alive and well. "I'm so glad you're here."

A lovely round table had been arranged in the shade of a few potted palms. Gold utensils and iridescent ivory china dressed the two place settings. Uldamar stepped aside as footmen came forward to pull out chairs for Ro and Violet. They took their seats, smoothing cloth napkins over their laps.

"Your ladyship, Madam Meadowcroft," Uldamar said. "I will leave you to your repast." He bowed, then looked at Ro. "I shall return with any news I glean."

"Thank you." Ro smiled across the table at her aunt. "I brought my two cats with me. Crossing through caused one of them to turn human. Or fae. Not completely sure about that yet. Anyway, it apparently happens sometimes. She broke out of her carrier, as you can imagine, and took off down the castle hall." Ro leaned forward. "She smelled rodents."

Violet laughed. "I'm not sure I hope she catches one."

"Me, either."

Violet sipped her water. "I never thought I'd see the day I became Madam Meadowcroft, but evidently that's what happens when your niece could potentially be queen."

Ro smirked. Violet didn't seem to mind the new title too much.

Two housemaids entered. One pushed a wheeled tea trolley, laden with sweets and sandwiches and steaming pots. The trolley was draped with white linen, and the handles were gold. The maids stopped tableside and curtsied.

Ro's stomach grumbled. The doughnut she'd had earlier, combined with the one she'd had for breakfast, were long gone.

"My," Violet said. "Doesn't that look lovely?" She was all smiles. "I've never had tea in the palace before. But then, I suppose not many people have."

One of the housemaids put a four-tiered stand of the same iridescent ivory china trimmed with a thin band of metallic lavender on the table. Each tier held finger sandwiches. Another four-tiered stand was added beside it, this one all sweets.

"Your ladyship," began one of the maids. "We have three kinds of tea. Sweet flower, iced clover, and spice bark."

Ro looked at her aunt. "What do you suggest?"

"Think chamomile, mint, and cinnamon," Violet answered. "Not entirely the same, but close proximities."

Ro nodded to the maid who'd offered. "Iced clover, please."

"The same for me," Violet said.

Tea was poured. Sugar and honey were added to the table.

Then the trolley's drapes were lifted to reveal the interior shelf, and three small but elaborately decorated cakes were brought out and displayed on the trolley's now mostly empty top.

The maids curtsied again and disappeared off to a far corner of the room.

Ro picked up the tongs and helped herself to a few of the sandwiches. "Do you know what all of these are?"

"Some things have different names here, but they taste the same. Those two on brown bread are slipper fish, which tastes just like tuna. The one on white bread is water gourd, or as you know it, cucumber. Much of the fruit and vegetables go by the fae name *and* the human name. Probably because of people like me, who end up here after what we thought was a lifetime in the mortal world. Anyway, if you ask for a tomato sandwich, you'll get a tomato sandwich."

Ro picked up one of the little sandwiches and took a bite. It was exactly like tuna and very tasty. "What was that like? Ending up here after … you know."

"Dying?" Violet said with a smile. "It was like being in a dream at first. I couldn't believe it was real."

"I feel the same way."

Violet laughed. "I suppose you do. But I adjusted pretty quickly. It's beautiful here. Like paradise."

Ro nodded. "What I've seen from the windows and the balcony has been like a painting of another time and place."

"Wait until you get into the village. It'll remind you very much of old England, but then, there are more fae in that country than anywhere else in the mortal world, so it makes sense. Apparently, the British Isles have the most fae portals and the very first one ever used. The fae have been traveling there for ages."

Ro thought about that. "It's making me wonder how many old fairy tales were really historical accounts."

Violet smiled, then leaned forward. "Fairy tales is fine, but don't call the fae fairies. They don't like it. It's a bit of a derogatory term, to be honest."

"Good to know. Now that I am one." Ro snorted. "Which I still can't fathom."

Violet's brows arched as she picked up a pink-iced triangle of cake. "Apparently, we come from a long line of them."

"Any Grym in our blood?"

Violet shuddered. "I hope not. But in all likelihood, there is. The two lines are more mixed than anyone likes to talk about, but you can see the signs everywhere. In the magic people can do. In the slope of their ears. Or the way they say certain words."

"It'll be a long time before I pick up on those things." Ro had eaten three sandwiches so far without making much of a dent in her appetite. She added a couple more to her plate.

Violet pointed her fork at the selections Ro had just made. "Cold roast venison and pork pate."

"Thanks."

Violet took a little tart in a paper cup off the sweet platter. The tart was filled with tiny red fruits the size of peas. Currants or grapes, maybe. "Are you really not going to take the throne?"

Ro finished the bite she'd just taken. "I don't see how I can. What about my job and JT?"

"Sweetheart, I know being queen would be a tremendous responsibility, but I do believe you're comparing apples to kumquats here."

89

"Aunt Vi, I'm going to be named curator on Monday."

"Oh, that's marvelous. I'm so happy for you! It's about time they recognized your work. I imagine you're making a tremendous amount of money then. Good for you."

Ro sighed. "It's not that much money, unfortunately."

Violet got a sly look in her eyes. "Summerton is a very wealthy kingdom. After all, they've had over a century with no ruler on the throne. I imagine they've had to build new vaults just to store all the gold that's not been spent."

Ro smiled. "I get it. Being queen would pay well."

"It's more than that, my darling. You would want for nothing. You would live a lifestyle previously unknown or unimagined."

"The royal apartment is pretty posh."

"And just think, you've yet to see the Winter Lodge or the Summer Palace."

Ro blinked. "There are other royal homes?"

"My dear." Violet shook her head. "I've never been to the Summer Palace, but from what I've heard, the walls are painted in pearl dust, the doorknobs are diamonds, and the floors are tiled in gold. It was the inspiration for Versailles. Or so they say."

Ro knew that had to be an exaggeration, but still. It was pretty intriguing. "Okay, so being queen is a better job. But that still doesn't account for JT."

Violet smiled and sipped her tea. "That's easy, dear. Bring him with you."

CHAPTER TWELVE

R o shook her head. "I don't know about that."

"You don't think he'd want to come?" Violet nibbled on a cookie no bigger than a quarter. The pale treat was flecked with pink zest.

Sandwiches gone and hunger mostly abated, Ro took one of the cookies for herself. It tasted like grapefruit shortbread, sweet and tangy with the kind of sandy texture that melted in her mouth. It was something she could easily imagine eating every day. "These are really good."

"You're changing the subject."

Ro smiled. She hadn't intended to, but she supposed she had all the same. "I think he loves the city and his life there too much to leave it. Not to mention he's got a pretty serious girlfriend who he's living with. A young woman named Jeanine. He definitely won't leave her." Ro didn't love Jeanine. She was a little too concerned with money for Ro's taste, but she wasn't about to tell JT that. "And all for a place he probably won't believe is real."

"Maybe that's so. But he could love life here, too. And find a new girlfriend."

"I'm sure he could." Ro rolled her eyes at Violet's suggestion. She just wasn't sure what JT would think of this place. If he even believed her when she told him about it.

"And if he decided not to come, you could still visit him. And he could visit you."

"I suppose." Ro hadn't considered that. But she didn't love that idea. What if JT and Jeanine got married and had kids? Did she really want to live a world away from them?

"Take the throne, Sparrow. You were obviously meant to. How else was it possible for you to remove that sword?"

Ro said nothing for a moment and just thought about what it would mean to actually become queen. Her as queen? Really? It seemed too fantastical to be possible. "Aunt Vi, I love that you think so highly of me and my abilities, but I wasn't exactly brought up to be royalty."

"Who is? You can learn."

"Sure, I could learn the protocol and the etiquette and all that, but what about the actual ruling part? I'm no diplomat. I don't have any kind of training in running a country. I can't even fathom what that would entail."

"The board of directors thinks you know enough to run the museum, don't they?"

"Yes, but that's different."

"Is it? Don't you deal with people and priceless objects?"

"Yes, but—"

"Don't you travel to other countries and meet with bigwigs to discuss the lending and borrowing of valuable artifacts?"

Ro pursed her lips. Her aunt was far too versed in the

job of assistant curator. "Yes. But you know very well it's not the same thing."

"What I know is that it's not so different." Violet leaned back, the set of her jaw a sure sign she wasn't about to let this go. "When you were a little girl, you used to solve all the problems on the playground, you know that? You were *known* for it. Even the kids knew it. Do you remember that time when Danny Hinkleman and Joey Fratelli came to see you so you could decide which one of them ought to have the Reggie Jackson baseball card?"

Ro laughed softly at the memory. "Yes, I do."

"Being queen wouldn't be that much different. The baseball cards may have changed, but the problems remain the same."

"You present a compelling case," Ro admitted.

Violet smiled. "And I haven't even started on how we'd get to see each other all of the time."

Ro nodded. "You didn't have to. It's been on my mind since I got here." She sighed. Could she really give this opportunity up? It was a once-in-a-lifetime chance in the most rare and unique way possible.

Queen Sparrow Meadowcroft.

She narrowed her eyes. "Say, if I were to become queen, what would that make you? Would you get a title besides Madam Meadowcroft?"

"I'd become a lady, I believe. Might make the bakery a little more popular. Not that it isn't doing just fine as it is." Violet was eying the cakes on the trolley. Suddenly, she looked back at Ro. "But JT would be a prince. Oh, Prince James Thoreau. Has a nice ring to it, don't you think?"

Ro hadn't considered that JT would earn a title, too. "That might appeal to him. Or he might think it's ridiculous and want nothing to do with it." Sort of how part of her felt. "Hard to tell with him sometimes."

"Maybe don't lead with that, then," Aunt Vi said. "What do you think about a slice of that coconut cake?"

"Looks good. Although I can't believe you still have room for that after all the sweets you ate."

Violet gave her a look. "I'm in the palace. I'm going to taste everything I can to see how their baker stacks up against me. Who knows? I might even pick up a few ideas. Those grapefruit butter cookies are definitely going to be on the menu."

Ro laughed. "Tell me about your shop. How did you end up with it?"

Violet sliced into the cake. "The work ethic here is very strong. Everyone contributes in some way. Although fledglings are given some time to adjust. The baker where I went to buy my bread was hiring, so I took the job. She and her husband moved to another village two years ago to be closer to their grandkids and offered me the chance to buy them out. I took it."

"Wow. That's very cool."

Violet looked proud. "I have three employees. One is a fledgling, like me. That's what they call those of us who arrive here for the first time."

"Would I be a fledgling?"

"No. You didn't die to get here. You'd be considered a crossover, I think. There are also prodigals, although that usually refers to fae born here who go to the mortal world for a long period before coming home again. Yes, you're probably a crossover, dear." She put a slice of the cake on Ro's plate, then a slice on her own.

Ro shrugged. "I'm sure someone will tell me. If I were to move here, I'd have so much to learn."

"That you would."

As Ro picked up her fork, Uldamar returned. He bowed as he reached the table. "Mrs. Wigglesworth has been found. Safe and sound, I might add."

Ro sighed in relief. "That's good."

"Mrs. Wigglesworth?" Aunt Violet looked confused.

"The cat I was telling you about that got transformed coming through the portal." Ro smiled. "I adopted her with that name." She looked at Uldamar again. "Where was she?"

"Asleep in the pantry, I'm afraid. The only damage seemed to be to a large container of dried fish flakes."

Ro made a face. "What are those used for?"

Violet answered. "Broth. Soup. Things like that. Quite tasty, too."

Uldamar clasped his hands in front of him. "If you'd like, I can have a guard carry her up to your quarters."

"Thank you. That would be fine. Then she'll be contained at least." Although now that Wiggy had opposable thumbs, what was to keep her from getting out of the royal rooms?

He nodded. "I'll see to it."

He bowed again and left.

Violet watched him go, her fork poised midair with a

bite of uneaten cake on it, a certain curious look in her eyes.

Ro studied her aunt and smiled. "You like him."

Violet blinked. "What? Who? No, I do not. I might find him handsome. A little. It's hard not to be intrigued by a man with that much power. But that's the end of it."

Ro nodded, unconvinced. "Sure. Is that because you're already involved with someone else?"

"I am well occupied with my bakery, thank you very much." Violet ate her forkful of cake. After a moment, she swallowed. "I do believe my coconut cake is better. This is very good, don't get me wrong, but the cake is just the slightest bit dry, don't you think?"

Still amused by Violet's reaction to Uldamar and the sudden change of subject, Ro nodded. "Just the slightest bit."

"What are you doing after we finish up here?"

"I don't think there's anything planned." Ro turned to look through the conservatory's glass walls. "What I'd like to do is walk in that garden. It looks amazing."

"I'd love to do that, too," Violet said. "As a commoner, I can tell you that being in the palace is a real treat."

"Then a walk in the garden is exactly what we'll do," Ro said.

CHAPTER THIRTEEN

Anyka set her cup of buca root tea down on its saucer and smiled at her daughter. Beatryce had become such a beautiful young woman. "How was your day?"

Bea smiled back. "Fine."

"Still working on that watercolor?"

Bea nodded and helped herself to a slice of carrot bread. "I am. I was thinking about sponsoring an art show. I wouldn't compete, of course. That would be unfair. But I would be happy to help judge. What do you think?"

Anyka nodded. "It sounds like a wonderful idea."

Bea smiled and tucked a strand of blue-black hair behind one ear. "Thank you."

Anyka sensed her daughter had more on her mind. Her smile seemed tense. "Is there something else you wanted to talk about?"

Bea shook her head and broke off a tiny piece of the carrot bread.

In the gentlest voice Anyka could manage, she said, "Please don't lie to me, Bea. I'm your mother. If you can't talk to me, who can you talk to?"

Bea nodded but had yet to look up. "I want ... more."

"More what?"

Bea sighed and lifted her head to stare out toward the sea visible beyond the solarium.

Such an absurd name for a room that got no sun.

"More of something. Anything." She finally looked at her mother. "Nothing I do matters. How many watercolors can I paint? How many samplers can I stitch? How many horseback riding lessons or fencing classes or language courses can I take? None of it will make a difference. I have a dressing room full of gowns, a vault full of jewels, and for what purpose? I am nearly thirty, and I have no real friends. No one I can trust."

Anyka arched a brow. "No one?"

"No one outside of you," Bea clarified.

Anyka felt for her child. "I understand, but—"

"I don't think you do. With all respect, Mother, you have a kingdom to rule. I have an afternoon class in making ribbon flowers." Bea frowned. "I want more."

Anyka really did understand. If Bea was anyone else, she'd have a husband and children by now. Close friends. A life of meaningful engagement. But she was First Daughter of Malveaux, the heir to the Grym throne, and that heritage had given her a very different life.

Anyka forced a smile. "I really do understand."

Bea was staring at her food again. This time, the carrot bread remained untouched. She looked utterly miserable. "I appreciate the sentiment, but I'm not sure you can. You have a life. You have a purpose."

"My darling, you have a purpose."

Bea looked up. "To one day marry a man who will bring our kingdom a choice ally and greater power?"

"You know I have never—"

"I know." Bea held up her hands. "But you cannot deny that such a thing might happen someday."

Anyka couldn't, so she stayed quiet.

"I might as well," Bea said. "There's no line of suitors at my door waiting to be turned away."

Nor would there be so long as Anyka headed them off first, although lately, there had been fewer and fewer requests for Princess Beatryce's hand. It took a very brave and confident man to want Anyka for a mother-in-law.

Although the lure of the Grym throne was still worth it for a few daring souls. None of whom Anyka had yet found remotely acceptable.

She straightened the fork beside her plate, her appetite greatly diminished by her daughter's unhappiness. "What can I do to help, my darling?"

There was almost nothing Anyka wouldn't do to make her only child happy. No lengths too far, no cost too great.

"There's no point in asking," Bea said. "I know you won't allow what I want."

Anyka frowned. "You don't know until you ask. What is it?"

Beatryce lifted her head, looked straight into her mother's eyes and made her request. "I want to spend my summer at Willow Hall."

Anyka opened her mouth to respond, then closed it again, as she had no immediate answer. "Willow Hall."

Bea nodded.

Willow Hall was the fae Summer Palace. A grand, sprawling manor house that had once been shared by both fae kingdoms. It sat on Celestial Lake, named for the way the water reflected the stars. The palace was surrounded by acres and acres of gorgeous grounds. But after the great divide, Willow Hall had stopped being a place the Grym felt welcome.

"No Grym has been to Willow Hall in centuries."

"I know," Bea said with more than a little defiance in her voice. "But there's no rule against it, is there?"

"No." It had just been understood that with the rift between the two kingdoms, such a joint undertaking would only lead to strife. The Grym had simply stopped attending. Anyka imagined the Radiant had welcomed that acquiescence.

No doubt, they had continued to make their annual pilgrimages there. Or perhaps they didn't. Anyka wasn't sure. She'd never bothered finding out, either. The Summer Palace just hadn't registered as that important. In part, she supposed, because she'd never been there herself. Heard tales of it. Been curious at one point in her life, but that had been a long time ago.

"You realize it might be full of Radiant Fae."

Bea shrugged. "And what will they do? Refuse to speak to me? Or, worse, try to befriend me for what it might benefit them? I am used to both here."

"Why do you want to go?"

Bea's lids fluttered, the near act of rolling her eyes. "For a change of scenery. To experience sun for once in my life. And for the rare chance that just maybe I might do something different with my days. It's only three months."

"You would go for the entire season?" Anyka pulled

back slightly. Three months without her daughter? Anyka shook her head. "You'd have to take an entire contingent of guards and valets and housemaids ..."

"Other than my lady's maid, I don't need any staff. I don't want to make some complicated royal event out of it. I just want to go and *be*. No one will care."

Did she honestly think that? "Out of the question. It's too great an ask, Beatryce. Too *big* of a risk. I'm sorry."

A storm cloud descended over Beatryce's lovely face. Her ice-blue eyes went stony, her mouth hard. She lifted the napkin from her lap, folded it and laid it over her plate. "I knew you would deny me."

"It's too great an ask."

"I am an *adult*." Beatryce's voice wavered. "I did not ask to be a princess, I did not ask for this life, and it is suffocating me and you do not care."

"That's not—"

Beatryce abruptly stood. "I have a class in making ribbon flowers I must attend. If you'll excuse me." Without waiting for an answer, she strode away from the table.

Anyka sighed and stared out the windows. The sea was dark and churning, capped with white. Her heart ached for her child, but Bea had to understand what a dangerous thing she wanted to do.

She would be completely vulnerable at Willow Hall, surrounded by Radiant Fae. There was no telling what might happen. Even with guards around her.

The very idea that she might go to the Summer Palace without guards was laughable. The fact that Beatryce even thought that could happen was also slightly worrying. Had

Anyka shielded her too much? Perhaps. But in Beatryce's own words, she was an adult.

Had the time come to show her what it was really like to rule Malveaux? Anyka wasn't sure. That felt like a door that, once opened, could not be closed again.

She hoped Bea would understand, and perhaps in time she would. Until then, no doubt Anyka would be given the silent treatment or the cold shoulder or some equivalent punishment. Whatever it was, she would take it without complaint.

Better to have a daughter who ignored her than a daughter who'd lost her life to the enemy because she wanted to spend her summer in a distant palace, cavorting with the very ones who wanted to do her harm.

And while that understanding should have been a comfort, Anyka's heart and mind remained unsettled. Something told her that this would not be the end of things with Beatryce.

If Anyka didn't find a way to distract her daughter, Beatryce would find her own way. She was too headstrong and tenacious to do anything else.

Such was the downfall of raising a child who was just like you.

CHAPTER FOURTEEN

The gardens outdid anything Ro had seen before. They were lush and intricate and full of plants new to her. Some were familiar, but some, like the white and purple variegated leaf vine with tiny pink flowers that smelled like honey, were a complete revelation.

Around every turn, she saw something new. The trees were tall enough in some places to provide a canopied walkway. Hanging baskets had been added to some of the branches, and more shade-loving plants grew around the trunks. The pathway was paved with a stone and shell mosaic. Small glass jars hung from knee-high shepherd's hooks along the route. Each one held a little greenery with a white flower that glowed with a soft light.

"What are those?" Ro asked. "I've never seen a flower that glows."

"Heaven's stars," Aunt Violet answered. "They're an air plant. Aren't they marvelous? I have them in the garden at my cottage."

"You have a cottage?" Ro laughed. "I mean, obviously, you must live somewhere. It just hadn't occurred to me that it would be a cottage. What's it like?"

"I love it. It's small, two bedrooms, one bathroom, a

little kitchen, and a living room. I have a table and chairs in the garden, too, which is where I usually have my dinner. You should come visit."

"I want to. Definitely."

Violet smiled. "I will do my best to stay up as long as possible. I hate to tell you this, but it's nearly my bedtime. I get up pretty early to make my breads and pastries."

"I bet you do. How about I come by for a quick peek but then visit your shop again tomorrow before I head back to the city?"

"You can come by my shop anytime." Aunt Vi fell silent for a moment. "Have you given any more thought to what you're going to do?"

"You mean about becoming queen, I know."

Aunt Violet nodded. "Yes."

"I haven't. I keep waiting for the right answer to come to me. Not sure it will, though."

"Maybe talking to JT will help."

"I'm sort of hoping it might." She hooked her arm through Violet's. "I wish you could come back with me and see him. He cried for a week when you passed. Totally inconsolable." They both had been. Aunt Violet had been a huge part of their lives.

"That poor boy." Violet sniffed. "After the joy of realizing my life was not over, I nearly sank into a depression knowing I'd never see you two again. I knew you'd take good care of him, but I also knew I was missing out on so many milestones of his life that had yet to come."

Ro welled up a little herself. "You were the best mother

to me I could have hoped for and the best grandmother to him."

Tears streaked Violet's cheeks. She pulled a handkerchief from the pocket of her dress and wiped her face. "Now you've done it."

Ro laughed, which helped her to not cry. "I guess someday my mother will show up here, hmm? She'll probably love this place."

Violet nodded. "She'll love it until she realizes she can't go back. Sheridan won't like that. She never did like being told what to do. Or doing what was expected of her. Sherry always had a problem with authority."

Ro hadn't heard her mother called by her real name in some time.

Violet cut her eyes at Ro. "When's the last time you talked to her?"

"It's been a while." Ro actually couldn't remember.

Violet frowned. "Did she come to my funeral? How was my funeral?"

"Yes, she came." Had that been the last time Ro had seen and talked to her mother? That had been ten years ago. Was that possible? She thought back. It actually might be. "Your funeral was well-attended. I bet there were three hundred people there."

"No!" Violet's eyes were sparkling again. "Was Aldus Feeney there? Did he cry? You know, I always thought he was sweet on me even if I was a few years older than him."

"He was there, and he looked weepy." Ro couldn't really remember if he'd cried or not, but then, who hadn't? And there was no harm in amusing Aunt Vi.

"I knew it," Violet said, grinning. "He might be fae. I wouldn't be surprised if he showed up here someday." She shook her head, slightly off in her own world.

Ro could hear water. They took the curve in the path and came to a pond. Half of it was shaded by trees, but the other half was in the sun. A bench under one of the trees beckoned. "Let's sit a minute."

"Fine by me," Violet said.

As they sat, pale shapes began to appear under the water. Ro leaned forward. "Look at those white fish. They're huge." They gleamed like pearls.

Violet pressed her hands together before her. "Those are the late king's ghost arakoo. His famous white carp. I think they were a gift from ... oh, I can't remember. Anyway, I've seen them on exhibition but never in their natural habitat."

"Are they pets? Or for dinner?"

Violet laughed. "Pets. The last king was crazy about them." Violet made a face. "And also actually crazy."

"What?" Ro leaned back. "Tell me more."

"I only know bits and pieces. Although Mrs. Fernbridge is a pretty good source of gossip if I get enough dandelion wine into her."

"Well, tell me what you do know."

"I will, but I can't vouch for its veracity."

Ro nodded. "Understood."

"The last king of Summerton, a man named Reedly Haythorne, had been on the throne for about fifty years when his wife, the queen, got very sick. Nothing the doctors tried made any difference. She got worse every day until she finally died. The professors all did their best to figure out what happened to her, and they came to the conclusion that she was poisoned."

Ro grimaced. "That's awful."

"It gets worse," Violet said, finger in the air. "Over the next three months, his son and daughter, the prince and princess, also died in the very same way. Two of the royal tasters died as well."

"Oh, no."

Violet nodded. "It was a very slow-acting poison, apparently. One that it seems could only be found in the Kingdom of Malveaux."

"So they were murdered?"

Violet shrugged. "Nothing could be proven. But the grief was more than the king could bear. He became obsessed with revenge. Two weeks later, the king and queen of Malveaux died at their only daughter's birthday party after drinking poisoned wine."

Ro gasped. "Haythorne killed them?"

Violet shrugged again. "I'm sure he didn't do it himself. He had someone else do the dirty work. He was the king, after all. But from the stories I've heard, he confessed to it. And the queen's mother confessed to making the poison."

"That's awful. All around."

"That's how the sword got in the stone."

"What? Explain."

Violet leaned in closer. "Uldamar was the First Professor of Magic back then, too."

"So I heard. How old is that guy?"

Violet laughed. "No one knows."

"Back to the sword."

"Right." Aunt Vi tapped a finger against her chin. "Where was I?"

"Uldamar."

"Oh, yes. He was the First Professor of Magic under King Reedly. And in an attempt to keep the Malveauxians from retaliating, he sank the royal sword into the stone and declared the Summerton throne would remain empty until someone with a kind heart, strong spirit, and an understanding mind could pull it free. Only then would Summerton have another ruler."

"And the Malveauxians were all right with that?"

"I guess so. There's been a tense peace between the two kingdoms since then. From what I know. But I'm sure they were busy with their own grief and their new teenage queen."

Ro stared out at the pond. How hard would that have been, to lose both your parents and then also have to take over the running of the kingdom? "That would be a much harder way to end up as queen than pulling a sword out of a stone."

Violet nodded. "It would. It's funny, but I think about that young girl quite often. Of course, she's not young anymore. But what a trial to go through. I wonder how she turned out."

"Probably bitter and angry," Ro said. "But maybe not."

Violet looked at her. "Are you bitter and angry that your mother turned you over to me and that you never knew your father?"

Ro smiled. "No, I'm not. I got you, didn't I?"

Violet smiled back. "Thank you."

Ro put her arm around her aunt's shoulders. "Thank *you*. You gave me a fantastic life."

Violet patted Ro's knee. "You did the same for me. I didn't know how I was going to raise a baby at my age, but I did. And having you in my house, and in my arms, reminded me of how much good there was left in the world."

Ro looked at her aunt. "You make it sound like you were going through something."

Violet nodded. "I was. I was in a bit of a dark place mentally. Then Sherry showed up with this gorgeous pink creature wrapped in a blanket and said she needed some time to get her head together and could I watch you?"

Violet let out a deep sigh. "I knew she wouldn't be back for a long time. I didn't want to take you in. You were *her* responsibility. But I'd known that child since she was born, and she'd never followed through on anything a day in her life. Leaving you with her seemed a far greater sin."

"You didn't want me?" Ro laughed at her aunt's confession. "I don't blame you. A baby is a lot of work."

"It wasn't because of you. It was because of me. I'd started to think I was past my prime. No good for anything anymore. I'd realized that, to the world around me, I had become invisible."

Ro understood exactly how her aunt had been feeling. She'd begun to feel the same way a couple of years ago. Invisible. She reached down and picked up a few of the acorns lying in the dirt around the bench. They were smaller than regular acorns, and the shell was more blue-green than khaki green. She tossed one into the fishpond. "You were having a midlife crisis."

Aunt Violet nodded.

"No wonder you didn't want a baby." She tossed another acorn. "But I'm so glad you changed your mind."

"So am I." Aunt Violet yawned. Then laughed. "Sorry for admitting I didn't want you."

Ro dropped the rest of the acorns. "No need to apologize if you're telling the truth. Maybe I could walk back to your cottage with you? Have a quick look around, then let you go to bed."

"That would be fine, but I didn't walk. It's a little too far. Someone sent a carriage for me. You could probably get them to lend you the royal carriage to take us back, seeing as how they're trying to woo you into taking the throne."

Ro got to her feet, smiling. "Good point. Let's go see about that."

CHAPTER FIFTEEN

The royal everyday carriage was fetched at Ro's request, although Uldamar had to give the footman the nod that it was all right.

They stood outside, under a stone portico held up by smooth pillars, waiting on it. The long drive was paved. Flowering baskets hung along the sides of the portico, where more potted plants abounded.

Ro turned to look at the castle, but they were so close to it that it was hard to see much.

Uldamar cleared his throat softly. "I hope you don't mind, but I believe it would be best if I rode with you. I won't interfere with your time with your aunt, but on the way back, I could show you some more of the village."

Aunt Violet nodded before Ro could answer. "You should do that. Get a little tour. Rivervale is such a lovely place."

"That's fine," Ro said.

The clip-clop of horses' hooves announced the carriage's arrival. It was a handsome affair with an open top, a rounded, cream-colored base, the whole thing trimmed in gold and lavender. The driver and the footman on the back were dressed in livery to match. But the horses were spectacular, a matched pair that gleamed in the sunlight, their coats such a warm, pale gray that they, too, looked lavender.

Or maybe they were. Nothing would surprise Ro about this place anymore. Their cream-colored manes and tails were braided, and they wore deep purple tack.

"That's a very nice ride." Ro wished she could snap a picture, but she had a feeling Uldamar would not approve.

Footmen came forward to open the carriage door and assist the women aboard. The seats were upholstered in teal brocade.

Uldamar climbed up front with the driver. The footman gave the ladies a bow, then took his spot on the back of the carriage and thumped his hand gently against the side.

The driver picked up the reins, clicked his tongue twice and the horses started forward.

Uldamar twisted to see them. "We'll go by your aunt's bakery first, so you can see it, then on to her cottage."

"Great," Ro said. Then she turned to look behind them. The farther they got from the castle, the easier it was to see what an enormous place it was. At least three stories, although there were two towers that looked like they went another two stories higher. In the sunlight, the pale golden stone almost glowed. Flags decorated the parapets, and here and there, banners hung from the windows.

Along some of the walkways, guards were visible making their rounds.

What would it feel like to call that place home? Surreal, probably. Although maybe it would seem commonplace after a while. She doubted that.

She turned back around. If not for the footman right behind her, she definitely would have snuck taking a few photos.

The carriage ride wound them through the castle's manicured side lawns and then under a scrolling metal arch that sat in front of two stone dragonflies on pedestals.

Ro leaned in toward her aunt. "Is the dragonfly the state bird or something?"

Violet nodded. "It's on the Summerton crest. I guess you could say it's the unofficial logo of this place." She smiled. "Speaking of, you should taste my dragonfly cake."

Ro made a face before she could stop herself. "Sorry, but I think I'll pass."

Her aunt laughed. "It's not made with dragonflies, you silly goose. It's a little like the hummingbird cake of the southern United States, but instead of being made with bananas, pineapple, pecans, and cinnamon, it's made with carrots, gold apples, kurra nuts, and cardamom. It's really good."

"That sounds a lot better than a cake made with bugs."

Aunt Vi rolled her eyes, making Ro chuckle.

Down a long, tree-lined drive, past a few rolling forested areas, they came to farmland. Sheep, horses, cows, goats, pigs, chickens … all the usual suspects were visible, along with some other animals that looked like alpacas, but they had longer faces, little curved horns, and fleece in shades of white, lavender, gray, rosy brown, and black.

"What are those?" Ro asked.

"Maralas," Violet answered. "Their fur is sheared and turned into the softest, most supple wools and yarns. It can be felted into thicker cloth or woven into sheer lengths as light as air."

Another couple of minutes and they approached the outskirts of the village. The stone cottages grew closer together, then pubs and shops cropped up until, finally, they were on cobblestone streets.

As they rolled through, everyone on the street stopped to stare. First at the carriage, then at Uldamar, then at Ro and her aunt.

She did her best to look nonthreatening. "I guess the royal carriage doesn't come to town that often."

"Not once in all the time I've been here," Violet answered.

"Did you get picked up in this?"

Violet shook her head. "No, that was a simple wooden carriage. Probably used by the palace staff for errands."

Ro looked at Uldamar, wondering if this was part of his plan to get her to stay. "Are the villagers going to think I'm … someone?"

"They might," Violet said.

A little miffed, Ro tapped Uldamar on the shoulder.

He turned. "Yes, your ladyship."

"Are the villagers going to think I'm someone special because I'm riding in this carriage?"

He looked confused. "But you are someone special."

"You know what I mean. Are they going to think I'm taking the throne?"

He shrugged as if he hadn't even considered such a thing might happen. "I don't know."

She frowned at him. "You're not as sly as you think you are."

With a little smirk, he turned back around.

Thankfully, the carriage came to a stop. The sign over the shop next to it said, "Flake & Crumble Bakery."

"I inherited the name," Violet said. "But I think it's kind of cute, so I don't mind it. Besides, flakes and crumbles are both kinds of desserts here in the fae realm, so it works."

"It's adorable."

The footman hopped down and opened the door for them, giving Violet a hand down, then Ro, to whom he also bowed.

Violet opened the shop door, making three little bells over it jangle. Ro followed her in. It was a small shop with just enough space for about five or so people in front of the counter area. Inside the long glass case, there was almost nothing left. A couple of cookies, half a tray of turnovers, and a single fruit pie.

Behind the counter were slanted wooden shelves. A few loaves of bread in paper bags remained, but that was about it.

An aproned young woman with freckles and a broom in hand came out from the back room. She waved to Violet. "Hi, Miss Vi."

"Hi, Ginny. Cleaning up?"

Ginny nodded. "Just about done, actually."

"Not much left by this time of day," Violet explained to Ro. "Which is why we close in less than an hour. Our busy time is the morning."

"Makes sense," Ro said.

Violet gestured at the young woman with freckles. "This is Ginny Lightfoot. Ginny, this is my niece, Sparrow Meadowcroft."

Ginny smiled bigger. "Nice to meet you. Have you just arrived?"

"You might say that," Ro said. "But I'm going back in the morning."

"I hope you enjoy your visit."

"Thanks."

Ginny's gaze shifted past Ro, to the royal carriage out front. Her face went slack. "Miss Vi, I think we're about to get a visitor from the palace."

Violet laughed. "No, we came in that."

Ginny's brows shot up. "You did?"

Violet nodded. "Long story for another time, but Sparrow is a guest at the palace."

Ginny looked back to Ro. "You must be someone very important."

Ro wasn't sure what to say to that, but she didn't want to give the young woman the wrong impression. Or start any rumors. "I just came across something that needed to be returned to the palace. In the mortal world. But I'm no more important than anyone else."

Violet gave Ro a look that she remembered very well from her childhood. She usually got it when she'd been caught in a lie.

"Well," Violet said. "We're off to my cottage. I'll see you tomorrow."

Ginny nodded. "Mrs. Frogsworth ordered a lime

chiffon pie. You'll see the note, but just thought I'd mention it."

"Thanks," Violet said. She tipped her head toward the carriage.

Ro waved bye to Ginny and headed out.

The footman helped them back in.

Violet settled into her seat. "You *are* more important. You shouldn't say you're not."

"I didn't want to start anything."

Violet sighed as the carriage rolled forward. "I hope you make the right decision."

Ro nodded. "So do I."

Violet's cottage was just two streets away. It was a gorgeous little two-story stone confection with bright blue shutters, a thatched roof, and climbing vines that spilled flowers all over the front and sides of it, including the trellised archway that covered the entrance to the front door, which was butter yellow.

There was no front lawn. Instead, large flower beds created a patchwork of color that made the place seem like something out of a storybook.

"Aunt Violet, this place is charming."

Violet smiled. "Thank you. I love my little home. Come inside. There's not much to see, but it's all I need."

Ro followed her in. The downstairs was really one large room split by stairs in the middle—on one side, an eat-in kitchen, and on the other, a living room with a nice-sized fireplace. Wood beams overhead, slate floors covered in rugs, and cozy furnishings made the place feel like somewhere Ro could stay for a long, long time. Under the steps was a powder room and a small closet.

Behind those steps was another exterior door, the top half glass so that it looked out onto the back garden.

Ro peeked through.

The garden beyond wasn't as showy as the front beds. There was a path that divided the space right down the middle. On one side, raised beds were set up for vegetables that had just begun to send green shoots through the earth. On the other side, things were wilder. It looked like all flowers and herbs. At the back were some fruit trees. At the very front was about ten feet of cobblestone patio. On it was a cushioned bench and a small round table with two chairs.

"I love your garden."

"So do I," Violet said. "It brings me a lot of joy. And feeds me. Let me show you the upstairs, then I can make us a cup of tea or something."

"I think after that, I should go. I know you need to get to bed soon." She didn't want to say it, but Violet looked a little sleepy. "I promise to come by in the morning before I leave. And to somehow figure out a way to visit you, no matter what decision I make."

Violet smiled, but there was disbelief in her eyes.

"Listen," Ro said. "I'm not going to find you after all these years of thinking you were gone for good, then never see you again. I promise you that."

Her aunt's smile widened a touch. "Come on. I'll show you the bedrooms."

CHAPTER SIXTEEN

Anyka sat in her favorite chair in the queen's library. Not only was it comfortable, but it faced the windows that looked seaward.

In the distance, Tenebrae rose out of the fog. A solemn reminder that unlawful actions had consequences. How many had she sentenced to that island during her time on the throne? Quite a number, she was sure, but she'd lost count. She had no doubt Orthor Penkeep, Minister of Accounting, could tell her.

The afternoon rains were well under way, the sky darker because of them, but it suited her mood. So did the lightning snapping in the distance. She stared out through the big arched windows, but her vision blurred as the thoughts in her head took over.

The fire had been stoked, the logs crackling and sparking as they burned. The heat felt good. If there was anything about the passing years that affected her, it was how much more the cold bothered her. Faraway thunder rumbled. She pulled her robes tighter. There was no escaping the incessant damp and cold.

For nine weeks out of the year, ten if the fates allowed, there would be a slight reprieve. Those weeks were quickly approaching, thankfully. The nights would still be cool, but the days would be dry and the temperatures as mild as they'd ever get. Occasionally, small patches of blue sky peeked through the clouds. They never lasted long, though.

Such was the climate of Malveaux. The wind whistled past as if making her point, sending a sheet of rain against the glass.

But a very different storm raged in her head and heart. What was she going to do about Beatryce?

Allowing her daughter to go to Willow Hall for the summer season was out of the question. Even if the Radiant Fae no longer went there themselves. She really needed to find that out. Maybe if she discovered that they didn't use the Summer Palace anymore, she could persuade Beatryce that there'd be nothing there to do.

But Beatryce clearly needed a distraction of some kind.

And Anyka was lost as to what that might be. She had to come up with something, though. And soon. If it was good enough, maybe she could dissuade Beatryce from Willow Hall altogether.

Anyka rapped her fingers on the arm of the chair, trying to think.

There was always the mortal world. Anyka didn't like that idea any more than she liked Willow Hall. The mortal world had its own dangers, and just like with the Summer Palace, she'd never allow Bea to go there alone. The princess would have to take at least two palace guards with her.

Guards who'd been to the mortal realm before. Nyko and Strom, maybe. They were loyal and trustworthy.

Would Bea go for that? She'd never shown any real interest in the mortal world, but then Anyka had done her best to convince Bea it wasn't worth her time.

The library doors opened with the faintest squeak. Anyka liked them that way and had commanded that they were not to be oiled. No one could surprise her when they squeaked.

She straightened in her chair. "What is it?"

Wyett, her personal valet, walked into her field of vision. He was a well-built man with a surprising amount of grace for someone of his size. He was smart and loyal and had the uncanny ability to move without making a sound, which made him a good protector. His skills with a sword were also impressive. He bowed. "Your ladyship. There is news."

Anyka nodded. "You wouldn't be here otherwise. Out with it."

"There is a rumor Summerton may soon have a queen."

She hadn't been expecting that. If it were true ... She smoothed her hand over her cheek as she thought. "Are you sure?"

"No. As I said, it is a rumor. But I wanted you to be aware of it all the same."

"Dig into it. See what you can find out through your usual sources. The moment you hear anything, you tell me."

He nodded. "I will do everything in my power."

"Good." She waved her hand, dismissing him. If there

really was a new ruler in Summerton, that could only mean—

Wyett hadn't moved.

She looked at him, brows raised in question.

"There is one more thing," he said.

"Yes?"

"Princess Beatryce has announced she is moving into the West Tower."

Anyka sighed. "If that's what she wants, let her. She won't like it. It's cold and damp." Much more so than in the heart of the palace, where they each had their quarters now. There were no heated floors in the tower, either. But then, the West Tower was as far from the queen's chambers as you could get in the palace while still having a decent place to sleep. She supposed Bea was making a point.

"She's tasked the staff with bringing things from storage. Rugs, tapestries, furniture."

Anyka nodded. "Humor her. Whatever she wants is fine. She's at loose ends right now. This will occupy her for a bit."

There was understanding in his eyes. "Anything else I can do for you, your ladyship?"

She stared out the window again. It had grown darker. As if the realm knew something was coming. "Pour me a blackberry brandy."

The liquor, produced in Summerton, was contraband in Malveaux. But she was the queen, and rules didn't apply to her.

"My pleasure." He went to the small rolltop bar,

pushed the top back, and got her drink. He brought the crystal glass to her on a small silver tray.

She took the drink, sipping a little of the sweet, deep purple liquor that tasted of what she imagined true summer must be like. "Change is coming, Wyett. I can feel it." Beatryce wasn't the only one who was restless, and Zephynia wasn't the only one who had premonitions about the future.

He tucked the silver tray behind his back. There was no need for him to answer her. It hadn't been a question. But she'd spoken to him, meaning he would stand there until he was dismissed again.

Anyka sipped her brandy again. "It worries me."

There were very few people in the kingdom she'd admit that to, but Wyett would go to his grave with her secrets. Although she sincerely hoped he outlived her. She liked him very much. He'd be impossible to replace. She'd once thought about taking him as a consort, but he was far too valuable as her valet.

Finding men to fill her bed was much easier than replacing a man like Wyett.

"You've faced adversity before," he said quietly.

She nodded. "I have."

"You've always come through it stronger."

She looked at him and smiled. "Thank you."

He bowed his head in acknowledgment.

"Go on," she said. "See if that rumor can be confirmed."

The silver tray was returned to the bar, and he was gone.

She drank a little more brandy and let her mind coast over her problems again. As if Beatryce wasn't enough, now she had the possibility of a new Summerton ruler to contend with.

What would that mean for Malveaux? Would there be war? It was generally accepted that the tenuous peace between the two kingdoms existed mainly because there was no opposition to anything Anyka did.

What was that curse about living in interesting times? It seemed they had arrived. Or were about to.

She tossed back the rest of her brandy and got up, leaving the glass on the small table beside her chair.

She might not know what to do about Beatryce just yet, but the possibility of a threat from Summerton was something she knew how to handle. She rubbed her hands together to warm them.

A trip to see General Wolfmane was in order. Perhaps even a surprise inspection of the barracks would be wise. First, she'd have to change into warmer clothing. Boots. Her fur cape, too. Although her sturdy marala wool might be a wiser choice.

She sighed as she left the comforting confines of the library behind. General Wolfmane was a useful tool in the defense and reputation of Malveaux. He kept her armies battle-ready, the men sharp, the armories well stocked.

She just hoped he'd bathed recently.

CHAPTER SEVENTEEN

After returning from her aunt's, Ro had every intention of going upstairs to check on Mrs. Wigglesworth and Benny, but Uldamar stopped her before she got more than a few steps into the castle.

"Would you like to see more of the palace? A small tour, I promise, because to see it all would take days."

She nodded. "I would. I was going to check on the cats, though."

"Of course. I'll meet you in the grand ballroom?"

"I don't think I know where that is."

"When you come back down, turn right and keep going until you come to a very large room. The guards can direct you, if you'd like."

"Okay, I'll meet you there." She headed off down the hall toward the royal apartment, which was something she did know the location of. She'd paid close attention for just that purpose.

She hesitated when she came to the guards, but they gave her short bows and made no attempt to stop her from going upstairs. Not that she thought they would after the instructions Uldamar had given them.

She jogged up the steps and went into the apartment. Amazing how beautiful this place was. She walked through and found both Wiggy and Benny asleep on the big bed, back-to-back. What was she going to do about Wiggy? Would she stay human when they went back through the portal?

Ro couldn't really fit another person in her apartment. Especially not one who was so poorly behaved. She needed to talk to Uldamar about that. If anyone would know how to return Edna to cat form, he seemed like the one.

The quarters were very quiet. Other than the soft snoring coming from the bed. There were no sirens, no honking, none of the ambient street noise that wafted up from the city even in the wee hours of morning.

The quiet might take some getting used to, but it was nice. Not that it mattered. She had no desire to be queen. On a whim, she went into the water closet. It was set up pretty much like any other toilet she'd ever seen, complete with toilet paper. Which wasn't shredded, thankfully.

She went back into the bedroom. All Ro wanted was the opportunity to come back now and then to see Aunt Violet. Uldamar would understand, wouldn't he? The high council would, surely.

Ro was not the person they needed for this job. Even if Vi thought she'd be great at it. Aunt Vi had once thought she'd be great at cheerleading, too, but Ro had sprained her ankle during the practice for tryouts, putting an end to that.

She glanced toward the balcony. She was alone. She went outside and took a few photos of Malveaux. Some more of the castle, too. Why not? If she never got to come back here, at least she'd have these to remember the place.

Inside, she took some of the apartment as well. In the dressing room, she trailed her hands over the clothes that remained. Beautiful, sumptuous garments. Silks and satins, velvets, leather, suede.

Her hand came to rest on a deep purple coat with ivory leather buttons and teal piping trimming the collar. It was as soft as Benny's belly. Was this marala wool?

More than a little curious about the royals who'd once lived here, she pulled the coat out and tried it on. The king had been a little taller than her, but not by much.

She looked at her reflection in the mirror. The coat looked pretty good on her. She admired it a moment longer, touching the fabric. Finally, she hung it back up. This was not her world. Even if her ears were pointed.

Hmm. Would they return to normal when she went through the portal? Now she had two things to ask Uldamar about.

She went back downstairs, turned right at the bottom of the steps, and went straight on. The hall curved slightly, and she passed several doors, but she kept going forward.

After one more bend, the hall ended in a pair of open double doors. Through them, she could see a large room. She walked in. Uldamar stood on the opposite side of the room, looking out one of the windows.

The room was enormous and projected past the doors in both directions. Closer to Uldamar, the room had a large fireplace. Two more sets of double doors, these painted to match the walls, flanked it. But on her end, the far wall curved out with windows all along the curve.

The walls were cream with panels trimmed in thin

lines of gilded molding. The floors were pale, polished wood. The ceilings were painted with picturesque scenes of fae life. A goatherd and his goats. An older woman with a younger one at her side, kneading bread with a man behind them putting loaves into an oven. Two more women spinning yarn, a marula just outside the window. A group of men on a boat, hauling up a catch of fish.

From the center of those murals dangled five massive crystal chandeliers with the largest in the center, then two smaller ones on either side. Crystal sconces sat between the outlined panels on the walls, but none of them were lit. The room had plenty of windows and plenty of natural light.

Chairs and settees lined the walls, all in the royal colors of lavender and soft teal.

She turned slowly, taking in the whole space. There was a balcony area over the doors she'd just come through. Maybe that's where the musicians sat.

It really was a grand space, and she could imagine the parties that must have been held here. All the people dressed in their fine, colorful clothing. The music playing. Couples dancing. The drinks being served. Just the thought of it made her smile.

"Quite a room." Uldamar walked toward her.

She nodded. "It really is."

"Sad that it's sat empty for so long." He sighed as he gazed up at the ceiling. "There used to be at least two balls a year here." Then he smiled and looked at her again. "I was thinking you might like to see the library and the gallery."

"Books and art?" She nodded. "I'm in."

"Then follow me."

It took nearly ten minutes to walk to the library, but that walk went through the gallery, during which Uldamar pointed out some of the past kings and queens, along with scenes painted by what he told her were famous fae artists.

The work was beautiful and, to Ro's practiced eye, as good as anything she'd seen done by humans. Some of them even better.

"Here we are," he said. "The library." More double doors. He opened the right-hand side a few inches, then paused. "Books and reading are very important to the fae people."

"They're important to me, too. I don't get to read for pleasure as much as I'd like but—"

He pushed the door wide and gestured for her to go in.

"Oh, this is fantastic." She took a few steps in, then stood still and just looked.

The library was about the same size as the ballroom but two stories tall with a walkway that went around the second story. There were two bridges that cut across the room as well. She must have been looking at thirty feet of books. Rolling ladders on the first floor allowed access to the higher shelves.

All throughout the room were seating areas illuminated by floor lamps and squat islands of shelves brimming with more books. There were three medium-sized fireplaces, and along the exterior wall, tall, narrow windows that spanned both floors let in natural light.

Otherwise, every inch of available space held books.

"Were these all written by the fae?"

He shook his head. "No. We send teams of librarians all over the mortal realm to bring back the best and most interesting books from around the world."

"Really? That's amazing." The urge to climb some of those ladders to have a better look was strong. "This collection is amazing."

"As I said, we value books and reading greatly. That's why we used to go to Willow Hall. The Summer Palace." He shook his head. "But that's of no import. The Summer Palace was closed after the king was exiled, and as you won't be here for the summer, there's no reason to go into all of that."

He had her attention. Exactly as he'd wanted, she was sure. She looked at him. "Exiled? Hold on. What does reading have to do with going to the Summer Palace?"

"It hasn't happened since we became rulerless, you understand, but tradition has always held that during the summer months, the royal court, along with a group of citizens selected by a lottery, adjourns to the Summer Palace to spend those months reading. Originally, both Radiant and Grym went. But that ended after the great divide."

She narrowed her eyes. "Just reading?"

He nodded. "That is the primary activity. In the evenings there might be some card games or music after dinner, although most gather to talk about what they've read that day. Occasionally, there might be a boat trip on Celestial Lake. But, yes, mostly reading. I'm sure that must sound rather dull to you, but—"

"It doesn't sound dull at all. It sounds like the perfect vacation." Was he kidding? He wouldn't kid about a thing like that, would he? It would be too easy to disprove. She could ask around and find out.

He chuckled softly. "It is quite enjoyable. The staff used to serve this fruit punch made with blackberry brandy in the afternoons. And then there were these little fruit and custard tarts they'd bring around. The perfect thing to eat one-handed. Although the skewers of marinated cheese and veg were quite good, too."

She crossed her arms. "Let me make sure I have this right. The royal fae vacation is you sit around reading all day while being served drinks and snacks? In a palace near a lake?"

"Yes, that's about right."

If he was trying to convince her to stay, he might have just done it.

Chapter Eighteen

Ro was so taken by the idea of spending her summer reading that they were several minutes into their journey to the kitchen, the next thing Uldamar wanted to show her, before she remembered to ask about Wiggy.

"Uldamar, about my cat, Mrs. Wigglesworth. She'll be back to her regular cat self once we go through the portal again, right?"

He pressed his lips together and shook his head. "There's not much chance of that. Once transformed, an animal usually stays transformed."

She stopped walking, which forced him to do the same. "Don't you have some magic you can use to change her back?"

"I could attempt it, but it would be tricky. And the likelihood that I would be able to cause a complete transformation is slim. She might still retain her fae ears. Or her voice. I can't say for sure what the result would be. When a transformation like this happens, it's because of magic that far surpasses what any fae is capable of."

Ro sighed and stared at the ceiling. "What am I going to do with her?" She put her hands on her hips and looked at him. "You saw my apartment. There's not a lot of room for another person in there. Not one with that kind of erratic behavior."

"No, no, not with her energy." He crossed one arm over his torso so he could lean his elbow into his hand and press his fingers into his temple. He went silent for a few long breaths as if thinking. "I suppose you could leave her here. She'd be perfectly safe. We'd find her a place to stay, make sure she was looked after, all of that."

Ro sighed. That didn't feel right. Just abandoning Mrs. Wigglesworth in a strange land? Although Edna seemed to like it well enough. Ro rubbed a hand across her face. "I need to think about it before I make a decision."

"Of course." He stood there as if waiting on her.

She waved her hand forward. "Go ahead, take me to the kitchen. I can think while I walk."

"Very well." He continued on.

The kitchen was busy. A lot busier than she expected for a palace that had no ruler. At least half a dozen cooks were occupied doing something. Dressed in white uniforms, they were stirring pots, chopping vegetables, icing cakes, basting meats, and carrying platters around. The smells made her mouth water.

"Happening spot." Stoves lined one side of the wall in the big room, then two large sinks with a counter space in between them took up the wall opposite. In the center was a long butcher block-topped island. A pot rack above it dangled all kinds of pans. "Who are they feeding?"

"They're preparing for tonight's dinner."

"All this for dinner? Seems like a lot. Or is this standard?" What did she know about what passed for a typical palace dinner? She glanced at him for further explanation.

"It's not standard, no. They're preparing for a banquet. For you. The high and low councils, along with a few other guests, are gathering in the royal dining room to celebrate *Merediem*'s removal from the stone and the woman who accomplished that feat."

"I see." Too bad Aunt Violet was probably already asleep. Ro would have loved to have her there. "That sounds ... nice."

He laughed. "I promise it won't be as boring as you might think. Official dinners can be, but there will be entertainment at this one. A few musicians, a singer, even a poet, I believe. The council wishes to show you more of our arts and culture."

"I'm all for that. I didn't bring anything fancy to wear, however."

"You mustn't worry about that. A seamstress will arrive at the royal chambers shortly to fit you with a gown for this evening."

She turned toward him. "You're going to an awful lot of work to sway me into staying."

A new light shone in his eyes. One that seemed like a mix of honesty and desperation. "You are worth an awful lot of work. Summerton is rudderless. We *need* a ruler. And *Merediem* has chosen you. It's my job to make sure you understand how full and rich and wonderful your life here would be."

She smiled, appreciating his efforts. "Thank you for that. You're doing a great job."

He snorted. "Not enough that you've changed your mind."

"I am thinking about it. I promise."

He nodded, but he looked a little dejected.

"I should probably go back up and see about that seamstress."

He smiled, the effort visible. "Yes, of course. Let me guide you back to the stairs."

"Thank you."

They didn't speak on the way. She was starting to feel bad, but the same argument played over and over in her head. How could she leave her son? And how could she leave the job she'd worked so hard for, especially with the promotion on Monday? Her whole life, all fifty-two years of it, had been spent in the city.

Moving to another realm wasn't something she'd ever considered, let alone thought possible.

He left her at the stairs, and she went up to the royal chambers, still trying to work it all out.

The seamstress was already waiting by the door. The woman, who looked about Ro's age, held a lidded basket in one hand and carried several long dresses over her arm. She bent low. "Your ladyship."

"Hi. You must be the seamstress, obviously. I'm Sparrow. But I suppose you know that."

The woman's smile was sweet and unassuming. "Yes, your ladyship. I'm Luena. It's a pleasure to meet you."

"You, too, Luena. Let's go in. I hope you're not allergic to cats. Or people who used to be cats."

"No, your ladyship."

Ro grabbed the door handle. "I'm not the queen yet. How about for now, you just call me Ro?"

Luena's brows bent in obvious uncertainty. "I don't think I can do that, your ladyship. My apologies."

"Then can you at least drop the ladyship? It just sounds so odd to me."

"As you wish, your ... ma'am."

Close enough, Ro thought. She opened the door and led the way in.

"It's so pretty," Luena said quietly.

"It is," Ro agreed. "I guess you've never been in here before?"

"No. Although my father was the king's tailor."

"Family business, huh?"

Luena smiled. "Yes. My mother is a seamstress, too. We have a shop in the village. Threadmaster's. My brother and his wife run the haberdashery."

Wiggy was still asleep on the bed, but Benny jumped down to greet Ro with a little chirp. He stopped a few feet away and did a big stretch. Ro scratched his head, then scooped him up like a baby.

"This is my cat, Benny, and the woman on the bed was my other cat, Mrs. Wigglesworth, but coming through the portal changed her. As you can see."

Luena nodded. "I've heard that can happen."

Ro gestured to the dresses Luena carried. "So do you want me to try those on, or how do you want to do this?"

"Whatever you'd like is fine, but typically the fitting process takes place in the dressing room."

"Right. That makes sense." Ro put Benny down. He

trotted off toward the lounge, where Ro had set up the cats' food and water. "It's back here."

In a few minutes, Ro had stripped down to her bra and underwear and was in the first gown. The dress was a silvery-gray chiffon with long, flowing sleeves, a deep vee neckline and trim of silver filagree, freshwater pearls and small faceted beads cut from some kind of gray stone that flashed blue when the light caught them just right.

Ro touched one. "What are these?"

"Trillianite. Aren't they beautiful?"

"They are. The dress is lovely, too. I would have been happy with one of the queen's old dresses, though. This seems like a lot of work."

Luena went over to the wall, took one of those dresses off the rack and held it up to Ro. It was about twelve inches short and four sizes too small.

Ro chuckled. "Never mind. I didn't realize the queen was so petite."

Luena put the dress back, still silent, as she had a few pins in her mouth. She had more at her wrist, where she wore a thick, padded bracelet that served as a wearable pincushion. She also carried a flat square of chalk, which she used to mark the dress. She walked around Ro, adjusting, pinning, chalking, and staring at the gown like it had secrets to tell.

Luena's last adjustment had tightened up the bodice, which had done wonders for Ro's bustline but had also put more of it on display.

Ro gazed into the big mirror across from the raised

platform she stood on. "That's a lot of cleavage, isn't it? Especially for dinner with the council members."

Luena glanced at the mirror. She'd used all the pins in her mouth. "I can change anything you like."

"Well, I'd like a little less boob on display."

Luena walked around to face Ro, hands lifted. "May I?"

"I'm not shy. Go right ahead."

Luena lifted and pulled and pinned. Then she stepped aside. "Better?"

Ro knew the gown still needed to be sown to stay as it was, but Luena was clearly adept at her job. Ro could see a few chalk lines, but the pins were barely visible. And Luena had closed the neckline by about three inches. The gown still showed off Ro's assets, but in a much more tasteful way.

She smiled. "Nicely done. It's perfect."

Luena nodded. "Thank you. Would you like to try on the next gown?"

Ro shrugged. "I'm not sure I need to. This one's pretty good."

Luena glanced at the two remaining dresses with such a curious expression that Ro realized that Luena had no doubt made all of these gowns and not getting to see them on Ro would probably be a disappointment. "Actually, I'd be happy to try on the other two."

The joy returned to Luena's face. "Excellent."

With Luena's help, Ro put the forest-green silk on next. It was more fitted but still flattering, with a high, empire waistline banded by a wide, intricately embroidered belt covered in dragonflies, each one adorned with crystals and beads. The belt reminded Ro of the slippers Maybelle had sent to the museum.

The gown was sleeveless but had a flowing capelet of matching green chiffon that gave some coverage to her upper arms, which were not her favorite part of her body. The cape was held at the shoulders with two more dragon-flies, these designed in metal and gemstones.

It was a little large in the chest, as the last dress had been, but very pretty. And very fairy princess. *Fae* princess, Ro corrected herself, remembering what Aunt Violet had said about the word "fairy".

"This is equally lovely," Ro said. "Now I don't know which one I like better."

"There's still one to go," Luena said.

Ro nodded. "I'll definitely try it." The last gown was made of thicker fabric with a sheen to it, like a thick sateen. It had a big floral pattern on a background of purple. The flowers were white with black and chartreuse centers, which were accented with little faceted beads in the same black and greenish-yellow. The fabric was bright and happy, but Ro had never been much on florals. Espe-cially not such overblown ones.

But she wasn't going to say that in front of Luena.

When the seamstress finished marking her alterations and putting in pins on the green dress, she helped Ro out of it and into the last gown, making Ro turn away from the mirror until she was dressed.

Luena zipped the back zipper, fluffed out the skirt and said, "All right. You may turn around."

Ro did. She looked at herself, shook her head, and laughed.

Luena looked horrified. "Is something wrong?"

Ro smiled. "As a rule, I shy away from florals. Especially big ones like this. As soon as I saw the fabric, I knew there was no way this would be my choice. But now? I think it might be my favorite."

Luena's face brightened. "I love this gown on you. It's a strong silhouette that makes you look powerful and yet it's a decidedly feminine fabric."

"And," Ro said, tucking her hands into the dress, "it has pockets."

Luena nodded. "I include them whenever I can."

Ro looked at her. "So you made these three dresses?"

Luena nodded, slightly hesitant. "Yes, your lady—ma'am."

"You are very skilled. They're all beautiful, and I would be honored to wear any of them." She looked in the mirror again. "But I think this is the dress."

CHAPTER NINETEEN

The next few hours passed in a blur. During that time, Ro took a bath in the massive pool, which was incredibly relaxing, then got out to find three more women waiting on her. Luena was in the sitting room, making the alterations to the purple floral dress.

One had come to do her hair and makeup. Another had come with a trunk full of shoes for her to choose from. The third had arrived with jewels to accessorize Ro's choice of gown.

"If you could pick your jewels first, your ladyship?" Diselle, the jeweler, asked.

"That's fine." Ro felt as though she finally understood what royal treatment meant. She'd also given up on asking them not to call her "your ladyship."

Helana, the hair stylist and makeup artist, immediately went into the salon and started setting up. Pearlina, the cobbler's daughter, began to unpack her trunk of footwear.

Ro followed Diselle into the formal sitting room and took a seat on one of the couches while Diselle pulled out several large, square suede and velvet pouches and laid them out on the table near where Luena was working.

"Jewelry," Ro said to Luena.

She looked up and nodded. "Excellent."

"I'd like your input," Ro said. Her go-to outfit for any museum affair was a simple black dress and a set of large Mallorca gray pearls she'd splurged on when she'd been in Spain. They were glass, not real pearls, but they were about as high-end as reproductions went.

Luena seemed surprised. "You would?"

"Absolutely," Ro said. "You made the dress, so you should have an idea of what will go with it."

Luena glanced at Diselle, then back at Ro. "Whatever you'd like."

Diselle untied the first pouch and unfolded the flaps to show off the jewelry inside. "This is the first suite of amethysts and diamonds."

Ro had a pretty good eye for jewelry. She picked up the necklace, a heavy piece of faceted purple beads with a large flower pendant. The beads were egg-shaped and about the size of two peas. Diamond rondelles separated each bead from the next. The pendant was made of smaller faceted amethysts set in gold. The weight was considerable.

She looked at Diselle. "These are real amethysts and diamonds."

"Yes, your ladyship."

Ro set the necklace down beside the earrings, bracelet, and ring that accompanied it. "Why are you giving me such expensive things to wear? I can't borrow these."

"But of course you can," Diselle said. "You're to be our new queen. You must be adorned as such."

What exactly had Uldamar told these women? Ro let out a soft breath and chose her words carefully. "I haven't agreed to take the throne."

Luena's stitching came to a halt.

Diselle looked stricken. "You … haven't?"

"No. And I'm sorry if you've been told otherwise. But it's not an easy decision for me to make. I have a life in the mortal world. You must understand that."

"Of course," Diselle answered. But she looked like a deflated balloon. She swallowed, then pressed her hand to her stomach. "You *could* be queen, though. Yes?"

"Yes. I could be." But the chances were highly unlikely. "I just …" Ro stopped. She didn't want to make promises she wasn't going to keep or give these women false hope. And yet she felt the need to explain herself further. She tried a different tack. "I have a son in the mortal world. I can't leave him."

She left her job out of the equation, then thought better of that. These were working women. Surely, they'd understand? "I have an important job there, too. One that's about to become even more important."

Nothing she said did anything to change the dejected expressions on their faces.

Ro felt bad, but the truth was important. "I'm sorry. I thought I should be honest with you. I understand that Summerton needs a ruler, but I don't think it's me. I don't know anything about being that kind of leader."

Luena spoke softly. "I don't suppose anyone does until they become that kind of leader." Her smile was kind but sad.

Ro nodded. "I really hope I'll be able to come back and visit. My aunt lives here. She runs the bakery in town. Flake & Crumble?"

Both women nodded.

"It's a lovely shop," Diselle said. "Excellent seeded bread."

Ro sank back on the couch. The mood had definitely shifted, and she wasn't sure how to get it back. Or if it was even possible.

"We've upset you," Luena said. "My deepest apologies. It wasn't our intention, I assure you. We just assumed that you were our new queen."

Ro nodded. "I understand. I'd be bummed, too."

"Bummed?" Diselle asked.

"Upset. Bothered. Disappointed." Ro exhaled. "It's too bad I can't be a part-time queen. Like maybe just on weekends."

She sat up. "I wonder if that would be possible? After all, wouldn't a weekend queen be better than none? I mean, you've gone, what, a hundred and thirteen years without a ruler on the throne, right?"

Diselle and Luena nodded.

The idea grew as a possibility. "Maybe it would work. I have no idea. The councils might not go for it, but then again, maybe they would. It would only be for the next fifteen years or so, until I can retire from the museum."

This was either a brilliant idea or a sure-fire plan to run herself ragged and end up hospitalized, but it was at least a plan. Ro smiled and rubbed her hands together. "Let's see the rest of the jewelry."

Ro was dressed, made up, and bejeweled with approximately fifteen minutes to spare before she was due downstairs to meet Uldamar and go to the dining room.

Helana had oiled Ro's hair, which had left it shinier than she'd ever seen it, then swept it back in three small braids on each side, leaving the rest to fall free. It was a very becoming style and nothing Ro would ever have considered for herself in a million years.

Her makeup was heavier than normal but deftly applied. Her eyes were the focus, done in smoky grays. But whatever Helana had done to Ro's skin had left it luminous. Additionally, her cheeks and lips were a dewy rose she wouldn't have thought possible.

For the jewelry, she'd gone with the first set, the amethysts. And on her feet were satin slippers in the exact same shade of purple as the background of the dress.

The dress. Ro sighed a happy sigh as she looked at herself completely done up. "I love all of this. You ladies have outdone yourselves, all of you, but Luena, this dress is beyond words." Her waist was nipped in, her bustline beautifully displayed, and the colors made her feel regal, even if she wasn't.

Luena bent her head, smiling. "Thank you, your ladyship."

Ro shook her head. "I've never looked this good in my life."

Helana's mouth turned up in a knowing smile. "You look like a queen."

Ro nodded. "I suppose I do. Thank you again. All of you."

That earned her more smiles.

"Now, I should go before Uldamar has to come up and get me. I hope you have a good evening. You deserve it after the work you've done." They bowed. She knew they still had to gather up their things before they could leave. "All I ask is that when you go, make sure Benny and Wiggy stay in, all right?"

Pearlina, who'd already had to remove Benny from her shoe trunk twice, laughed. "We will be sure of it."

"Thank you." With that, Ro headed out to meet Uldamar, holding the hem of her dress up slightly and feeling every inch like a new woman. Well, not new exactly, but she certainly wasn't her old self, either.

She couldn't imagine what this dress or these jewels were worth. The shoes, too.

Uldamar was at the bottom of the steps, speaking to one of the guards. He looked up when he heard her footsteps.

For a moment, he said nothing, and his expression registered nothing. Then he stepped back and bowed. "Behold, the chosen queen of Summerton."

That caused the guards to bow, too.

She frowned. He really needed to stop that. "Rise. Please."

All three straightened.

Uldamar smiled at her. "You look truly royal, your ladyship."

"Thank you. The women you sent were exceptional. Worth twice whatever you paid them."

"I'll make a note of that." He gestured ahead of them,

in the same direction as the grand ballroom. At least she thought it was the same direction. "Shall we?"

"Absolutely." And she was right. They passed the grand ballroom and went into the room next to it, which was only about half its size. Meaning it was still enormous.

The dining room was decorated in much the same style as the ballroom, but the walls were teal and the accents were cream, gold, and dark blue. The table could have been a landing strip, it was so long. At first glance, it might have seated forty or fifty. Maybe more.

Crystal chandeliers illuminated the space, as did tall candelabras on the table, one for about every seven or eight chairs.

No one was seated, however. They were all milling about with cocktails in hand or chatting in small groups. A small group of musicians, tucked into one corner, played softly.

The milling and chatting stopped abruptly when she entered behind Uldamar. The crowd turned toward her. She recognized the council members she'd already met, but the rest of the faces were brand new. And most of them weren't quite as friendly. She felt a slight twinge of nervousness under their judging gazes. She lifted her chin and put on a Mona Lisa smile, her way of combating what she was feeling.

Uldamar wasted no time with the introduction. "Ladies and gentlemen, may I present Lady Sparrow Meadowcroft, the fae who freed *Merediem* and is now the chosen ruler of Summerton."

After a long few seconds of silence, Professor Spencer

Cloudtree stepped forward, raising his glass. "To Lady Sparrow Meadowcroft and the future of Summerton!"

She exhaled. At least she had one friend in the crowd. It didn't surprise her that it was the First Professor of History.

A housemaid approached with a tray of crystal wine-glasses filled with a pale lavender liquid.

Ro took one and sniffed it.

"Sparkling blackberry wine," Spencer said. He'd joined Ro along with a petite woman whose silver hair was wound on top of her head like cotton candy.

"Thank you." Ro took a sip. It was pretty good. Sweet, but a little tart, too. And under the circumstances, very drinkable.

"Lady Sparrow, this is my wife, Althea."

Ro hadn't seen a lot of handshaking, so she just held onto her wine. "It's a pleasure to meet you, Althea."

The woman smiled. "You, too. It's so exciting that you're here!"

"It's exciting to be here." Not a lie, Ro thought as she sipped her wine. She really was enjoying herself. Although that enjoyment faded a bit when she thought about how many people she was going to disappoint when they found out she was turning down the throne.

The dining room doors opened, and a footman came in. "Professor Gabriel Nightborne."

Ro turned to look, but not before she noted the eager expression on Althea's face.

The man who walked through the doors caused Ro to

forget everything else for a moment. He was a full head taller than her and broad-shouldered. His square jaw was covered in a dark dusting of stubble that made his piercing green eyes stand out even more.

His black hair was braided back at his temples, then fell to his shoulders. Streaks of silver in that hair and the lines fanning from the corners of his eyes said he was older than he looked, but he had the lean musculature and posture of a much younger man. He wasn't so much standing as he seemed coiled to strike.

He wore a sword on his hip and a dagger tucked into his boot. He scanned the room like he was looking for something. Or someone. When he turned his head, she noticed one ear tip bore a small tattoo.

From beside her, Uldamar spoke. "Nightborne is the First Professor of Palace Security." Then, with a little exasperation in his voice, "He's also late."

Ro nodded, still staring. Professor Nightborne looked perfectly capable of securing just about anything he wanted. And to her, he seemed right on time.

Uldamar cleared his throat softly, as if trying to get her attention.

"Mm-hmm," she said. "First Professor of Palace Security."

"Yes," Uldamar said. "As queen, you'll work very closely with him. In fact, he will be your personal guard and see to it that you are well protected at any event you attend. He is an extraordinarily dangerous man. Thankfully, he works for the Crown."

Ro took a breath. Maybe the wine was stronger than what she was used to, but she felt a little lightheaded suddenly.

"Come," said Uldamar. "I'll introduce you."

CHAPTER TWENTY

Ro had never been happier that she'd gotten professional help to get ready. Maybe it was vanity, but she really wanted to make a good impression on Gabriel Nightborne.

Uldamar led the way to him.

Gabriel had just refused a drink from one of the housemaids.

Uldamar greeted him. "Nightborne."

"Darkstone." Gabriel spoke to Uldamar, but his gaze was on Ro. "You must be the one who freed *Merediem* from her stone."

Ro nodded, not sure what to make of this man just yet. "I did."

"She is the chosen one," Uldamar corrected. "She is due our respect."

Gabriel finally glanced at him. "I have shown her nothing else so far."

"You were late," Uldamar countered.

"Because of a security issue." There was a challenge in Gabriel's eyes. "And this party was a bad idea."

Uldamar frowned, and Ro was left to wonder what Gabriel had against dinner parties.

Gabriel returned his attention to Ro. "It's a pleasure to make your acquaintance."

"Yours, too." Out of habit, she extended her hand.

He took it, lifted it to his mouth and brushed his lips across her knuckles, barely touching her skin, but his hot breath raised goosebumps down her arms. She inhaled. He smelled of woodsmoke and rain. Once again, she forgot everything else going on around her.

She regained her senses when he let go.

She wasn't sure which was sadder—how long it had been since she'd had such intimate contact with a man, or that such a brief connection had affected her so much.

Uldamar made a little noise of consternation, and for a moment, Ro thought it was because of her reaction to Gabriel, then realized he was looking toward the other end of the room. "I must excuse myself. I need to talk with Professor Morehouse."

She nodded. "No problem."

He glanced at her. "Or perhaps you'd like to come with me? You haven't met her yet. She's the First Professor of Arts. I'm sure you'd—"

"I'd like to get to know Professor Nightborne first, thank you."

Uldamar's gaze went to Gabriel. To Ro, it seemed less than approving, but maybe she was reading too much into it. "As you wish."

Gabriel waited until Uldamar was out of earshot. "Please, just call me Gabriel."

She smiled and sipped more of her delicious wine. "Is that allowed?"

"If you're the queen, you can do whatever you like."

She nodded. "Good point."

His eyes narrowed, but there was no malice in them. "Except you don't plan on becoming queen, do you?"

She didn't know quite how to react to that. Truth might not always make people happy, but at least it was nothing to apologize for. "No, I don't."

He looked away. "No one else here understands that."

"It doesn't seem that way. Although I haven't been quite that upfront with them just yet."

"They don't make it easy. But then, that's the point." He looked at her again. "It's none of my business, but can I ask why you don't want the throne? Other than it's a lot of responsibility over a great number of people and an incredible amount of land you have no real attachment to."

She tipped her wineglass at him. "That's not entirely true. My aunt lives here."

"But it's not enough for you to take the crown."

She sighed and let her gaze roam the crowd. "I have a life in the mortal world. And a son. It's not that easy to walk away from all of that."

When she looked at him again, he was nodding. "I understand. I suspected that would be the case with anyone who pulled the sword free."

"How did you know? About my decision toward the throne?"

He shrugged. "It's my job to read people and anticipate what they're going to do next."

She held her glass close. "Then tell me how this crowd

is going to react when they find out that I am not their new queen."

He took a quick look around, then his gaze came back to her. "I am not a seer, merely a student of life. Some will be angry. Some will be bereft. A few will understand. A few will be happy the new queen isn't a crossover."

"And you? How does it make you feel?"

He smiled, which completely changed his face. He looked far more approachable. Much less like a man who knew ways to kill you without leaving a mark. But then the smile was gone. "All that matters to me is what's best for my country. If you aren't it, then you do the kingdom a favor by not ruling."

"That's a wise assessment. Anyone who becomes a leader begrudgingly is liable to do a bad job."

He nodded. "I will escort you back to the mortal world tomorrow and make sure you're safe."

She made a face. "Why wouldn't I be safe?"

He slanted his eyes at her. "You're still the de facto queen of Summerton until someone else can remove *Merediem* from her stone."

She stared at him. "Even if I refuse the throne?"

"Refusing doesn't change the fact that you pulled *Merediem* free. That didn't happen because you were pure of heart or imbued with magic or any other nonsense. It happened because the sword *chose* you. You will be the chosen one until the sword chooses another. Until then, it's possible the enemies of Summerton will view you as a threat."

"What enemies?"

He looked at her like she wasn't all there. "Have you not seen the kingdom across the sea?"

"Yes, but—"

"Queen Anyka would love nothing more than to take control of Summerton before you take control of Malveaux."

Ro made a face. "Even if I was queen, I'd have no reason or desire to rule Malveaux, too."

Gabriel shrugged. "There's a Malveauxian prophecy that says otherwise."

Ro rolled her eyes. "If this queen wants Summerton so badly, then why hasn't she done something about it in the last century when there's been no ruler here?"

"Because a hostile takeover would only cause the citizens to rise up and fight. War will destroy villages, tear up the land, and leave many dead. Queen Anyka would rather do things in a way that would leave no question about her legitimacy. Not to mention preserve Summerton so that she could reap the most benefit from it. And that's by taking possession of *Merediem* for herself."

Ro thought. "I'll just stick it back in the stone. Then she won't be able to have it."

His expression didn't change. Then one brow cocked. "And there's nothing she could do to make you free it once again and hand it over?"

Ro opened her mouth to say no but knew that wasn't true. If this woman put her son or aunt in danger, Ro would absolutely turn the sword over to her. She took a breath. "Why did you say this party was a bad idea?"

"Because it announces you to the realm. Very few here

are going to keep quiet that they dined with the new chosen queen. In a matter of days, the news will spread throughout the kingdom, regardless of your decision."

She sighed in frustration. "I wish I'd never touched that wretched thing."

"You and me both."

She glared at him. "How do you know so much about this queen and what she wants to do?"

He kept his eyes on the crowd as he answered her. "Because I grew up under Queen Anyka's reign."

CHAPTER TWENTY-ONE

After her conversation with Gabriel, which had ended thanks to Uldamar stealing her away to meet more people, Ro's appetite was nearly nonexistent. She ate enough to be polite, nodding at the right spots during the various discussions going on around her, commenting on the entertainment, and doing her best to look engaged.

But her mind was elsewhere. Gabriel's words played over and over in her head. The thought that JT or Aunt Violet might be in danger because of this whole affair was really upsetting.

"Lady Sparrow?"

Ro blinked and brought herself back to the present. She looked at Uldamar, who'd been seated at her right. Gabriel was across and two seats on her left, but he'd said little since the first course had been served. "Sorry, I was lost in thought."

"So I noticed. Is everything all right?"

Nothing was all right, but she couldn't exactly discuss it here, could she? She smiled as best as she could. "I'm fine. Just tired. And a little overwhelmed."

"I'm sure. Dinner will be over soon, although I expect

some of the guests will want to bend your ear over cordials and coffee long into the night."

Ro shook her head. She didn't have the patience for that. "I'm sorry. I can't. I'll fall asleep in my chair." She wasn't that tired, but it was as good an excuse as any to end the evening.

"Understood." He glanced at Gabriel, then back at her. "Are you sure nothing's upset you?"

She studied the old wizard, because that's what he was, after all. An old man filled with magic and mystery and secrets. If that didn't make him a wizard, what did? "I have a lot on my mind. That's the best answer I can give you right now."

He bowed his head slightly, and that was the end of the conversation. For now, anyway. Something told her he wouldn't let things go that easily.

Dessert was served, individual dishes of sweet custard topped with fruit and chocolate shavings. It was really nice, but after a few spoonfuls, it tasted like nothing to Ro. She wished she could go home tonight, but that would mean missing the chance to see her aunt one more time.

Maybe that was Ro's answer. Maybe talking to her aunt some more would help her figure this out. There wasn't an issue Aunt Violet hadn't been able to solve when Ro was a kid. Even if Violet had said Ro was the problem solver, the only way that was true was if Ro had learned it from Violet.

The idea gave Ro some comfort. She took another bite of the custard. It really was good.

On her direct left were Professor Cloudtree and his

wife, Althea, then Gabriel across from her. Althea had been trying to engage Gabriel in conversation all night. He'd responded in grunts, glares, and snorts until she'd finally given up.

Cloudtree had been rattling on about a previous king and his ruling on a grain embargo, and Ro's nods had only kept him going. But she was done. She wanted to strip off all of her finery and collapse into that big bed.

Traveling to this realm was by far the strangest and most interesting thing that had ever happened to her. But she was ready for it to be over and for that sword to be back in the stone.

She smiled at Professor Cloudtree, who'd started up again as soon as Uldamar had stopped. This time about the historical significance of the Brightwater Bridge. Something clicked in her head. "Excuse me, did you say Brightwater Bridge?"

He nodded. "Yes. That's the name of bridge that spans the Whistling Sea."

Brightwater was also Maybelle's maiden name. And Ro wasn't a big believer in coincidences. "Why was the bridge named that?"

Spencer looked thrilled to have found a subject Ro was interested in. "It was named after the engineer who designed it—Atllus Brightwater—which isn't usually how such things are named, but he died during the construction. A terrible accident. Seemed only fitting that his name should live on as part of that beautiful bridge. Of course, it's not in use anymore."

Althea leaned in. "Lovely people, the Brightwaters. Terrible shame about Atllus."

Ro nodded. "I'm sure. About the bridge ... is there a law against using it?"

"Oh, no," Spencer said. "But no one does. It would be foolhardy. Malveauxian archers are stationed day and night in their watchtowers."

Althea wrinkled her nose. "Summerton's got archers on our side, too. Fair is fair."

"Are there Brightwaters who still live in Rivervale?"

Spencer looked at his wife as if to confirm.

Althea shook her head. "Last I'd heard, they were all gone. Moved to Brookridge or Woodburn. Can't remember which it was. Anyway, I guess living in sight of the bridge got to be too much, so they just retreated to the country. Not that they were going to be farmers or anything. They had a country home out there."

"I see."

Althea smiled. "You know what I mean by a country home, don't you?"

"I'm not sure," Ro said.

"I mean the kind of place you could billet an army in. Fifteen or twenty bedrooms set on acres and acres with private hunting grounds, stables, estate workers, all kinds of staff. I'm not saying they went out there to reconnect with their roots or live off the land, you understand. Their home is more like a smaller version of this place."

Ro nodded. "And they've never come back?"

This time Althea looked at Spencer. "Not that I've heard. You?"

He shook his head. "Nope. Don't know why they would, honestly."

"Thank you. I appreciate that information." Was Maybelle one of those Brightwaters? If so, that might explain why no one had known who she was. After she'd died and returned here, she'd probably ended up in the country where her family had moved to, which made sense.

Tomorrow she'd ask Aunt Vi about the Brightwaters, see if she knew anything. Ro covered her mouth as she felt a yawn coming on. She really was tired. Maybe there was a jet lag equivalent to traveling between the two worlds, because the sense of exhaustion had suddenly come on pretty strong.

She leaned toward Uldamar. "I'm ready to go. Should I say anything or just get up and excuse myself or what?"

"If you were queen, you'd simply rise, thank everyone for coming, and leave."

"I can do that. After I leave, can you meet me upstairs? I'd like to talk to you before I turn in."

"I will do that."

"Thanks." Ro pushed to her feet. She smiled at those around the table. The musicians ended their song. "Thank you all for joining me this evening. It's been my pleasure to get to know you. I apologize for cutting this short, but today has been quite a day, as you can imagine, and I am at the end of my energy."

That got her lots of smiles and nods.

"I wish you all a safe trip home. Good night."

Everyone stood as Ro left. She found her way back to

the stairs. The guards had been replaced by a different pair, but they seemed to know who she was and merely bowed their heads as she passed them.

Once again Gabriel's words came back to her about the news of her arrival spreading throughout the kingdom. He was right, of course. If the guards knew, wouldn't they tell their friends and families? Even if it was just the small contingent who stood watch at the steps, they hadn't been sworn to secrecy.

She didn't blame them for sharing. Summerton had been rulerless for so long that there was no way the news of a long-awaited prophecy coming true would remain a secret. These people had been waiting over a century for someone to pull that sword from the stone.

She entered the royal chambers.

Wiggy was pacing but stopped when she saw Ro. "I'm hungry."

"Did Benny eat all the food?"

"I'm not sharing with him. Besides, I want people food."

Ro sighed. "I suppose you would. All right, we'll get you something. What do you want?"

"Tuna," Wiggy said.

"I think the best they can do is something called slipper fish."

Wiggy made a face. "Maybe. Or chicken."

"Okay. I'll see what I can do." As Wiggy headed off toward the lounge, Ro glanced at the rope that Uldamar had told her would summon help. She went over and pulled it. A moment later, soft chimes rang.

She frowned. She hadn't expected to hear anything, imagining that whatever bell the cord rang would be closer to the staff quarters.

Then the chimes sounded again.

She went to the foyer and opened the door.

Uldamar stood on the other side. "You wished to talk?"

"Yes. Thanks for coming. This won't take long." She walked through as far as the first sitting room and stopped. "Why didn't you tell me about the threat from Queen Anyka? And about the Malveauxian prophecy that says the next ruler of Summerton will overthrow the Malveaux throne? Don't you think that's kind of important information?"

For a breath or two, he said nothing. "Yes, it is important, but I didn't feel it was prudent to tell you those things so soon. That prophecy is one of many. Also, you have yet to accept the crown. There is much that cannot be shared until you officially become our new queen. You must understand that."

"Sure, I get that you don't want to turn over the combinations to the royal vault or give me signing privileges on the official checkbook, but threats? That seems like something I should know about."

He shook his head. "The threat is nebulous. She will not act. At most, she will prepare for any action the new ruler might take, but unless you plan to invade Malveaux, then there is nothing to worry about."

"Gabriel said—"

Uldamar snorted. "Nightborne. I should have known. He likes to stir up trouble."

"I don't think he was stirring up anything. Just giving me some information. And I appreciate having as much pertinent information as possible going into this decision."

Uldamar tipped his head. "Then you are still trying to decide?"

She wasn't. And she didn't want to lie. "No. Not really. I guess I just didn't want to rule out any possibilities, you know? Although I was thinking about a possible solution."

"Oh?"

The chimes rang again.

She glanced toward the door. "I pulled the bell to get a housemaid. Wiggy's hungry. Just give me a minute." She answered it and found a housemaid there.

The young woman curtsied. "You rang, your ladyship?"

"Yes. Could I get some boiled chicken? Maybe a little fish, if you have it? No bones. It's for my cats." She couldn't leave Benny out. That would just be cruel. "But bring silverware, too. And an extra dish." She had no idea how Wiggy planned to eat it but better to be prepared.

"I'll see to it, your ladyship."

"Thank you."

The young woman left. Ro shut the door and went back to Uldamar.

"You said you had a possible solution?"

"Right." She put her hands on her hips. She was ready to get out of this dress. "I was thinking maybe I could be queen part-time? I could come here Friday night, then leave Sunday night to go back to the mortal world. Would that be enough?"

He stared like he was thinking. "I don't know. I'm not

sure what the councils would think of that. I am inclined to believe they wouldn't care for it. Neither would the citizens, I fear. Ruling in such a manner might make them feel you weren't taking the job seriously. Like they weren't your first priority. Which they wouldn't be."

She nodded. "Right. I can see that. I was just trying to come up with a way to make things work."

"I believe in the mortal world that's what they call having your cake and eating it too."

She frowned. "I wasn't doing it for my benefit. I was trying to help."

He held his hands up. "Forgive me."

"What have you got against Professor Nightborne? You really don't seem to like him."

"I like him well enough. But we have different philosophies about life and how it should be lived."

Ro crossed her arms. "So it has nothing to do with the fact that he was born in Malveaux?"

Uldamar's expression hardened ever so slightly. It was obvious Nightborne's heritage had a *lot* to do with Uldamar's feelings about the man. "One's birthplace means nothing in comparison to one's character. Now, I should leave you to your rest. As you said, it's been a long day. Good evening, your ladyship. I'll see myself out."

Chapter Twenty-Two

After the visit to General Wolfmane, Anyka's appetite for dinner was significantly reduced. It had been good to see just how prepared Malveaux was for war, but spending time in the barracks was like being bathed in brute male essence.

It was stimulating at first but very soon became unbearable.

Her mood wasn't helped by the fact that Beatryce remained aloof. Not a word from her only child. Not even a note to say she'd moved into new quarters.

Anyka had sent word to the kitchen that she would dine in her chambers and only to send hot soup, fresh bread and butter, and a flagon of wine.

The kitchen did exactly that but had included three petite iced chocolate cakes and a pot of spiced cocoa, too. Each cake was about an inch across, and the cocoa, one of her favorite warm drinks on a cold night, smelled divine.

Normally such a blatant disregard of her orders would be grounds for a reprimand, but she was willing to overlook it this time. She smiled. The head cook, an older man named Bartlam, would have to do much worse to earn her wrath than send her desserts.

He'd been running the kitchen and cooking for Anyka

since her parents' Minister of Spirits had been executed for allowing their poisoning, and the cook, his wife, banished.

Anyka trusted Bartlam a little more than she trusted most people. After all, he'd had many opportunities to end her and yet, she lived. Although in truth, Trog would have been the one to perish, as he was not only her guard but her taster.

She ate her soup of beef, vegetables, and lentils, dipping torn pieces of bread into it. She fished out a few hunks of meat and tossed them to Galwyn, who perched on the edge of the table. He gobbled them down with great enthusiasm, which amused her.

Trog was stationed at the door to her chambers. Trolls had the uncanny ability to sleep standing up, and she often wondered how much he slept while on duty. Not that it mattered much to her. He had whip-fast reflexes and had never once failed to respond to a disturbance. Even if most of those disturbances were Galwyn's caws.

And the first time Trog slept through a threat, he'd be done. Sent to Tenebrae, or worse. If she were still alive to make sure of it, that was.

She sat back. Her bowl remained half full, but she'd lost interest. She tossed Galwyn a bit of bread. He ruffled his feathers and picked at it. Bread was not his favorite.

Maybe she should have invited her uncle to join her. Ishmyel was sometimes good company, but most often, he was too much.

After the day she'd had, he probably would be too much. No doubt wanting to chime in on how to handle Beatryce. Or how to proceed if Summerton did have a new ruler. Anyka had no patience for any of that. Even from her father's younger brother.

She preferred to keep him at arm's length. Which was why she often sent him on delegations to the farthest lands in the kingdom. Maybe she should send him back with the trolls as an envoy.

The rain had stopped at least, and the skies had cleared enough to let a few stars shine through. The village below glittered where streetlamps, lanterns, candles, and the glow of magic illuminated the night.

Even Malveaux could look beautiful now and then.

A soft rapping at the door turned her head around. Trog gave her a look she knew well. She shook her head. "I wasn't expecting anyone."

But maybe it was Beatryce, come to make amends.

Anyka held out hope as Trog faced the door, blocking the sightline of whoever was on the other side with his width. He opened it. And grunted.

Then moved aside to let Wyett through.

Good, she thought. If he was here, maybe she'd engage him in a game of hounds and wolves.

He bowed as he stood before her, waiting to be acknowledged.

"Wyett."

"Good evening, Your Highness. I have news about the matter we spoke of in the library."

Eager to hear, she nodded. "Go on."

"It has been confirmed. *Merediem* has chosen a new ruler. A woman pulled the sword from the stone. She has not yet been established as queen, but a coronation will undoubtedly take place soon. My sources say she is from the mortal world."

Anyka let that information sink in. "Not Summerton born then?"

"No. Mortal born. A crossover. She knew nothing of this realm until she pulled the sword free and was transported."

What a shock that must have been. Anyka's jaw shifted to one side as she thought. A woman like that might be as useless on the throne as a glass hammer. Pretty to look at it but easily shattered under pressure. "I doubt she'll be much of a threat then. Or much of an opponent."

"I cannot speak to that. The information I gleaned is thin, at best."

"When is the coronation?"

"No word on that, either, but it would be terribly rude of them not to invite you."

She smiled. "It would be, but I won't hold my breath. Anything else you can tell me about her?"

He nodded. "She has a child in the mortal world and an aunt in Rivervale."

"Interesting. Very interesting." Her appetite was returning. But not for soup. She picked up one of the little chocolate cakes. "I want to know more about the aunt."

Wyett nodded. "I've already sent a few feelers out."

"Good. What about Beatryce?"

"She's completely moved into the West Tower. She had dinner in her new chambers with two of her ladies-in-waiting and had a troubadour in to entertain them."

Anyka rolled her eyes and laughed. "Playing house will soon lose its appeal, I think."

"I imagine it will."

She took a bite of the cake, eating half of it. It was soft and moist and deliciously sweet. "Stay and play a game of hounds and wolves with me."

He nodded. "As you wish. Shall I set the board up here?"

"No, let's play in the lounge." She ate the last half of the cake. "But first, have the kitchen send up more of these. In fact, have them send a whole platter of sweets and fruit."

"I'll see to it."

The sugar had improved her mood, making her feel generous. "What would you like to eat, Wyett?"

He looked surprised but only for a moment. He didn't answer, though.

"Go on," she said. "Hounds and wolves can take hours. You ought to have something to sustain you."

"I do enjoy those nut and fig cookies."

"Then get some. And another pot of spiced cocoa. This time with a little kurra nut liquor in it."

"Very good." His mouth curved up, making him even more handsome. "Thank you."

She smiled. "Don't thank me yet. My wolves are about to tear your hounds to pieces."

CHAPTER TWENTY-THREE

Twenty minutes or so after Uldamar left the royal chambers, the housemaid returned with a tray of food for the cats. Ro let her in, and she carried the tray into the lounge and set it on the table. There were three platters covered with silver domes.

"The kitchen prepared boiled chicken, poached white fish, and a dish of plain steamed shrimp." The housemaid took the domes off as she spoke. "I hope that's to your liking."

Wiggy came zipping in. "I smell chicken."

Benny trotted in behind her, announcing himself with a plaintive meow.

Ro laughed. "I think it will be to everyone's liking. Thank you."

The young woman nodded. "You're welcome."

She started to leave.

"Wait," Ro said, walking with her. "Can you have Professor Nightborne sent up? I need to speak with him."

"I will send a footman."

"Oh. Does he live far?" Ro realized it might be a bigger inconvenience than she'd imagined. She didn't want Gabriel mad at her. Getting on his bad side seemed like an unwise decision.

"No, your ladyship. He lives on the grounds."

"Okay, fine. Thank you." Made sense, Ro thought. He was in charge of palace security.

She checked in on Wiggy and Benny. Wiggy was sitting at the table with the plate of chicken in front of her, eating with her hands. Benny was sitting on the table, eating from a dish that had chicken and fish on it.

Wiggy must have put it there for him. While Ro watched, Wiggy put a shrimp on Benny's plate.

That made Ro smile. She sat in a dining chair next to them. "How is it?"

"Good," Wiggy said.

"You put that dish of food on the table for Benny?"

Wiggy nodded but was apparently too busy eating to say anything.

"Thank you. That was very kind of you."

"He's not very smart."

"No? He seems pretty smart to me."

Wiggy cut her eyes at Ro for a second, then went back to eating. "He doesn't have thumbs."

"You realize you only have thumbs because going through the portal changed you into a human being. Or fae being. You know what I mean, though, right?"

Wiggy shrugged and stuffed a shrimp in her mouth.

"Would you like to live here? Or do you want to go back to the apartment that we came from?"

Wiggy had no problems talking with her mouth full. "No way. This place has room to run. That place is too small. And it doesn't have any rodents."

"I'll tell the landlord." Ro shook her head. She'd see about securing Wiggy a place in the morning.

The chimes rang again.

Nightborne was at the door when she opened it. He'd changed out of his formal clothes and now wore a loose, white linen shirt with tan trousers tucked into soft leather boots. His sword was still on his hip and his dagger still in his boot. "You summoned me?"

She couldn't tell if he was bothered by that or not. He was very hard to read. "Remind me never to play poker with you."

"Poker?" He stayed just outside the foyer.

"It's a card game. Anyway, I'm sorry to disturb your evening, but I was hoping to talk to you again."

"I am at the queen's beck and call. It's my job."

"But I'm not the queen."

A hint of a smile played on his mouth. "No, you are not. Unless you've called me here because you've changed your mind?"

"No. I just had some more questions. And I thought you were the one most likely to tell me the truth."

That got her a real smile. He nodded. "I will."

She backed away from the door. "Please, come in."

He hesitated. "If you want to talk, perhaps this is not the place to do it."

That surprised her. Were the royal chambers bugged in some way? "What do you suggest?"

"The gardens are quite pleasant in the evening. A stroll?"

"All right. But I'd like to change first. If you don't mind waiting in the sitting room." She gestured toward the room behind her.

"Not at all." He came in.

She walked with him into the sitting room, then kept going toward the dressing room. "Be right back."

She hadn't brought a lot of clothing with her, figuring it was just an overnight stay. She put on jeans, a T-shirt, and a cardigan along with the woven ballet flats she'd worn here. She hung the gown up and carefully put all of the jewelry on the island in the middle of the dressing room, leaving the slippers next to it.

She left her hair and makeup as they were and went back out to get Gabriel. "I'm ready."

He stood, taking in her outfit. "Very good."

She started toward the door.

He shook his head. "Not that way."

She stopped. "Then how?"

He smiled. "I'll show you."

He led her back through the bedroom and into the dressing room. He went about three-quarters of the way toward the back wall, then parted the clothing hanging there. "Closer. So you can see how to do this."

She stood next to him.

He put both hands on the wall, fingers spread, and pushed.

The wall panel sank in with a click and hinged open an inch on one side.

"A secret passageway." She grinned. "Very cool. And in

a place like this, I should have known there'd be one. All the best castles have them."

"This isn't the only one, either. This place is full of them." He lifted one shoulder. "Of course, I probably shouldn't be showing you this since you're not—"

"Really queen. I know. I get it. You and Uldamar."

Gabriel's brows lifted. He put a finger to his lips as if she shouldn't say anything else, then pushed the door open and motioned for her to follow.

The light from the dressing room leaked into the passage enough to show her there were curving stairs, but as they descended, darkness surrounded them. She put her hand out in front of her, keeping the other on the wall for guidance.

Her fingers brushed against Gabriel's muscular back.

A few steps down, and a breeze drifted past. She sensed a large opening to her right. Another passageway?

Before long, they were on flat ground. They came to a stop. Gabriel opened a door in front of them, and she could see again thanks to the stars and moon overhead. They were outside, obviously, but she wasn't sure where. It didn't seem like the garden she'd been in with Violet.

"This way," he whispered.

She grabbed his hand, a reflex.

He held on and guided her, keeping them along the castle's curved walls. They went through another door, this one wooden and set into a thick hedge.

Then they were in the garden, the air thick with the perfume of night-blooming flowers and pulsating with the hum of insect life.

The garden looked so different at night. The colors were muted by the darkness, turned into cool, jeweled shades of their former brightness. And everywhere she looked there were glowing things. Flowers, insects, patches of moss. The garden seemed lit from within.

"It's so beautiful," she breathed out.

He let go of her hand and nodded. "The private gardens are something special. King Reedly built these for his queen. Before her death, obviously. He went quite mad after losing her and his children."

"Whatever happened to the king after the sword was put into the stone? Uldamar said something about exile."

Gabriel held his hand out. A luminous white moth landed on it. "Yes. He and the queen's mother were exiled. Punished for their roles in the deaths of Queen Anyka's parents."

Ro nodded. "I heard about that. But not what had happened to the king. Where were they exiled to?"

"The mortal world." He looked at her as the moth walked along his knuckles. "I don't think you'll run into them, though. I believe they were sent to Canada."

"Good to know. But when they die, won't they come back here?"

He shook his head. The moth took flight again. "Their magic was stripped before they were exiled. When they die, they die."

"That's kind of sad."

"Actions have consequences."

She knew that. And she agreed with it. "Were they tried and found guilty? Or just accused and that was that?"

"They confessed to a judge. In fae society, that's enough." Gabriel stuck his hands in his pockets.

She shook herself. "I know perfect doesn't really exist, but this place looks like it should be."

"It's not," he said. "No place is." He jerked his chin at the path ahead of them. "Would you like to walk? And ask me your questions?"

"Yes." She kept step beside him. "But some of them I've already asked."

"What's left?"

"I was wondering if it would be possible for me to visit here on occasion. You know, my Aunt Violet lives here now, and it would mean so much to me to be able to see her again. And maybe even bring my son here."

His brow furrowed. "Of course. You're fae. That's not going to change if you turn down the throne. I would have thought you'd have been given a ring by now. And shown how to use it."

"You mean one of those rings with the gemstones on it? Uldamar showed me how to use his. Sort of. I put it on and used it to bring us back to the castle from my apartment. But he hasn't given me one yet. Maybe he's going to do that tomorrow before I leave."

"Maybe."

"You don't sound very certain."

"The old wizard and I don't see eye-to-eye on a lot of things."

Ahead of them was a flower bed filled with orangey-red lilies that looked like little fiery torches, in part because their throats glowed like they were full of live embers. They were held back from the path by a low, wrought-iron fence.

She reached out to touch one, but Gabriel grabbed her arms, pinning them to her sides and putting himself face-to-face with her.

CHAPTER TWENTY-FOUR

"No." The word was a stern rebuke. He shook his head. "Don't."

"Don't what?" She stared into his eyes, inhaling the smoky scent of him. He had quite a grip on her. That had to be the reason she suddenly felt so breathless.

Certainly not because her body was pressed up against his. Although that could be the reason she felt so weak in the knees.

She really needed to get out more.

"Don't touch those flowers." He released her and took a step away. "I'm sorry for grabbing you like I did, but those things will kill you."

She took a breath as she stared at the beautiful blooms. "Those?"

He nodded. "Fire lilies. That's what the queen's mother used to make the poison that killed Queen Anyka's parents."

Ro shuddered to think she'd been seconds away from taking hold of one. Gabriel had saved her life. "Why on Earth is there such an enormous bed of them growing here then?"

"Because no one's lived here since the king and queen

were exiled. The gardens have been maintained, but that's it. They might have also been left to serve as a reminder. I don't know. You'd have to speak to the gardener."

She backed away from the lilies. "If I were in charge, I'd have them destroyed."

"So would I."

"Thank you for saving me."

"It's my job." He nodded toward a point up ahead. "Come on. I know a place we can sit for a minute."

She walked with him, sending one backwards glance at the flowers. "Is it by the pond with the ghost fish? I sat there earlier with my aunt today. It's a great spot."

"It is. And you should see it at night."

They rounded the bend, passing by the enormous trunk of a smooth-barked tree, and came into sight of the pond.

The fish glowed eerily underwater, although there was nothing scary about them. They looked like flying ghosts, gliding through the water.

Ro grinned. "I can see why they're called ghost fish now." She went over to the bench and took a seat.

He joined her, and they sat in silence for a moment.

Ro glanced at him. "I had an idea about how I could keep my life in the mortal world *and* be queen. I could come here on weekends. But Uldamar nixed it. I guess it wasn't such a great idea, to be a part-time ruler, but I did try."

Gabriel wasn't looking at the fish. He was scanning the area around the pond. "It's not such a bad idea, but I don't think the people would like it. After so many years of going without, they want a ruler who's fully invested. They want a ruler who will provide them with guidance and stability."

"I can understand that."

"There's a chance they might accept a part-time queen, if that's the best you can manage right now, but it would have to be presented as a temporary solution. That's my opinion anyway."

She shrugged. "Uldamar kind of shot it down, so it doesn't matter."

Gabriel snorted. "He's not in charge, you know."

"He's not?"

"No. No one is. That's the problem."

She thought about that as she watched him. He fixed on a spot across the water, gave it a few extra seconds of consideration, then moved on again. "You really think I could be in danger?"

"I don't think there's a ruler in any country in any realm who isn't in danger at some point. Sometimes from themselves. Power makes people do crazy things."

"That's certainly true."

He turned to look at her for a moment. "You don't strike me as the type to let power go to your head, but then, I've been wrong before. Not often. But it does happen."

She almost laughed. "Good to know you're not as perfect as you seem."

He shook his head slowly. "I am a deeply flawed man, but I am good at my job, and that's all that matters." His brows lifted slightly. "Any more questions?"

"Just about a million, but my head feels full enough already."

"May I ask you one?"

"Sure." She hadn't been expecting that.

"What do you do in the mortal world?"

"I'm an assistant curator at the Museum of Historical Arts, but on Monday, the board is announcing the new curator." She smiled. "Me. I've been working toward this job all of my adult life."

No smile, but he nodded. "And that's why you don't want to give it up to come here."

"Right. That job and my son. I'm very much a part of his life, and I would miss him terribly if I left."

"But not your husband?"

She smirked. "There is no husband."

"You're widowed?"

"No. Not divorced, either." She stared at the pond, watching the fish again. "I had an affair with a man I shouldn't have. I regret that but not the end result. JT is the best thing that's ever happened to me. Hands down." She snuck a peek at Gabriel. "I suppose the citizens of the realm might not like that I have an illegitimate child?"

"The citizens of the realm understand that trials and tribulations happen to everyone. It's how we deal with them that defines us."

"Good to know." She liked Gabriel. And not just because he'd saved her life. He might be flawed, in his own words, but he seemed like a good man to her. "I'm sorry you won't get to be my head of security."

He took a deep breath, then let it out before answering her. "So am I." He leaned forward, grabbed hold of one of his fingers and wiggled the ring off it. He held it out. "Here. Hold onto this in case Uldamar doesn't give you one."

She took it. The ring had a lot more of the thin inner bands set with gems than Uldamar's had. "Thank you, but won't you need it?"

He shook his head. "I have others. And I want to make certain you can return when you want to."

"I appreciate that. Unfortunately, I still don't know how to use it other than lining up all the gemstones."

He nodded. "That will always take you to the castle portal. The same one you came through."

"You'll be with me tomorrow when I leave, right?"

"I will be."

"Maybe you could show me how to get to my aunt's then? That's really all I'll need."

"I'll work out the coordinates."

"Thanks." She studied him, trying to see the Grym Fae in his features.

He made a face. "Do I have a bug on me?"

She snorted. "No. I was trying to figure out how to see the Grym in someone. You are Grym, right?"

"I am."

"Well, right now, everyone looks the same to me." Although he was significantly more handsome than any other man she'd seen.

He tapped a finger against his ear, the movement somehow bringing him closer. "Grym ears curve around the skull more and point back more than up. Radiant ears stand out from the head a bit and the points go up."

"Anything else?"

"Yes, but those things are subtle and take more time and experience to learn."

And she wasn't going to be here, so why should he bother teaching them to her? At least she had to wonder if that's what he was thinking. She wouldn't blame him if he was. But it made her a little sad.

"Are you completely sure you're going to renounce the crown?"

Ro nodded. "Yes, I am."

He leaned in and kissed her. The firm press of his mouth lingered, softening, teasing, then pulling back. There was a light in his eyes. And a hint of wicked amusement as his mouth curved up on one side. "That was nice."

She was breathless and jumbled but managed to nod. It was very nice. And very unexpected.

He looked past her, focused on the woods again. "We should probably get you back."

She was still reeling from the kiss. "Okay."

She was about to stand when his hand snaked out and grabbed her arm, holding her in place. Was he going to kiss her again? She was all right with that. "What?"

He shook his head, his gaze pinned to a spot beyond her. Something rustled in the brush. She froze, fear sluicing through her veins like ice.

"Look," he whispered.

She turned.

And saw a mama skunk walk out of the bushes with three little ones behind her.

Ro smiled and exhaled out the fear. It tickled her that Gabriel had wanted her to see that. The mama led her babies down to the water to drink.

"They're very cute," Ro whispered back. "I hope they don't spray us."

"Agreed," Gabriel said. "This is my last clean shirt."

CHAPTER TWENTY-FIVE

The kiss had left Ro in a bliss cloud, floating along on autopilot. She brushed her teeth, cleaned her face, put on her nightgown, then settled into the giant bed. It was very comfortable, and the sheets were soft and silky. Royal quality, apparently.

Benny hopped up next to her, attacked her feet through the covers, then wedged himself against her thigh to make some biscuits on the mattress before settling down to sleep.

Wiggy showed up next. She climbed up onto the bed, then curled up at the foot and eased down with a big yawn.

It was a little strange to have an elderly woman sleeping nearby like that, but Wiggy had been sleeping at the bottom of Ro's bed since Ro had adopted her and Benny. It would have been strange *not* to have Wiggy there.

"'Night, Benny. 'Night, Mrs. Wigglesworth."

"'Night," Edna said.

Benny, of course, said nothing. Thankfully.

Ro extinguished the oil lamp next to the bed and lay there watching the shadows develop as her eyes adjusted to the dark. Once again, she was struck by how quiet it was here. There were almost no sounds, but if she listened closely and let herself sink into the quiet, she could pick up some small, vague noises.

Animals in the distant fields. The faint chirp and buzz of insects. The almost imperceptible hum of the castle itself. Maybe the sound of the sea.

What little light there was seemed clear and crisp compared with the warm, artificial glow that seeped through her windows in the city. But the light here was from the moon and stars, not from the twenty-four-hour bodega on her block.

This would absolutely be an easy life to adjust to. Except for the ruling part. That part, if she was being honest with herself, scared her.

Despite what her aunt thought, it wasn't anything like being in charge of a museum. Being queen meant making decisions that affected peoples' lives. That was *very* different than deciding which pieces of ancient Peruvian pottery they'd be able to view during an exhibition.

Being queen meant a kind of responsibility she hadn't had since JT was a baby. But on a much broader scale, of course. In a sense, she'd become the mother of Summerton. Maybe that was being overly precious about the whole thing, but wasn't it kind of true?

The citizens expected someone they could look to for guidance and stability. Gabriel had used those exact words. Wasn't that what a child looked to a parent for?

She sighed. Gabriel was a whole other vortex of thought. One that would be with her a long time. Sleep was tugging at her, but just barely. There was so much on her mind that shutting it down felt impossible.

Why was she even thinking about being queen, though? It wasn't going to happen. Nothing about it fit into her life. She was about to be curator, and that was going to take everything she had for a while. It might not be a requirement of the job, but her own personal work ethic meant she would spend the next year or so proving that the board had made the right choice in giving her the job.

She'd work extra hours, spending time at home on the details of new exhibitions or thinking up new ways to increase traffic even further. The museum was about to be her kingdom, and she could only rule one at a time.

But she'd be back to Summerton, especially now that Gabriel had given her his ring. Spending time with Aunt Violet would be the perfect way to unwind. Maybe she'd get to see Gabriel again, but he'd probably be busy protecting whoever pulled *Merediem* free from the stone next.

Or maybe that wouldn't happen for a while. It had taken over a century for her to do it. Or was that just because the sword and stone had been tucked away at Maybelle's house? And if that was true, then why?

Had Maybelle's family been purposely trying to keep Summerton rulerless?

It was such a strange idea and one Ro couldn't work out an answer for. She finally fell asleep in the throes of the dilemma.

She woke up more rested than she'd expected to be. The room was filled with warm, peachy light, and the windows across from the bed showed a broad expanse of golden sky streaked with luminous orange clouds reflecting the rising sun.

No matter how long she lived in the city, that wasn't a view she was ever going to see in the morning.

Benny was still curled up next to her. He chirped and curled up a little tighter, stretching one paw sleepily toward Ro. She gave it a little shake. "Good morning to you, sleepy boy."

Wiggy was nowhere to be seen.

Then she came running into view. "You're up? Good. Let's eat."

"I only just woke up."

"Now. Come on. I'm dying."

Ro shook her head and threw back the covers. Wiggy as a person wasn't much different from Wiggy as a cat.

She went over to the feeding area and put a bowl of cat food down. At the sound of the can being opened, Benny bounded over and happily went to work on breakfast.

Wiggy stood by, hands on her hips, nose wrinkled. "I want salmon. And chicken. And some of those little shrimps again."

Ro shot her a look. "You sure have gotten demanding. No, I take that back. You've always been demanding." She laughed. "I guess you like being a person, huh?"

Wiggy looked slightly confused. "I've always been a person."

Typical cat. Ro went over to the bell pull and gave it a tug to summon a housemaid. "We'll get breakfast ordered."

She wouldn't mind some coffee and food herself. She'd

only picked at her meal last night. She wondered what a typical fae breakfast looked like.

The chimes sounded, indicating someone was at the door. That was fast. Maybe they'd been anticipating she'd want something to eat. Ro got her robe on and went to answer it. A young woman, in the uniform of the household staff, curtsied.

"Morning. I'd like to get some breakfast."

"Anything you like, your ladyship."

"Great. For the cats, a plate of salmon, if you have it, along with some chicken and some shrimp. Kind of like what the kitchen made up for them last night."

The woman nodded. "Very good."

"And for me, coffee, definitely. I don't suppose you know what a mocha latte is, do you?"

The woman shook her head, looking very apologetic.

"It's basically coffee with chocolate syrup mixed in, but I don't expect the kitchen to go overboard on my account. Coffee with cream and sugar will be fine."

"Very good."

"I don't know what the standard breakfast is in Summerton, but I'd be fine with a few pastries or a bowl of cereal. Honestly, whatever people usually eat is great. I don't need a lot, because I'm going to visit my aunt, and I'm sure she'll try to feed me, too."

"I'll make sure the kitchen knows."

"Thanks. How long do you think? I need to get ready, and I don't want to be in the middle of things when breakfast arrives."

The woman bit her lip. "Twenty minutes, maybe?"

"Okay, that's perfect." She could be showered and ready by then. Or bathed, rather.

The woman curtsied again and took off down the steps.

Ro shut the door and went to get ready. As soon as she ate, she was going to see Violet one more time.

She went into the bath, shut the door behind her, and looked around. There was no shower that she could see, but she'd make do. She set her shampoo, conditioner, and soap on the pool's edge, then stripped down and walked in.

The water was steaming hot and felt amazing. She sank all the way under to wet her hair but only came back up as far as her shoulders. Her bath last night had been pretty quick and would have to be again today, but she could see how easy it would be to spend an hour or so soaking in this thing every day.

No wonder the fae considered bathing a social experience. Although she hoped that included suits of some kind. She should have asked Gabriel. But she could imagine hanging out in here with a couple of girlfriends and a nice bottle or two of rosé.

A fae spa day.

She shampooed and conditioned her hair, soaped up the rest of her, then rinsed thoroughly before getting out and grabbing one of the towels off the nearest bench. She wrapped her body, then took another one and wrapped her hair in it.

She stayed that way while she moisturized and added a little makeup. Tinted SPF, a flick of mascara and a dab of blush. Not bad, but whatever Helana had done last night had been better. Unless that had literally been fae magic. There was no way Ro could reproduce that.

She put on a bit of eyeliner and penciled in her brows a touch, too. That helped. She'd add some lip color after she had her coffee and brushed her teeth.

But what she really needed was Helana on call.

Ro thought about that. If she were queen, that would probably be a given.

She put on the same outfit from last night, leaving the cardigan on the bed for later. Jeans, a T-shirt, and flats. Back in the bathing room, she towel-dried her hair and finger-combed it into place. Without a hair dryer, there wasn't much else she could do. Maybe that's why so many of the women wore braids. Those could easily be done on wet hair.

She'd just snapped her second hoop earring into place when the chimes announced her breakfast had arrived.

"Come in," Ro shouted. She wasn't sure she could be heard from this distance, so she headed toward the foyer.

The door opened as she reached the sitting room. The young woman from before was accompanied by two more young women, all in the same uniform. Each one had a tray of covered dishes, along with utensils. On one tray there were two steaming teapots, cups, spoons, and saucers as well as smaller covered pots. Sugar, maybe?

Ro moved out of the way to let them in. It looked like a lot more food than she had ordered.

The first young woman asked, "Your ladyship, where would you like us to set this up?"

"The dining table in the lounge would be fine. No,

wait. I'd like to have my breakfast on the balcony. The cats can eat in the lounge." The last thing she needed was Wiggy trying to leap off the balcony.

"Very good."

The young women busied themselves setting all that up.

Ro felt like she ought to tip them, but mortal world money wouldn't do them any good, and they probably weren't allowed anyway. Instead, she thanked them profusely as they left.

The young woman who'd originally shown up said, "I'll be just outside, ready to clean up when you're through."

"You're welcome to have a seat in the sitting room if you want to wait there."

The woman blinked at her, speechless.

Ro nodded. "I'm sure it's not protocol, but it's okay."

Then she went to check on the cats. Well, *the* cat and Wiggy. Both were happily munching down on the plates they'd been brought. Benny was going to have a hard time getting used to just cat food again once they got home.

She went out to the balcony. The table had been dressed with a tablecloth, which she hadn't seen on any of the trays. Two covered dishes were arranged along with two pots of what Ro assumed was coffee. A small pitcher of cream and a small, lidded dish of probably sugar were there, too, as was a crock of bright yellow butter, a crock of dark purple preserves, utensils, and a cloth napkin. A cup and saucer completed the setting.

She sat down at the table. This was definitely more

than she'd asked for, but what else could she do but see what had been brought? She started with the first pitcher and poured it into her cup. Not coffee. It looked and smelled more like hot chocolate.

She took a sip. It was hot chocolate, but it was something else, too. It had more depth of flavor. In fact, it tasted a little like chai seasonings had been added to hot chocolate. It was very good. She drank the rest, then poured from the second pot.

That looked and smelled like coffee. She tasted it. A hundred percent coffee. Then she wondered if they'd brought her both so she could mix them together. That would be something like a mocha latte.

She did just that and added a little splash of cream. The hot chocolate was sweet enough so she didn't think the drink would need sugar. She tried it. And smiled. It was different than the mocha latte she usually got every morning at City Donuts. But it was really, really good.

Cup in hand, she lifted the dome off the first dish. Underneath was an array of pastries. Hand pies, turnovers, tarts, biscuits dotted with bits of dried fruits, and some flaky buns that reminded Ro of square croissants. They all looked great.

She took the dome off the second dish and found scrambled eggs, sausages, a small pot of pink beans, fried potatoes, and a wedge of cheese. Her stomach rumbled, and she was suddenly starving.

So much for not eating a lot of breakfast. With eager anticipation, she picked up her fork and dug in.

CHAPTER TWENTY-SIX

Ro arrived at her aunt's bakery by way of an unmarked royal carriage. She'd specifically requested that in an attempt to stay incognito and not cause any further speculation about what might be happening at the castle.

Gabriel's words of warning had stuck with her just as much as his kiss had.

Because of his warning, she'd even had the carriage drop her off a street away. She passed a florist and thought about bringing her aunt some flowers, then realized she had no local currency. Kind of a bummer. She'd need to get some for when she came back to visit. It wouldn't do to let Aunt Violet pay for everything.

After the florist, she passed a butcher and a sewing shop. She stopped to look in the window. The fabrics on display were beautiful. She glanced across the street. There was a tea shop where it looked like you could buy loose tea but also sit and have a cup. Next to it was a dentist's office, and beside that was a general mercantile with everything from pots and pans to stepladders on display.

The whole place was so sweet and charming. She could absolutely see spending long weekends here with Violet.

Of course, Violet would still have to run the bakery, but

maybe in time that was something Ro could help with. Not by working there but by giving her aunt some money to hire another employee.

With the promotion to curator, Ro would be getting a decent raise. She could definitely spare a little of that every month if it meant making her aunt's life easier. She needed to talk to someone about how to get local currency. Maybe there was some kind of exchange.

She headed for Flake & Crumble, surprised to see a line out the door. She grinned. She was happy to see that line. Busy was good. She peeked in. Violet was behind the counter, as was a different young woman than the one Ro had met yesterday afternoon.

Both of them were hustling to take care of the customers. There was no way Ro could expect her aunt to take a break in the midst of rush hour.

Ro had a plan, though. She went around the block and found the back of the bakery. As expected, there was another entrance. The main door was open, leaving a wooden screen door to block out bugs but let air through. Ro slipped inside.

An older man was working at a long marble counter, preparing pies. "Can I help you, miss?"

"Hi. I'm Sparrow Meadowcroft. Violet is my aunt. I'm just here visiting, but she looked pretty swamped. I was thinking maybe I could throw on an apron and help."

He smiled. "Sure, if you want to get stuck in, have at it. Aprons are there by the door."

Ro found them on a hook. She took off her cardigan and hung it, then slipped the apron over her head and tied it behind her back. She went to the nearest sink and washed her hands. "Anything I can take out there?"

He used his elbow to point to a tray of sugar cookies on a rack. "Those can go."

"On it." She grabbed the tray and pushed through the swinging doors to the retail side.

Her aunt turned, a pie in her hands, and stopped. "Sparrow! What are you doing here?"

"We were supposed to meet this morning, remember? But I can't take you away from this. So I thought I'd help, instead."

"Of course I remember." Smiling, Violet shook her head. "But you shouldn't have to do that."

"I want to. And it's a great way to spend time with you. Now, where do these cookies go?"

"Top shelf, third column over. Daisy, this is my niece, Sparrow."

Ro nodded at the young woman. "Hi, Daisy. Nice to meet you."

"You, too." Daisy was putting plump muffins into a box for a customer.

Ro slid the tray of cookies into their spot. "If you need help, just tell me what to do."

Daisy looked over the counter. "Mrs. Crabapple is next. Can you help her?"

"Sure." Ro spoke to the woman in line. "What can I get you, ma'am?"

Thirty minutes later, the rush was over, and the cases were nearly depleted. Ro leaned against the back counter feeling a little like she'd run a marathon. "Is it always like that?"

Aunt Violet nodded. "Always, and I'm thankful for it. There will be another smaller rush around lunch, then right before we close, a few stragglers who forgot to get bread for dinner."

"Are you able to take a break now?"

Violet nodded. "I am. Let's go sit in the back and have a cup of tea."

Ro hesitated. She'd been hoping for a more private place to talk. "Is there a bench or something outside where we could sit? I'd love to see the village a little more."

"Sure. Daisy," Violet said. "You've got the shop."

Daisy nodded. "No problem."

Violet pushed through the doors to the back room. Ro followed. "I guess you met Mack."

"Not formally."

"Mack, this is my niece, Sparrow."

Mack was now forming thin ropes of dough into twists. He smiled at Ro. "Pleasure to be formally introduced." Then he looked at Violet. "Pies are just about done, and breadsticks will be next, then I'll get the meat pies finished."

"Perfect," Violet said. "Ro and I are going out for a bit. Daisy's got the front."

"We'll be fine," Mack answered.

"Come on," Violet said to Ro. "There's a park near here. We can sit there, by the fountain. Lovely spot. And sometimes there's a frozen custard man there."

They walked a few blocks away and found the park. It

was gorgeous. Large green lawns were ringed by tall trees that gave plenty of shade around the edges. Set back in that shade was a gazebo that looked very much like the portal at the castle. In the park's center was a fountain with a paved area surrounding it. Benches offered plenty of spots to relax. A few women had their young children there, splashing in the pool around the fountain.

Violet picked a bench with some shade. "This all right?"

"It's great."

They sat, and Ro dug the ring Gabriel had given her out of her pocket. She held it flat on her palm to show Violet. "I'll be coming back."

"Oh, that's marvelous." Violet pointed toward the gazebo. "There's a portal right there. Closest one to me, by the way." She leaned in. "Hold on now. That's quite a ring. That's not something most ordinary fae get. Does this mean you're accepting the crown?"

Ro shook her head. "No. What's so different about this ring?"

"Look at how many of the thin bands it has. With a ring like that, you could go just about anywhere, I imagine." Her aunt lifted the chain around her neck, pulling it free of her blouse. At the end dangled a similar ring. She held it out. "See?"

Ro inspected it. Vi's ring had about a third of the gemstone bands. "I do. Well, this one was given to me by Professor Nightborne."

Violet's eyes widened. "You met him?"

"I did. There was a dinner party last night at the castle.

I wish you could have come. I met both the high and low councils and some other folks." Ro smiled. "After the party, Gabriel and I went for a walk in the garden."

Ro decided to keep the bit about almost offing herself with poisonous flowers a secret for now. Same went for the kiss. Both were liable to elicit over-the-top reactions from her aunt.

Violet's brows lifted and her eyes gleamed with curiosity. "*Gabriel* Nightborne? You're on a first-name basis with the most dangerous man in the kingdom? What exactly happened on this *walk?*"

Ro laughed and tried very hard not to blush. Her aunt had always been a little too perceptive. "He was just showing me around. He answered some questions for me, things like that." Her smile disappeared. "I hate to tell you this, but I have to. You need to know. You might be in danger because of what I've done. Pulling the sword from the stone, I mean. Gabriel thinks that agents working for the queen of Malveaux could come after me to get the royal sword."

"As a way of bloodlessly taking Summerton."

"That's exactly right." It was good to know her aunt had a fair understanding of kingdom politics. "Gabriel said you and JT could be threatened as a means of making me turn the sword over. I just want you to be extra careful. If anything were to happen to you, I don't know what I'd do."

Violet patted her hand. "I'm sure I'll be fine, dear." She sighed. "I'd be better if you were queen, but I don't suppose asking again will help."

Ro squeezed her aunt's hand. "I'm sorry I can't be

queen and keep my life in the city. I really am. I tried to come up with a way to do that, but neither Gabriel nor Uldamar thought a part-time queen would be very popular with the citizens."

Violet chuckled. "No, I don't think people would like that much. But it's all right. You have to live your life. And watch over our boy. You'll bring him to visit, won't you?"

"You bet I will. I'm not going to keep this from him. I'm not sure he'll believe me until he sees it for himself, but I'll have him here as soon as possible."

"Wonderful." Violet craned her head. "Look, the custard man." She waved at him. "We'll take two."

The man pushed his striped cart toward them. An umbrella stuck up from one corner, shading him, but he still wore a straw hat with a striped band that matched the cart. "Afternoon, ladies. What'll it be?"

"Two vanilla with chocolate shards." Violet looked at Ro. "Is that all right?"

"I won't know until I try one, but it sounds good."

"Cups or cones?" the man asked.

Violet glanced at Ro again.

"Cones," Ro answered.

Violet dug coins out of her apron pocket and handed them over.

The man took them, then flipped up the big lid on his cart. He scooped up two fat cones of creamy yellow vanilla custard. He opened the second, smaller lid and rolled them in a dish of chocolate shavings, then handed them over with a couple of napkins. "Enjoy."

"Thank you." Ro took a cone from him.

With a nod, he went on his way.

The cone looked very much like a waffle cone, and it was wrapped in a sleeve of brown paper. She took a bite of the ice cream, instantly glad her aunt had suggested this. "Wow. This is one of the best things I've ever eaten."

Violet nodded. "You can't beat a frozen custard on a warm day."

"Life here is really nice, isn't it?"

Violet nodded. "When I first came here, after I got my bearings, it felt like I was living in a fairy tale. It still does some days. Not saying it's all sunny days and roses, but I don't miss the mortal world at all. You and JT, absolutely. But the rest of it? Not a bit."

Violet shook her head before having another bite of ice cream. She swallowed that quickly. "I'm not just saying that to sway you, either."

"I understand. Are you doing all right here? I mean, it seems like you could use more help at the bakery."

Her aunt laughed. "And normally I have it, but Wren is out sick today."

"Oh. Well, that's good. Not that someone's sick. I mean that you have more help. I was worried."

Violet smiled. "I promise, I'm getting on just fine."

"How did you get money when you first got here? I'm thinking I could use some for when I come visit. Is there an exchange?"

"Just about any bank will take mortal funds and exchange them. Although I think they have a daily limit. Anyway, it shouldn't be a problem. People on this side need mortal currency for their trips to the other side, too."

"That works out then. I should get a little before I go back."

Violet seemed to be concentrating on her frozen custard, so Ro did the same. It wasn't a hardship. The stuff was truly delicious.

Then Violet spoke. "You're going back today, hmm?"

"Probably not long after I get back."

Violet took a deep breath that seemed to lift her entire body.

"I'll be back. I promise."

Violet nodded, but her lower lids were rimmed with liquid.

Just the sight of her aunt nearly in tears made Ro weepy, too. "Please don't cry, Auntie Vi. We will see each other again before you know it."

Violet nodded. "I know," she said softly. Then she laughed. "I honestly don't know if I'm happy or sad. I'm just a silly old woman who's all mixed up inside."

Ro sniffed and shook her head. "No, you're not. I feel the same way. Happy I've found you. Sad I'm leaving. Happy I'll be coming back. Sad I won't be able to stay."

"All of that," Violet said. She managed a smile. "We should head back."

"Okay. I can eat and walk."

They strolled back to the bakery, taking their time and finishing their cones. When they arrived, Ro said her good-byes outside. She hugged her aunt tight, inhaling the scent of her perfume and the lingering aromas of baked goods, relishing Violet's soft embrace, and doing her best to absorb every atom of the moment into her memory.

She would be back, she knew that. But leaving her aunt after just finding her again was harder than she expected.

Violet patted Ro's cheek. "You go on home now. Tell JT all about me, okay?"

"I will. Then we'll both be here to see you."

Violet smiled through tears. "I can't wait."

Ro kissed her aunt. "Soon as I can. Maybe even next weekend."

Violet nodded. "Looking forward to it."

With a wave, Ro started back toward the street where the carriage was parked. She turned once to see if Violet was still standing there. She was. Ro teared up a little more, and a sob tore through her chest.

Maybe she was being a fool by not taking the throne. What did a job matter compared to family? She'd just have to talk JT into coming here. She couldn't leave him. She couldn't. Ro blew out a breath and did her best to get her emotions under control.

Could she really turn down the curator's job after all these years of working toward it? She didn't think she could. Maybe ... maybe she'd just be curator for a year or two. At least that way she wouldn't have any what-ifs.

She shook her head. It ached from so much hard thinking. Was there even a right decision to make?

CHAPTER TWENTY-SEVEN

Ro's bag was packed, the cat things were in the tote, and Benny was tucked into his carrier. Wiggy was sitting on the bed, brushing her hair, something she'd recently figured out she could do now that she had thumbs. She seemed to be slowly putting herself to sleep with the brushing.

Ro went over and hugged her. "I'll be back, Wiggy. You behave yourself, all right?"

"I'll be fine," Wiggy said. "The food here is good."

Ro didn't love leaving her, but there weren't many other options. She patted Wiggy's head. "I'll see you soon."

"Okay. See you soon." Wiggy went back to brushing her hair. Then she stopped. "You promise you're coming back?"

"I promise."

"With JT?"

"That's the plan."

She went back to brushing.

Uldamar and Gabriel were out in the formal sitting room, waiting on Ro. She should probably get moving before they came to see what was taking so long. She took one last look around. She was pretty sure she'd gotten everything. It wasn't like she'd unpacked.

She rolled her bag and the carrier out to the sitting room. "I guess I'm ready."

Gabriel and Uldamar both got to their feet. Uldamar had the sword, which would be returned to the stone shortly, then it had been decided that Uldamar would be bringing both back here.

The men had agreed it would be safer for everyone if Ro and the sword were not in the same realms. She was good with that. It wasn't like she could have displayed it at the museum anyway.

Gabriel took her weekend bag. "I'll carry that."

"Thanks." Was that really the same man who'd kissed her last night? He was so businesslike now. But maybe that was how things had to be in front of Uldamar. Made sense. Or maybe that kiss had meant absolutely nothing to him.

She hoped that wasn't the case.

They walked to the portal together, got into it, then Uldamar, making sure Ro was holding on to him and Gabriel on to Ro, began to set his ring.

"Wait," Ro said. "What are the coordinates to get me home?"

"Sapphire," Uldamar answered. "It'll bring you closest to your home."

"Thanks."

He turned the sapphire inner band to line up with the notches.

In a dark flash, they were back in the city.

Ro frowned as she recognized her surroundings. The smell was unmistakable. "We're in a subway station?"

Gabriel, who was now wearing dark jeans with boots, a

gray T-shirt, and a black leather jacket, answered. "Subway stations are never closed, safe from weather, and permanent. Using their coordinates makes the most sense."

"I can see that."

"Shall we?" Uldamar said. He was back in the old blue suit he'd had on during their return trip to the mortal world.

"Sure." This station was right by her apartment. "We're going to my place first, right? I don't want to haul all of this stuff to the museum. And pets aren't allowed anyway. Only service animals."

"That will be fine," Uldamar answered.

Gabriel seemed to be scanning every face that went past. "I'd like to check it for security purposes."

"That won't take long," Ro said.

She led them straight there with no stop at City Donuts. When they were inside, Gabriel looked around with a confused expression. "Where's the rest of it?"

"This is all of it." She put her hands on her hips. It did seem smaller than she'd remembered after spending time in the royal chambers. The bed she'd slept in last night wouldn't even fit through the door. Or in the apartment.

Amusement filled his gaze. "Yes, I can see why you'd be so reluctant to leave all of ... this."

She narrowed her eyes and responded to his sarcasm with a quick, fake smile. "Just drop the bag there. I'll deal with it later." She stood the carrier up and let Benny out. He hopped down, scratched the carpet a few times, then trotted off toward the bedroom.

She made sure she had her work badge, which was on

her dresser where she'd left it. "All right. We can head to the museum."

As they walked, she thought about the best way to get them in. If she brought them with her through the employees entrance, there'd be a record of them. Visitors' names were written down and they were issued badges. Better they come though the main lobby, pay the admission fee, then meet her inside.

From there, she could bring them down to the basement.

"Do either of you have mortal world money on you?"

Gabriel nodded. "We both do. None of us cross over without means."

"Okay, good." She'd get some fae coins for herself the next visit. "You both need to come in through the regular entrance. I'll meet you inside by the giant globe in the center of the rotunda. You can't miss it. It's straight ahead of you after you pay and come through security."

"Whatever you think is best," Uldamar said.

She walked them to the front. The museum was busy today, but it always was on Saturdays. "Up those steps, pay your admission, then straight through. I'll meet you there shortly."

"Got it," Gabriel said. He was still scanning faces.

She gave them a wave, then went around the side of the building to her usual entrance.

Kwame was off today. Jeremiah was in his spot.

The older man gave her a smile and a wink. "Dr. Meadowcroft. Coming in late, huh?"

She laughed. "I know. I'm not scheduled to be here."

Although it wasn't unusual for her to work on a Saturday. Not when there was a recent acquisition. To be honest, she'd worked a lot of Saturdays the past few years. All in the name of earning the promotion she was about to get.

He scanned her badge and let her through. "Don't work too hard, now."

"I won't. Not today. I'm meeting my son for dinner later."

"Good for you."

She went straight out to the main floor and found Uldamar and Gabriel staring up at the giant, spinning globe. "Gentlemen? This way."

She led them as discreetly as she could to the staff elevator, which she accessed with her keycard. She exhaled as they got in and the doors closed. She pushed the button for Basement One. Something about this whole thing made her feel like she was pulling a heist. Not that she'd ever done that, but in general, the museum's basements weren't meant for visitors.

Too many valuable things down there.

The car descended, the doors opened, and she held her hand up, peeking out first. Neither Estevan nor Salifya would be here. The warehouse guys only worked during the week. On the rare occasion one of them was needed, it required overtime. Something the museum didn't really budget for.

She stepped out. "Coast is clear."

Uldamar and Gabriel left the elevator. Uldamar reached into his jacket and pulled the sword free where it had been hidden down the side of his trousers. He went straight to the stone and embedded the sword into it.

She wondered if the warehouse guys had noticed the sword missing. If they had, hopefully they just thought she'd managed to get it free and had taken it to her office for more research. Or something. She had a feeling they had noticed, though. The stone hadn't been packed up like all the other Clipston pieces had.

He stepped back. "Gabriel, if you'd like to test it so that we might be sure it is truly secured."

Gabriel went over, grabbed the hilt, and pulled. Nothing. He sighed with a great deal of showmanship. "Still not king."

Uldamar set his hand on the hilt. "I'll get this back and leave you to your work."

Ro took a few steps toward him. "Uldamar?"

"Changed your mind, your ladyship?" His eyes were hopeful.

"No, sorry. But weren't you supposed to give me a ring so that I might return?" She assumed that Gabriel hadn't said anything about the one he'd given her last night.

Uldamar gasped. "For sooth, you're right. Forgive me." He dug into his pocket and produced such a ring, holding it out to her. "There's a portal near your aunt's cottage and bakery."

"The one in the park with the fountain?"

He looked a little surprised. "Yes, that's the one. Simply line up the peridot and the emerald and you'll be taken there."

"Peridot and emerald. Got it. Thank you. And thank you for showing me around and being so patient with me."

"You're very welcome, your ladyship. I wish you all the best."

"Thanks. You, too."

With one hand on the hilt of the sword, he used his thumb to shift the bands on his ring, and a second later he and the sword in the stone were gone.

"Good thing you asked him," Gabriel said.

She glanced over at him. He was studying a painting that was about to be restored. "Even so, I have the ring you gave me. Or did you want that back?"

He walked back toward her. "Keep it. You never know when it might come in handy."

"Okay." She doubted she'd need it, but who knew. Maybe she'd give the ring Uldamar had given her to JT. "I guess you'll be heading back, too?"

"No. I need to make sure you're safe first. Just because the sword is back in Summerton doesn't mean there might not still be a threat against you."

"You really think so?"

"Yes." There was no question in his eyes.

"What do you need me to do?"

"What would you normally do on a Saturday?"

"Work here a little. Maybe clean my apartment a bit. But today I'm going to be meeting my son for dinner." She looked at her watch. It was later than she'd realized. "In about two hours, actually."

A low rumble from the elevator shaft announced the car was on its way down.

She turned to look, then realized she was going to have to explain Gabriel to whoever was on their way down. She turned back to tell him to go along with whatever she said. Except he was nowhere in sight. Had he hidden? Taken off?

The doors opened, and she couldn't worry about him anymore. "Chairman Peters." What on Earth was a member of the board of directors doing down here?

"Dr. Meadowcroft." He smiled as he got off the elevator. "I thought I might find you here. Your work ethic is to be commended."

"Thank you. Were you looking for me?"

"I was, yes." He adjusted his glasses. "Just curious how that Clipston bequeathment is coming along."

Had he really come to see her about that? Interesting, if true. "I've only just dug into it, but unfortunately, I don't think it's going to turn into the treasure trove we'd hoped. At first glance, some of them appear to be replicas."

"I see. That is disappointing. You put quite a lot of time and effort into that, didn't you?"

"I did." Was this going to reflect badly on her? She couldn't very well explain that Maybelle's items weren't of this world. Peters would think she'd lost it.

"Well, these things happen." He gave her a curt smile, then headed for the elevator.

"I'll be sure to let you know Monday if I find out anything different."

"Monday? Oh, yes. Monday. Very good. We're going to need you more than ever on Monday." He shuffled onto the elevator, tapped a button, and disappeared behind the closing doors.

She stared after him. Had he actually forgotten for a moment that Monday was the day they were announcing her as the museum's new curator? Maybe he ought to be stepping down and making way for a younger person to join the museum's board of directors. He'd covered nicely with the comment about needing her, though. Always good to hear.

With a shake of her head, she turned. And nearly bumped into Gabriel.

She let out a soft shriek. "What—don't do that. You scared the daylights out of me. Where were you?"

"Right here. Hiding." He jerked his chin toward the elevator. "Who was that?"

"Chairman Roland Peters. He's a member of the board of directors, which is like the museum's high council. The same board that's going to make me curator on Monday."

"You look ... concerned."

She shrugged. "Maybe I am. A little. The bequeath-ment he came to ask about is a big nothing burger, and I worked on securing it for a long time. I'm really hoping he doesn't look at that as a failure on my part."

Gabriel narrowed his eyes. "Nothing burger?"

"I mean that I thought it was going to be full of all kinds of wonderful, interesting antiquities. Instead, it was filled with fae odds and ends. That's where the sword in the stone was. And obviously, that's very valuable, but I can't exactly display fae objects in a mortal world museum, can I?"

"No."

She waved her hand as if to dismiss the subject. "Anyway, it doesn't really matter. He's only one person on the BOD. And I've done a lot of other important things here at the museum. I'm not going to give it another thought. Not when I've got to get home and get ready for dinner with my son."

He nodded. "And I have surveillance to do."

CHAPTER TWENTY-EIGHT

Gabriel left Ro at the door to her building, promising he'd see her before he left. She went upstairs to get ready for dinner, starting with taking a quick shower to perk herself up a bit.

She had no idea what Gabriel meant by surveillance, but he was welcome to do whatever he needed to make sure Queen Anyka hadn't sent any thugs after Ro.

She almost smiled. Summerton seemed a little less real now that she was back home. She knew she'd been there, knew she'd spent real time with Aunt Violet, but somehow, away from the fairy-tale perfection of Summerton, surrounded by the gritty reality of this life ... it felt like a dream.

She turned the water off and got out. She peeked at the two rings sitting on her dresser. Would those really take her back there? She would test them out very soon.

Or maybe this was a dream and she just needed to wake up. She pinched herself. Ouch. Okay, not a dream.

Impulsively, she dug into her purse and pulled out her phone. She scrolled through to the gallery and looked at the pictures she'd taken. They were all there. Her battery was also about to die. She plugged the phone in to charge while she finished getting dressed.

Black slacks were paired with a black and white patterned blouse. She laid the black leather jacket she planned to wear with it on the bed. The jacket was a gift from JT. He'd bought it right after he'd gotten the job at the architectural firm. His way of saying thank you for supporting him.

Such a good kid. Although he was thirty, so she probably shouldn't think of him as a kid, but she couldn't help it. He would always be her baby.

She did her makeup with more attention to detail than usual, trying to recreate a little of what Helana had done. Then she flat-ironed her hair, put on some different jewelry, and took a look in the full-length mirror on the back of her bedroom door.

She pulled her hair back on one side just to be sure her pointed ears were gone. They were. She ran her finger over the top. Had they really been pointed? She should have taken a picture of herself as a fae.

Would have been nice to have a picture of herself looking like that. Now she looked a little flat and dull. The sparkle was gone. She sighed. Not much she could do about it unless she decided to spend some of her anticipated pay raise on serious time at a med spa.

Maybe she *should* start doing a little more. Not Botox, exactly. But maybe a monthly facial. And a little something extra with her hair. And maybe no more morning sugar high from City Donuts. She was about to be curator. She needed to represent the museum in the best possible way.

Starting Monday, she'd get more serious about taking

better care of herself. Right now, she needed to head toward the restaurant.

Satisfied that she looked the best she could, she pulled on her leather jacket, slipped her feet into black flats, gathered up her purse, phone, and keys, and headed out. She stopped at the door and, on impulse, went back for the ring Gabriel had given her.

When she hit the street, she looked for him. She had no idea where he was or what he was doing, but since he'd promised to say goodbye before he left, she sort of expected to see him. She didn't.

Maybe he'd gone already. The thought made her a little sad. She shrugged it off and started for the subway. She'd probably take a cab or an Uber back, depending on what time it was, but since it was still light out, she felt all right taking the subway.

She'd never had any issue on the subway, although she'd seen some crazy things—who hadn't—but after dark, she thought as a woman alone she was better off with less public transportation.

She arrived at Malone's at five-thirty on the dot. The restaurant was very much a traditional steakhouse with dark wood paneling, white tablecloths, and the warm glow of Edison bulbs. She approached the maître d' stand with a smile. "Hi. I'm meeting my son. Reservation is under Meadowcroft?"

The older man behind the stand consulted his book. "Ah, yes. Your son is here already. Right this way, ma'am."

She followed him back and saw JT sitting in their favorite little demi-booth. She grinned. "Hi, sweetheart."

"Enjoy your meal," the maître d' said, leaving them alone. A server swooped in and left a glass of water for her. JT already had one.

Her son got up and gave her a big hug, but not before she noticed that beside his glass of water there was another drink in front of his seat and it looked half gone. He held onto her a second or two longer than he usually did, his embrace tight and needy.

Something was wrong.

She kissed his cheek before letting go of him, then took her seat. Menus were already on the table, but she wasn't interested in them right now. As JT sat across from her, she studied him. "What's going on, honey? You don't seem like yourself."

He took a deep breath, which he let out in an equally deep sigh. "Things are … not good."

"Tell me."

"I got passed over for junior partner, and because of that, Jeanine broke up with me."

Anger was Ro's first response. Anger that her son hadn't been given the promotion he'd been promised and anger that his girlfriend could be that shallow and unsupportive. Ro had always known that girl was too focused on money. "If she broke up with you because of that, she's obviously got some serious character flaws."

He sighed and swirled the ice cubes melting in his drink. "I knew you'd say that."

"Well, it's true. And whoever decided not to give you that promotion is an idiot."

"That would be the senior partners."

"Then they're all idiots."

He smiled a little, but it was just a passing thing. His morose expression quickly returned. "I feel like a loser."

"Oh, honey, you are not a loser. You're one of the smartest men I know. You're handsome and funny and kind. You're the total package."

He shot her a skeptical look. "You're also my mother. You have to say that."

"No, I don't. If you were a jerk, I'd tell you."

He snorted. "Yeah, you probably would." He shook his head, still clearly despondent. "I'm trying to take it as a sign."

"What kind of sign?"

"That I need to do something different."

He'd spent a lot of time and effort getting to where he was, but if he wasn't happy, none of that mattered. So she nodded. "Maybe you do. Is there something else that speaks to you? Something that resonates in here?" She touched her heart.

He hesitated. "Don't laugh, but—"

"I would never laugh at you."

"No, you wouldn't." His smile was genuine this time. "I was thinking maybe I'd go into teaching."

"Really?"

He nodded. "I'd have to go back to school to get my certification, but I could do that in two years."

"What grade were you thinking?"

He shrugged. "Middle school, maybe? I'm not sure."

"What subject?" Although she had a feeling she already knew.

He made a little face. "English." Then he shrugged. "What else?"

"You always did love reading and writing." She flattened her hands on the table. "I love that idea."

"You don't think it's an easy way out and that I wasted all that time getting my architectural degree?"

"No one's path in life is a straight line."

"Now you sound like Aunt Violet."

"Speaking of—"

"Good evening." A trim, middle-aged man approached the table. "My name is Arthur, and I'll be your server this evening." He looked at Ro. "Can I get you something to drink, ma'am?"

"House red, please."

"Very good." He looked at JT. "And for you, sir? Another bourbon?"

JT put his hand over the glass. "I'm good, thanks."

"All right, I'll be back with that red in just a minute. Our special tonight is a forty-two-ounce tomahawk ribeye that can absolutely be shared. It's cooked to your liking and carved tableside and served with two of our signature sides."

"Thanks," Ro said.

Arthur left, leaving her free to speak again. But now she wasn't exactly sure how to broach the subject of Aunt Violet and everything that went with it. JT was clearly in a vulnerable place. Maybe now wasn't the right time to share that she'd almost accidentally become queen of a non-human realm.

He downed the last of his drink, then pushed the glass

aside. "What were you going to say about Aunt Vi?"

Ro smiled. "Just that she'd be proud of you, no matter what you did. Same goes for me."

"Thanks, Mom." He rubbed his forehead. "I can't believe Jeanine broke it off. I was thinking about asking her to marry me, too."

"Maybe you can look at that as a potential disaster averted?"

"Yeah, maybe."

She really wanted to tell him about Summerton. Then another thought popped into her head. "So is Jeanine moving out?"

He flicked his gaze at her, then went back to staring at the table. "No. Her name's on the lease. She said I can stay until I find a place, but I'd love to get out sooner. I need to make some decisions soon. Like in the next few days. Wherever I end up moving, it should be close to whatever school I'm going to go to."

"Makes sense. Where are you thinking?"

He frowned. "Probably not in the city. It's just too expensive to go to school, pay rent, and not have a full-time job. Because if I have to work full-time, it'll take me longer than two years to get my certification. I don't want to delay things any longer than I have to."

Her heart sank. "You're going to move away?"

He looked at her. "I don't think I have a choice."

Arthur returned with her glass of wine. They placed their orders, deciding to share the tomahawk ribeye with sauteed mushrooms and garlic mashed potatoes.

As Arthur went off to send their order to the kitchen, a new, probably crazy idea came to Ro.

She took a sip of her wine for courage. "What if … you stayed with me for a while? I know my place is small, but the couch pulls out, and we could make it work until you were back on your feet. You wouldn't have to pay rent or anything. And if you don't have to work while you're going to school, you might even be able to get done faster."

"Mom, your place is tiny."

"I know. But is a little sacrifice the worst thing?"

He seemed to think about that for a moment. "No. You really think we could manage to live in that postage stamp and not make each other crazy?"

"Sure. If we worked at it. Plus, I'm about to be curator, which means there will be a little more travel on my schedule. And I'll be making more money, so the increase in my grocery bill would hardly be noticeable."

He laughed. "That's pretty cool of you to offer. I just need to think about it. I really don't want to cramp you."

"Cramp me? Please! You lived in my body for nine months."

He grimaced even as amusement danced in his eyes. "Do you have to say things like that?"

She laughed. "I'm your mother. It's my right."

He shook his head. "Don't you ever think you might want to date somebody?"

For some reason, her mind went to Gabriel. She ignored that thought. "Maybe, but it's not like there's anything pending, so there's no reason to put that into the equation now."

JT sat back, stretching a little and shifting in his seat. "You know what I really wish?"

"What's that?"

"That I could go back in time and start over. Start with teaching to begin with. Maybe work on that novel I always thought I'd try to write. Just do things differently."

Her thoughts returned to Summerton, but that wasn't really starting over so much as it was starting something completely different. "I think we all wish that at some point in our lives."

CHAPTER TWENTY-NINE

Ro hadn't said a word about her experience with the fae during dinner. Instead, she'd mostly let JT talk. He needed it; she sensed that. She also sensed that trying to explain something as fantastical as traveling to a different realm might be too much for him right now.

He was already dealing with a lot. No reason to add to that load. There'd be plenty of time to tell JT once he made some decisions and knew what he wanted to do.

Besides that, she worried that if she told him, he'd want to go immediately. And she wasn't ready to go back. Not yet. Not with Monday being such a big day.

She was fully prepared for him to move in with her, though. Yes, it would take some getting used to, but if it was for her son's future, then it was a sacrifice worth making.

At the end of the meal, they shared a dessert, just an apple dumpling with vanilla ice cream. Ro didn't say anything out loud, but the dessert didn't compare to anything she'd eaten in the fae realm. She really couldn't wait to take JT there. The timing just had to be right.

When the meal was over and she had paid the bill, they walked outside.

JT gave her a hug. "Thanks for dinner, Mom. I really appreciate it. Thanks for listening, too. It was good to talk it all out. I'm going to walk home."

"Are you sure? I don't mind sharing a cab."

"I'm sure. Besides, we're going in different directions." He looked around. "You ever feel like you're being watched?" He laughed. "I thought maybe the Google car was going by. Anyway, the air will do me good."

"Okay, honey. I might walk a little bit, too, then grab an Uber. I'll talk to you soon, okay? Let me know as soon as you make a decision about what you want to do."

"I will, promise. I love you."

"I love you, too." She kissed his cheek, then they parted ways, each going in a separate direction. She didn't plan to walk far, but she wasn't in the mood for small talk with a random driver, either.

Walking was one of those great autopilot activities that let your brain work through all sorts of problems. It was also something she didn't do enough of. She headed uptown. She was many blocks from where she lived, but she'd only go a little ways. There were plenty of people around, as well. It was Saturday night, and the weather still held the coolness of late spring, so everyone was out and about.

She tucked her hands in her pockets and walked, thinking. Having JT move in with her would definitely be an adjustment. She thought about how she could rearrange the living room to give him the most space. She could even utilize the little alcove where her desk was. But actually, turning her living room into his bedroom wasn't what was going to take getting used to—it would be sharing the bathroom. She'd have to straighten that up a little, consolidate her things a bit. Clean out the medicine cabinet, which was long overdue anyway. Maybe get a caddy for each of them to keep their personal items in?

And she'd have to remember not to dry her unmentionables over the shower rod. But that small sacrifice would be worth it to help her son. She'd do anything for him. It didn't matter what it was or how old he was. Taking care of him had been her life's work. It always would be.

He'd make a great teacher. He'd probably make a great writer, too. He'd always written stories when he was a kid. All she really cared about was that he was happy.

Although she wouldn't mind the opportunity to tell Jeanine what a mistake she'd made and what a shallow, heartless woman she was for breaking up with a man because he'd lost a promotion.

Didn't that make her a gold digger? Ro snorted in disgust. JT was better off without her, that was for sure. She just hoped he understood that and didn't try to win Jeanine back.

Her mind shifted to Monday and the new job. She couldn't help but smile. She had wanted to be curator for so long, and now it was about to happen. She thought about what she'd wear to work on Monday. Maybe her black pinstripe suit. It always felt so dressed up that she didn't wear it that often. But Monday seemed like the perfect opportunity.

As her mind worked over the many things before her, she lost track of where she was. Still headed in the right direction, but there weren't so many people around now that she had gotten away from some of the shops and restaurants. Probably time to get an Uber or a cab. She walked to the corner and looked down both sides of the street, but there were no cabs in sight. She pulled her phone out to call an Uber.

What she did catch sight of was a man about twenty feet behind her, walking in the same direction. He stopped, too, ducking into the doorway of an apartment building to just stand there. He was in a tatty wind-breaker, with a ball cap pulled down low over his eyes. His jeans and sneakers were both dirty and showed signs of age.

The little hairs on the back of her neck stood up for reasons she couldn't identify. With her phone still out, she walked on to the next street.

After a few seconds, he followed.

Her inner senses sent a trill of warning through her. She never discounted those feelings, but now she wondered if that sixth sense was more than just an instinct. Maybe it was part of being fae?

She stopped at the curb and looked at him, making eye contact to show him that she was getting a good view of him. Enough to describe him to police, if need be. Of course, that meant she couldn't look at her screen to order the Uber, either.

He kept shuffling toward her with a dead-eyed stare. Straight toward her. He wasn't veering at all to go around. She went closer to the curb. Where was a cab when you needed one? Or a police car?

The man's gaze shifted to her purse, and the warning going off inside her got louder.

"There you are, sweetheart." Gabriel was suddenly at her side, hands on her shoulders. He positioned himself so that he was between her and the approaching man, facing her but his side to the man. "I've been looking for you."

"Where did you—"

He kissed her on the mouth, then put his arm around her and got her walking again. He glanced over his shoulder, eyes on the man.

She looked back. The man was just standing there, staring after them. She had no idea if he'd intended her harm or not, but if he had, Gabriel had thwarted his plans.

"Thanks," Ro said. "But seriously. Where did you come from?"

"I've been in the vicinity."

That was a non-answer if ever there was one. "I didn't see you."

"You weren't supposed to."

"I'm surprised you're still here."

"I told you I wouldn't leave without saying goodbye."

So that was what this was. His goodbye.

He took his arm from around her shoulders but stayed close beside her. "How was dinner with your son? Did you tell him about Summerton?"

"Not yet. I wanted to, but he had a lot he needed to talk about. I will soon, though." She glanced at him. "Were you watching me during dinner?"

"Not so much watching you as keeping an eye on your surroundings."

She thought about that. "And? Am I being stalked? Am I in danger?"

"Outside of that guy who was going to make a grab for your purse, no."

"Good news, then. Was he fae?"

"No idea. I can't tell what people are unless it's someone I already know to be fae or troll or whatever."

"Troll?" She shook her head. "Never mind. I guess you'll be headed back?"

He nodded but didn't look happy about it. "I will be. Soon. You'll know before I go." He frowned. "Once I'm gone, if you think anyone's watching you or feel like you're in any danger, you use that ring and get to Summerton immediately. Promise me."

The seriousness of his tone made her quickly agree. "I will."

"Good. What are your plans for tomorrow?"

What were her plans for tomorrow? "I guess I'm going to be doing a thorough cleaning of my apartment. It's time to purge some stuff." Honestly, it was long overdue, but if JT was really going to move in, a hardcore spring cleaning had just become critical.

"You won't be going out then?"

"Other than to haul stuff to the trash chute or down to the curb, probably not."

He gave a nod. "Good."

She heard a little noise that might have been his stomach. "Did you eat dinner?"

He shoved his hands in his pockets and grunted something that she took as a no.

"You have to eat."

"I will. I need to keep watch over you for a little while longer yet."

"Then do it from inside my apartment. I'll make you something."

"You don't have to—"

"No, I don't, but I want to, so let it be." There was a subway entrance ahead. "Come on. We can hop on and be back to my place in twenty minutes."

And a few minutes after that, they were walking through her front door. "Make yourself comfortable. I'm going to change."

She put a pot of water on the stove first, figuring she could easily whip up some pasta. Nothing fancy. Boxed noodles and jarred sauce, but it was better than him going hungry.

Then she went into the bedroom and changed into leggings, a thin, tunic-style sweatshirt, and knitted slippers.

She went back out and got to work on his dinner. She added salt to the pot of water, then found a couple of frozen Italian sausages in the freezer, so she sliced them and tossed them into a pan to fry.

Gabriel was standing by the window. Right in front of it actually.

She smiled. "If anyone is stalking me, you're going to scare them off."

"That's the point."

"Good job then."

At the smell of the frying meat, Benny came running

out of the bedroom, meowing.

She shook her head at him. "This isn't for you."

She leaned against the counter near the stove. There wasn't much for her to do until the water boiled. "You want a glass of wine?"

He glanced over and shook his head. "I'm on duty."

"Suit yourself. I'm having one." Just a small one though. She did *not* need to lose her head around him.

The water boiled. She tossed the pasta in, a box of bucatini, gave it a stir, then set a timer so she didn't get distracted and let the noodles cook too long. She poured herself half a glass of wine but left the bottle out to add a splash to the sauce to fix it up a little.

She walked over to the couch and sat down. "You can take your jacket off, you know."

He looked over his shoulder. "Right." He shed the jacket, laying it over the arm of the couch, then went back to looking out the window.

From her position, she could see him in profile. It was a very handsome profile.

She thought about how he'd disappeared so quickly at the museum. And how he'd shown up so suddenly on the street. And then about how Uldamar had told her all fae had magic. "What kind of magic do you have?"

The brow closest to her cocked. "The kind that makes me well suited to this job."

"Meaning?"

A little half smile answered her, and he glanced over. "It's not polite to ask what kind of magic someone has."

"It's not? Why?"

"Because they might not want to talk about it. If they want to tell you, they will. If they don't ..." He shrugged.

Then they wouldn't. Like he didn't want to talk about his. She got the message. "I was just wondering what kind I might have."

"Your aunt might be able to help you figure it out."

"So it runs in families?"

"Sometimes. And sometimes there's no rhyme or reason to it."

"What kinds of magic exist?"

"Pure magic. Like what Uldamar has." Gabriel put his hands up. "Not that he's told me. That's just my assumption based on his apparent abilities. It's usually those who wield that kind of broad magic who end up rising to any kind of position, anyway."

"Makes sense. What else?"

"Earth magic. Fire magic. Water, wind, light, animal, mineral, alchemy, divination, chaos, healing ..." He shook his head. "There are many kinds. And within each one are more deviations. For example, someone with animal magic might be able to talk to animals, or command animals to talk, or transform into an animal, or cause an animal to transform, or any variation of that."

The timer went off. She got up. "Well, now I have more questions than ever."

Chapter Thirty

nyka was in no mood for anything, but if Wyett had news, the least she could do was listen. Beatryce had yet to answer Anyka, despite the fact that Anyka had sent both a note and a housemaid with a message.

Wyett stood before Anyka now, in her private sitting room outside of her bedchamber. She'd been about to go to sleep. The wine she'd drunk playing hounds and wolves with him had done its job. But he'd returned not even an hour after she'd bidden him good night. "What is it?"

"My source tells me the Summerton queen is gone."

"Gone? Where?"

"Back to the mortal realm."

That wasn't really news to Anyka. "So she's gone to get her belongings. I don't see why this is noteworthy."

"My source says she's gone for good, with only plans to return on occasion to visit her aunt."

Anyka tightened the sash on her robe. "All right, that is curious. Would she really turn down the crown?"

"It appears she has."

"And what of the sword? They can't have let her take *Merediem* with her."

"It was carried back to the mortal world with the Professor of Magic."

"This is interesting but nothing I can act on. Unless there's more you haven't told me."

"No, your ladyship. I have eyes watching but nothing more to tell you. Other than Nightborne guards her."

Anyka blew breath through her nostrils in a hard burst. "Traitor." She waved her hand to dismiss Wyett. "Keep me apprised."

"I will." He turned to go.

"Wyett?"

"Yes, Your Highness?"

"Any word on Beatryce?"

He shook his head. "Nothing new. Has she not answered your letter?"

"No." Anyka stared off at the pitch-black windows.

"Perhaps you should go visit her tomorrow. Extend the hand of compromise."

She looked at him, brows arched. "Have you ever known me to extend the hand of compromise to anyone?"

"No, Your Highness. But Beatryce is not just anyone."

Anyka paused. He was speaking boldly, but his words were also the truth. "No, she isn't. Sound counsel. Good night."

Wyett bowed, then left.

Anyka returned to her bedchamber. A housemaid was stoking the fire so that it would last the night, but the room was already warm enough. Or maybe Anyka's mood had caused the rise in her temperature.

Or perhaps it was her age. She knew that was a possibility, but she preferred to ignore such things.

"The fire is good enough. Leave it."

The housemaid nodded, put the tools back, and scampered off.

Alone at last, Anyka shed her robe and climbed into bed. The lamp on her bedside table still burned. She picked up the book she'd been reading and found her place but couldn't concentrate.

Had Summerton's chosen queen really turned down the chance to rule? Why would she do such a thing? Was her life in the mortal world that impressive? Was she already wealthy? Did she live in a palatial home?

This woman and her decision intrigued Anyka. How could they not? She had refused the throne.

Who did that?

Anyka let that thought unfurl in her mind. What would that be like? To not be royal? To not have the weight of such responsibilities? To live an ordinary life.

She didn't know. She supposed she never would. But the thought was as intoxicating as the wine she'd drunk.

Maybe she should take a trip to the mortal world and see this woman for herself.

Ro didn't ask Gabriel any more questions so that he could eat in peace. She was happy that he at least came to the counter and sat in one of the two stools there. She worked in the kitchen, cleaning up and drinking the last sip of wine in her glass. Maybe a tiny little bit more wouldn't hurt.

He stabbed another sausage coin with his fork and used it to scoop up some bucatini as well. "This is good."

"Thanks. It's nothing fancy."

"Still good. And still made by your hands. Thank you for feeding me."

He ate with a lot of gusto, so he'd either been hungry or he really did like the food. Either way, it was nice to feed an appreciative man. She supposed that would happen a lot more in the future if JT moved in.

She emptied the rest of the pasta into a large, lidded glass container. "Do you want more before I put this away?"

He nodded and held out his plate. "Yes, please."

She gave him two more hearty scoops. "What's your plan for the rest of the night?"

"More surveillance."

She made a face. "You're going to stand at that window all night?"

He shook his head. "Outside. Across the street."

"No, you are not doing that."

He looked at her. "Why not?"

"Because that's silly. No one is after me. The sword is back in Summerton. Citizens are probably lined up right now to see if they're the one capable of pulling it free. You can sleep on the couch. I'll get you an extra pillow and a blanket."

"But I need to keep watch."

She tipped her head toward the door. "Look at that door. Look at the locks on it. You really think someone's going to get through that? And if they do, shouldn't you be here with me instead of trying to get across the street?"

He frowned. "That is a lot of locks. But it's not standard royal protocol."

"And as I keep reminding you, I am not the queen. So maybe SRP doesn't matter so much."

He closed his eyes briefly and nodded. "Right. Perhaps I should return to Summerton now."

She hadn't expected that. "I think it's fine if you want to stay the night. I'd feel safer. Which is not to say I feel unsafe now, but …" She put her hands on her hips. "Just stay. You can leave in the morning."

"All right."

She yawned without meaning to, which made him smile. She laughed. "I'll go get you that pillow and blanket, then I'm going to turn in. You don't mind, do you? Sorry if I'm not being a good hostess."

"You've fed me and given me a place to sleep. There is nothing more I could ask."

"Okay." She hesitated. "The bathroom is the door right in front of my bedroom. I'm a heavy sleeper, so if you need to use it in the middle of the night, go right ahead. You won't wake me."

"Thank you." He got up and took his dish and silverware into the kitchen.

She went into the bedroom and got the extra pillow and blanket off the top shelf of her closet. She had a lot of work to do tomorrow to get this place ready for JT, but she was excited about doing it, too.

Having him close would be nice.

She carried the pillow and blanket out and put them on the chair, then started pulling the cushions off the couch.

Gabriel's eyes narrowed. "What are you doing?"

"I'm going to pull out the couch. It turns into a bed."

"You don't need to do that. The couch is fine as it is."

She straightened. "You sure? It would be more comfortable as a bed."

"I'll be fine. Thank you."

She put the cushions back. "Suit yourself. I'm just going to change and brush my teeth, then the bathroom's all yours."

She left him to do whatever he was doing and went to the bedroom. She grabbed her nightgown and went into the bathroom, straightening up as she got ready for bed.

When she came out, the lights in the living room and kitchen were off. Gabriel was stretched out on the couch, his head on the pillow, the blanket tossed over him, his eyes closed.

On the chair beside the couch was his jacket. His boots were on the floor.

She tiptoed over and quietly shut the blinds, then made her way back to her room. She stopped at the door and whispered, "Good night."

He said nothing. She turned the lights out and slipped into her bed. She lay there, listening to the noise of the city. A distant siren whined, fading as it grew farther away. A car alarm went off. Someone yelled.

She grabbed her phone and set her sleep app to play forest sounds. Insects humming, wind shifting through branches, a softly trickling stream. The occasional soft coo of a bird or throaty ribbit of a frog.

If she closed her eyes, she could just about imagine she was back in Summerton.

CHAPTER THIRTY-ONE

R o woke up stuck in a slight fog. For the briefest of moments, she couldn't understand why there were no windows across from her bed and no view of the glorious morning sky.

Then she remembered where she was. And that she wasn't alone.

She pulled on her robe and padded out to the kitchen, but there was no need to be quiet. Gabriel was already up. He was standing by the window again. Back in his jacket and boots. The blanket was folded, and the pillow sat squarely on top of it. Benny was sprawled on the windowsill in front of Gabriel, who was mindlessly stroking the little cat's back.

"Morning," she said softly.

He turned, almost smiling. "Morning."

"Did you sleep all right?"

He nodded. "I did. You?"

"Fine." She didn't tell him she'd woken up thinking she was back in Summerton. "Coffee?"

"Yes, please."

She scooped grounds into a new filter, added water to the reservoir, and pushed Brew. "If you want the bathroom, now's your chance. I'm going to shower in a minute."

"Thanks." He went to use it.

She leaned on the counter, listening to the coffeemaker do its thing. She wasn't quite awake yet, and as she stood there, she realized she'd dreamed of Summerton. What was the dream?

Something about walking through the garden at night but seeing eyes in the bushes. That's all she could remember.

She yawned again and pushed her hair out of her face. The amount of work ahead of her was daunting, but she had all day to get it done. She wondered if JT had made any decisions yet. Maybe she'd text him later just to check in.

She got two mugs down and took the half-and-half out of the fridge. The sugar and fake stuff were already on the counter by the coffeemaker. She ought to offer Gabriel some breakfast. Would he eat Special K with almond milk? That seemed like a weak breakfast for a guy like that. Especially after seeing the breakfast the palace kitchen had prepared for her. He was probably more into eggs and bacon.

He came back out. His hair was a little damp.

"Are you hungry?"

He stopped at the counter. "I could eat. But only if you're already making something for yourself."

"I'm good with coffee, but I'd be happy to make you something. It's no trouble." Behind her, the coffee machine sputtered out the last few drops. She filled the two mugs she'd gotten down, then put one in front of him. "Cream and sugar?"

"Sugar."

She gave him the bowl and a spoon. She added a packet of the fake stuff to hers, along with a good splash of half-and-half. "So? What would you like to eat?"

He looked at the refrigerator like he could see what was in there. "I liked the dinner you made me last night."

She smiled. "You want leftover bucatini?"

He nodded. "That would be fine. But I don't need to eat. I can eat when I get back."

"Sit and drink your coffee. It won't take long to heat up a plate in the microwave." She got out the leftovers and put some on a dish, then stuck it in and set the timer. "You must be looking forward to getting back."

"Not really."

That surprised her. "No?"

He drank his coffee, then set the cup down. "I won't have much to do outside of an occasional shift guarding the sword, which is considered palace property. Not the most challenging work."

"Oh." She laughed. "Does that mean I'm challenging?"

"You are ... not boring."

The microwave dinged, making Benny look up from his spot on the windowsill. "I'll take that as a compliment." She put the plate in front of Gabriel and got him a fork. "Be careful. It's probably hotter in some places than others."

He used the fork to stir the food. "I will be careful."

"I'm going to grab a shower. Don't leave until I get out, okay?"

He nodded, already lifting a bite of bucatini to his mouth. "Promise."

She showered fast, then brushed her teeth and got dressed in the same leggings and oversize sweatshirt she'd had on last night. They were comfortable clothes for the work she had ahead of her. She towel-dried her hair, then clipped the damp strands up in a twist.

Lastly, she moisturized and thought about putting on a little makeup. She didn't. But she thought about it.

When she rejoined Gabriel, his plate was in the sink, and he was rinsing his coffee cup. "That was fast."

"I didn't want to make you wait too long."

He smiled. "Remember your promise."

She had no idea what he was talking about. "My promise?"

"If you think you're in danger, you will come back to Summerton immediately."

She nodded. "Right. I will."

His smile was gone. "I should go. Thank you for your hospitality."

"Thank you for keeping me from getting mugged last night."

"All in a night's work." He lifted his hand, his fingers going toward the ring on his middle finger.

"Wait. What would I dial if I want to come to the portal closest to you?"

"Garnet and Nepheline." He pointed the stones out. Wine red and a milky gray flecked with black.

She nodded. "Garnet and Nepheline." She smiled. "G and N. For Gabriel Nightborne."

He smiled. "Yes. Goodbye, Sparrow Meadowcroft, almost queen of Summerton. It was a pleasure getting to know you. Perhaps our paths will cross again someday."

"Bye, Gabriel. It was a pleasure getting to know you, too. Will you check on Wiggy for me? Make sure she's okay? Assuming she's still in the palace."

"She is. And I will." He twisted the bands into place. And disappeared.

She stood there for a few long moments, staring at the empty space where he'd just been and feeling bereft in a way she couldn't quite explain. She set her coffee cup down as it came to her. With him gone, she no longer had a connection to the fae realm.

Sure, she could go there using one of the rings, but that would be a different experience. She wouldn't be staying at the palace or be spending time with Gabriel.

Spending time with Aunt Violet would be fantastic. And she was so looking forward to that.

But Gabriel was...Gabriel.

With a sigh, she gave herself a little shake. She had too much to do to mope around over a man she'd known less than forty-eight hours. She picked her cup up again and refilled it. He was a really good kisser. She wasn't about to forget that.

She had a bowl of Special K with almond milk along with her second cup of coffee, and by the time she'd finished that, she was ready to get to work.

After getting a small start on the bathroom because of

Gabriel, she decided to keep going in that room. She kept a list of things she needed, mostly containers and the two caddies she planned on buying.

Under the sink was a mess. A couple of shelves in there would go a long way. She filled half of her trashcan with expired medications, dried-up nail polishes, shades of eyeshadow she had never worn and would never wear, the old shower head she'd replaced about three years ago, and tubes of various creams that were now dried up and sticky.

The medicine cabinet was slightly better because it was a smaller space. The worst of it was yet to come. Namely the kitchen and the small area next to the living room that she pretended was her office.

This was going to require more coffee.

CHAPTER THIRTY-TWO

A nyka hadn't been to the castle's West Tower in many months. She'd had no need to. Now, however, she had a need. Her daughter.

She'd chosen her blue velvet gown with burgundy trim and burgundy slippers. Her hair was braided around the crown of her head and secured with a lapis pin. She wore her dark blue marala wool cape, anticipating the tower's chill.

She'd completed the outfit with her lapis and platinum circlet, a rather informal nod to her status but a reminder that she was queen, all the same.

She thought about taking Wyett with her, but she wanted Beatryce to think this was more of a casual visit. Although Trog would be accompanying her. Trog went everywhere with her. As queen, she couldn't be too careful.

Even in her own home.

She gave Galwyn his breakfast of chopped fish. "I'll be back soon, my pet. Then perhaps we'll go out for a ride. What do you think?"

He cocked his head to look at her, then attacked his fish.

She left her chambers. Trog was at his post by the door.

She didn't wait for him. Just started walking. He fell into step behind her.

The West Tower was quite a walk, but it was a good opportunity to see how other parts of the castle were being maintained. She stayed to the hallways but on occasion detoured through various salons and sitting rooms just to cast her eyes over them.

Everything seemed to be in its place, and when she drew her finger along the top of the harpsichord in the music room, she gathered no dust.

Impressive. It pleased her that the staff were maintaining things with such diligence.

She reached the tower some minutes later. She gathered her skirts to ascend, then paused. She didn't remember the steps having a runner, and yet, they did.

Royal blue trimmed in a gold keyhole pattern. It was old-fashioned, something that had gone out of style ages ago. The carpet was held in place with polished brass rods.

She pursed her lips. The West Tower hadn't been this well decorated in ... well, ever. Beatryce had obviously commandeered more staff than Anyka had realized.

She started up the steps, Trog behind her.

Beatryce's new apartment was on the next floor. Oil lamps flickered along what had once been a dark hall, and another rug had been laid. This one led to a pair of dark wood doors.

Anyka knocked but didn't announce herself. She wasn't sure Beatryce would answer if she knew her mother was at the door.

Beatryce's lady's maid opened it, a young woman named Sylvia or Sysia or something like that. She went wide-eyed at the sight of Anyka and dropped into a curtsy.

Anyka waved her hand for the girl to move. "Is your mistress in?"

"Yes, Your Highness. She's in the solarium."

Anyka frowned. The West Tower did not have a solarium. That was a room meant to take advantage of the sun, something Malveaux didn't have in great enough quantities to take advantage of.

She strode through. Trog followed. She stopped and gestured to him. "Stay at the door."

He nodded and went back out, hand on his sword.

Before starting forward again, Anyka looked around. The furnishings were mostly older pieces, taken from storage, but had Beatryce taken all of them?

Rugs overlapped in places. Seating areas were piled with extra pillows. Draperies were double hung, and tapestries covered every inch of bare stone. It was almost … cozy.

Crackling fires and flickering candles along with oil lamps and lots of mirrors made the space surprisingly bright. And warm.

Anyka untied her cape and tossed it to the maid, then she strode forward. "Beatryce? My darling, I've come to visit."

Beatryce came out from a door. "Mother."

The word was said with a great deal of surprise but, thankfully, no animosity. Anyka smiled. That was a good start. "You've turned this apartment into quite a cozy space."

Beatryce nodded. "I've had a lot of help."

"I can imagine. To do as much as you've done in such a short time, I'm surprised you didn't borrow troops from General Wolfmane."

Beatryce cracked the tiniest of smiles. "The palace staff is remarkably hardworking and resourceful."

"So I see." Anyka gazed toward the room Beatryce had come out of. "You like it all right here?"

Beatryce nodded. "I do. And it's given me a way to occupy myself." Her smile flattened. "At least for the time being. I was just about to sit down to breakfast. Would you like to join me? There's plenty."

Anyka had left early enough that she'd hoped for a breakfast invite. "Thank you. I'd love to join you."

Beatryce stepped back and held her hand out toward the room behind her. "Then please, come in."

Anyka stepped through, amazed by the room before her. It was at the very front of the tower, looking out over the sea, and had windows facing it and making up part of the sloped roof. She shook her head. "I don't remember the tower having a room like this."

"Neither did I. The windows were covered with tapestries. We took them down to clean them and found all of this."

The room was not nearly as warm as the one Anyka had just left, although the fireplace on the opposite wall was doing its best to keep up. Thankfully, the table and chairs for breakfast were set close to the hearth.

This room would be unbearably cold in four or five

months, but Beatryce would have to find that out for herself. "How marvelous." She took Bea's hand. "All of it is. You've done a wonderful job."

"Thank you." Beatryce's smile was back.

They took their seats. A housemaid poured tea, piping hot.

Beatryce added sugar to hers. "I'm surprised you came to visit."

Anyka swirled honey into her tea. "I couldn't leave things as they were."

"Does that mean you've changed your mind about Willow Hall?"

Anyka almost sighed but held herself back. "No. My concern for my only child's safety remains first and foremost."

Beatryce frowned. "As does my concern for my mental well-being."

"I understand that, my darling. I really do."

"I don't know how you can. You have all kinds of things to keep you occupied. I have nothing. Nothing of value. No real purpose."

"Your purpose is to represent this kingdom. You are a princess. It might seem like you're not doing anything now, but your day will come." Many, many years from now if Anyka could help it. She reached across the table and put her hand over Beatryce's. "Speaking of things that keep me occupied, something has come up. I must make a trip to the mortal world. And I was wondering if you'd like to come with me."

Beatryce's lips parted, and new light shone in her eyes.

"The mortal world? But you've always said it was too dangerous for me—"

"We'd be together. And we'd have guards. And Wyett. Just for a day or two. It would be a short trip. Long enough for a little sightseeing and some shopping, perhaps." Anyka shrugged. "But if that doesn't interest you …"

"No, it does." Beatryce grinned. "I would love to come."

More housemaids came in with trays of food and began placing dishes in front of them. The smell of sweet and savory items made Anyka's mouth water. Her plan was working, and that did wonders for her appetite.

The housemaids left, and Beatryce leaned in. "When?"

Anyka made a show of looking at the clock on the mantelpiece. "Say in about … three hours?"

"Three hours?" Beatryce almost shrieked. "That's so soon."

"Sometimes being queen means one must act quickly. Is that too soon for you? Or can you be ready?"

Beatryce, still grinning, nodded. "I can be ready."

"Excellent." Anyka picked up her fork. A trip to the mortal world would be the perfect way to do some investigating concerning Summerton's chosen queen but also a way to alleviate some of Beatryce's boredom while allowing Anyka to prove to her sweet, sheltered child just how dangerous the world beyond the castle's walls could be.

Hopefully, the lesson would be something Beatryce would bring home with her. A lesson that would end her desire to go to Willow Hall once and forever.

A healthy fear of what could happen when one was

away from home was not such a bad thing to have. Especially for a princess.

CHAPTER THIRTY-THREE

Ro hauled the last of the trash out to the chute and went back to her apartment. Things didn't look that different, unless you opened drawers and cabinets. She'd managed to clear half of a kitchen cabinet, which would give JT a place to put his own food.

She'd made space in the medicine cabinet, too. One whole shelf. Amazing how much stuff got accumulated over time. Old prescription medications, expired over-the-counter items, a box of Band-Aids that only had two left in it … so much junk she no longer needed.

It was good to do a deep clean like that. Not only was she getting her place more organized, but it was giving her new enthusiasm to tackle the museum's basements. Granted, that was a much bigger job, but she'd have help there.

Maybe she'd even be able to hire an assistant curator once her promotion was official. They'd have to fill her spot, wouldn't they? If so, she could put that person in charge of organizing the basements. With help, of course.

She walked over to the small area just beyond the living room. Benny had left the windowsill to eat, but he was back there now, staring down at the puny humans below.

A single step led up to the space. It was roughly eight by six and held only a few things. An old desk she'd found on the street, a small office chair she'd bought at a flea market, and a plain white shelving unit bought at the same flea market two weeks later.

She considered it her office, but she never used it. Which made it wasted space.

If she got rid of the desk and chair and pulled the shelving unit forward to act as a divider, she might actually be able to get a mattress in there. Not exactly a bedroom but sort of. And it would be better than JT having to use the living room. Pulling the couch out every night would get old.

And this way he'd have a small area to call his own. In fact, if they turned the shelving unit around so that the shelves faced in, he could use that for storage. Clothes, books, shoes, whatever. Maybe she could find a hanging rack for the rest of his clothing, too.

And if he didn't move in, maybe she could turn the space into a little reading nook. It ought to be used for something.

She really needed to touch base with him and see what was going on. She didn't want to pressure him, but it would be good to know. Her stomach rumbled. The Special K with almond milk had lasted about twenty minutes.

She didn't know why she ate that stuff. It was more like a punishment than food. What she needed was a trip to City Donuts. And she could call JT on the way.

A glance in the mirror said she was reasonably appropriate for public consumption. She had no makeup on, she looked like she was in the middle of a project—which she was—and it was Sunday, so if anyone expected polished perfection, they could just mind their own business. "Headed out, Benny. Keep an eye on things."

If he missed Wiggy, Ro couldn't tell. It was certainly quieter without her in the apartment. Too quiet. JT would change that. If he moved in.

She grabbed her purse and phone, stuck her feet into slip-on sneakers, and headed out, locking the door behind her. Not all the locks, though.

Most of them were for show, despite what she'd told Gabriel. There was no way she was locking and unlocking all of those every time she left or came home. But they looked impressive. Whoever had lived in this apartment before her had been extra careful.

The air still held a little coolness, which was nice. In a few more weeks, summer would be here along with the stifling heat that made her long to escape the concrete oven the city became for those months.

Thankfully, the museum was kept blissfully climate controlled. Had to be, to ensure the proper preservation of its many antiquities.

She texted JT. *Morning. How are you?*

She was hoping his answer would tell her more than his state of mind.

City Donuts had a small line, but it moved fast. She got her usual, a mocha latte, and went with the doughnut of the day, Coconut Cream Pie. It was just a regular filled doughnut with coconut cream filling and coconut shavings sprinkled on the glaze. Very tasty though.

She ordered a Boston cream, as well. To take home for later. She'd already worked hard, and with more hard work ahead of her, a little reward seemed appropriate.

Her phone pinged as she walked back, but both hands were full. As soon as she finished the doughnut, she fished her phone out of her purse. She'd just arrived at the door to her building, too.

She stood there, enjoying the sun and checking her screen. JT had answered.

All good. Pretty sure I'm going to take you up on your offer.

Ro smiled. *Great! How soon?*

Soon.

You're welcome to bring things today, if you want.

Might do that. Maybe later. Need to draft my resignation letter first. Then I might pack a bag.

Let me know if you need anything.

Will do. Love you, Mom. Appreciate you and all you do for me.

Ro sniffed as she sent him a smiley face with hearts for eyes. She just wanted to hug him and tell him everything was going to be all right and that he was brave for following his heart. He was going to make a great teacher.

She went inside and got back to work with renewed vigor, determined to clear out the small space so she could show it to him when he came by.

Anyka didn't have a lady's maid. She didn't want someone around her that much. Instead, she directed a pair of housemaids to lay out her things before they packed her bags. Enough for two nights, although she only planned to stay one. All the same, she wanted to give the selections her final approval.

While they did that, she went into her vault. It had been many years since she'd travelled to the mortal realm. She trusted that the money she had would still be good.

She had a credit card and a thing called a driver's license, both of which had been made by Nazyr, her Minister of Magic. Perfect replicas but that didn't mean they'd still be viable.

Things changed in the mortal world far more quickly than they did in this realm. Humans were too much in love with progress, in her opinion.

She chose several stacks of paper money from one of the shelves. That should be enough. Although part of the mortal world's progress included increasing prices. On everything. She took one more stack to be sure.

She'd promised Beatryce some shopping, but the credit card would handle that. The bill would never be paid, nor would it ever be sent to anyone, but she was reluctant to overuse it lest it cause her mortal identity to come under scrutiny. Two or three stores, no more.

After this trip, perhaps she'd have Nazyr make her a brand-new card and ID. That might be best. She tapped them against her hand, wondering if she should have him make an ID for Beatryce, too.

But that might open a door Anyka would be unable to close. Beatryce would want to keep the ID. And then she'd think having such a thing meant visiting the mortal world whenever she liked.

Anyka frowned. Not the intended outcome of this trip.

She tucked the credit card, license, and money into the small bag she'd brought, then went to the section of the vault that held the royal jewels.

She went to the top drawer first. At the very back of it was a velvet pouch that held a significant piece. A necklace that would help her with a particular task she hoped to achieve. She wouldn't be wearing the necklace. It would, instead, become the key that opened a door for her. If all went well.

From the very bottom drawer she selected a few simple but impressive pieces. A gold watch, diamond earrings. A gold necklace, a gold and diamond bracelet, a few rings. All designed to contribute to her disguise as a wealthy mortal woman out for a few days of fun with her daughter.

Her last selection was an item referred to as a designer handbag in the mortal world. Such nonsense, she thought. How a few symbols on the outside of a purse meant anything about a person's status or place in life was beyond her.

If such a thing held true in this realm, she'd emblazon her own name on everything she wore. She laughed at the idea. But there was no need for that. Everyone already knew she was the queen.

As she exited the vault, she found Wyett in her sitting room. "Ready?"

He stood and nodded. "Whenever you are, your ladyship."

"Beatryce has yet to arrive, but I'm sure she'll be along shortly. Everything is in place?"

He nodded again, but she could tell by the look on his face that he wasn't pleased. She didn't really care. "It is. Although—"

"I know. You have your doubts. Or you don't think it's wise. Or you just want me to know that these things can go sideways."

His mouth was tight with disapproval. "Yes. All of that."

"If the plans were made properly, none of that will happen."

His eyes narrowed. "No matter how well laid out the plans are, we will still be in the mortal world. There is no way to correctly factor in the havoc those surroundings might cause. The people are highly unpredictable."

"It will be fine."

"And if it isn't?"

She stared at him pointedly. His boldness was barely tolerable. "If it isn't, you will do whatever you need to do to make it right."

As expected, that did nothing to appease him. "Let us pray that nothing happens, then. And if it does, that the errors are not fatal."

"This is a lesson. Nothing else. Nothing untoward will

come of it. And that is the end of what I want to hear about it."

He bowed his head. "As you wish, Your Highness."

She went to check on the clothing selections, her irritation aroused. She knew there was truth in what he said. The mortal world was extremely erratic. That was one of things she found so fascinating about it. Authority was often flouted. Individualism was prized, although in truth those who rebelled against the system, as they called it, all seemed rather alike.

But all Anyka wanted to do was scare her daughter a little. Just enough to make her realize how safe she was at home. And want to stay there.

Chin lifted, she surveyed the outfits the handmaids had laid out. They stood off to the side, awaiting her nod before they packed the items.

She rolled her eyes. Their understanding of what passed for fashion in the mortal world was slim at best. She changed out two of the jackets and one pair of pants, added different shoes to one outfit and a scarf to another.

Then she shook her head. "No hats. Women don't wear them like they used to."

The hats were put away.

"All right, pack this. Plus a sleeping gown and robe."

They curtsied and got to work.

Behind her came the sounds of Beatryce's arrival.

Anyka put on a happy face and went to greet her daughter. "There you are. All packed and ready for our little adventure?"

Beatryce had three bags with her. "I think so. It's so

exciting. But I'm not sure I've brought the right things. Will I need a coat? I only brought my cape."

"Capes are generally reserved for special events," Anyka said. Unless capes had suddenly fallen into daily wear fashion. Hard to tell with the mortal world. "But don't worry about it. If you need something, we'll just buy it."

Beatryce smiled. "All right." She looked at Wyett. "I'm glad you're coming with us."

"Thank you, Princess. I'm honored to accompany you."

Trog stood at the door. He'd already been outfitted for the mortal world: a black suit, which Anyka thought must have taken an extraordinary number of yards of fabric, along with a white shirt and black tie, a large watch, an earpiece that did nothing but looked impressive, and a dark pair of sunglasses.

Private security chic in the mortal world.

Anyka held her hands up. "All right then. To the portal we go."

Chapter Thirty-Four

J T showed up around five with a suitcase, a backpack, and duffel bag. "Hi, Mom."

"Hi, honey. Come on in." Ro was proud of all the work she'd done. Exhausted, a little sweaty, but proud. "I can't wait to show you what I did."

"What you did?" He walked in.

Benny jumped down from the sill and trotted over to say hello.

JT dropped his bags to scoop the cat up. "Hi, Benny boy. How's it hanging?" He looked around. "Where's Wiggy?"

"She's, uh, staying with friends." Not entirely a lie. "Carry Benny over here and have a look at the space I made for you." She led him over to her former office space. She'd hauled the desk down to the street, moved the shelving unit to work like a room divider, and left the chair in the corner. "What do you think? I figure we can get a mattress in there. I know it's not a real bedroom, but—"

"Hey, that's great. I can't believe you did that for me. What about your office, though?"

"I never used it. That desk was just wasting space. Besides, I have an office at the museum. That's all I need."

He shook his head, smiling. "Thank you."

"You're welcome. Did you get your letter drafted?"

"I did. I started filling out the enrollment forms for school, too. I found out they have a summer program that starts in a month. If I can get into that, that would be awesome. I'm not putting in my notice until I find out, because if I can't do the summer program, I won't be able to start until September. And I figure I should work at least until then. Save as much as I can, you know?"

She nodded. "Smart. And you should be able to save a good deal if you're living here."

"That's what I was thinking."

"What are you going to do with your stuff?"

He put his hands on his hips and studied the space in front of him. "My bed I'll bring. After I measure to make sure it'll fit."

"I measured the space," Ro said. "It's eight and a half feet by six and a half feet. Unless you have a king-size bed, it should fit."

"Queen."

She smiled. "That'll work. There won't be room for much else, but you won't have to sleep on the pullout couch every night."

"Or go through the hassle of setting it up every night."

"That either." She glanced at his bags. "What did you bring?"

"Some of my casual clothes and some books. I'll have to get a big Uber to bring the rest. I'll sell what I can. None of that old furniture means anything to me anyway. Maybe I'll even donate it."

"Jeanine knows you're moving out?"

He nodded. "I told her this morning that I'd be gone in a week. That's okay with you, right?"

"It's perfect with me."

"Thanks. I'm going to unpack this stuff, then bring one more load over. Probably take about an hour. After that, maybe we can get some dinner. In fact, I have some food I need to bring over. Soup, rice, a couple boxes of pasta. Nothing much."

"Dinner sounds great. That little Italian place around the corner makes great pizza." She went into the kitchen and opened the cabinet she'd partially cleared out. "Your food can go in here."

"You cleared out a cabinet for me? Thanks." He hauled his things over to his makeshift bedroom.

While he unpacked into the shelving unit, she took a critical look for anything else she could get rid of. Or another way to make more room. There wasn't anything that jumped out at her.

JT came out. "Hey, I was thinking maybe I should invest in one of those bed platforms that has drawers under it."

"Or you could put your bedframe on risers and just get some big containers that will slide underneath. They make containers specifically designed for that purpose. I think some of them even have wheels."

"Yeah? Cool. I'll do that."

She grabbed her pen. "I already have a list started. I'll add them. And while you go get more stuff, I'll take a trip to the hardware store and get you a key made."

"Good idea. Then we'll get pizza. My treat."

"Sounds good."

An hour and a half later, they were sitting down at Luigi's, waiting on the pizza they'd just ordered and sipping their drinks. Water for Ro, Coke for JT. They had paper plates and napkins in front of them, ready to go.

Luigi's was a hole in the wall, but they had a brick oven and did a pretty good carry-out business, based on the traffic.

The restaurant's small dining room was a little busy but not so crowded they couldn't carry on a conversation without feeling like they were having it with everyone around them, too.

To Ro, it felt like the right time to tell JT about Aunt Violet. And Summerton. It still wasn't going to be an easy thing to explain, but she didn't want to put it off any longer. "So, listen, I need to tell you something, and you're probably going to think I'm crazy but just hear me out, okay? And keep an open mind."

He made a funny face at her. "Okay. What's going on?"

She started at the beginning, because jumping into the middle would only make things more confusing. "We recently got a bequeathment at the museum. One I'd been working on securing for some time. Anyway, one of the things in that bequeathment was an old sword in a stone."

He grinned. "Like the Disney movie."

"And the Arthurian legends that movie is based on, yes."

"Cool. Did you pull it out and become queen of something?"

She stared at him while she breathed and tried to think

of a way to answer that in which she wouldn't sound snarky or like she was joking. She nodded and remained serious. "I did."

He frowned. "What?"

She drank some water. "I know how this sounds. Completely implausible. But that's pretty much what happened."

"You're not really making sense."

"Let me give you more details. There was a grouping of things in the bequeathment. A large, beautiful tapestry. Some jewelry. A trunk. A vase. A pair of silk slippers. And the sword in the stone. I thought for sure that was just a fun conversation starter. A curiosity, you know? So I ignored it to examine the other pieces."

She took a breath. "None of them were quite right. The vase looked like celadon, a distinctive jade-green ceramic glaze, but didn't fit cleanly into any of the ages it should have. The people in the tapestry weren't quite human. The trunk looked—"

"Back up. Weren't quite human?"

"They had slightly pointed ears."

His brows pulled together. "So they were ... elves?"

"Fae."

His look of skepticism remained. "Mom, if you're trying to distract me from the job and Jeanine, I really appreciate it, but I'm not a little kid anymore. You don't have to make up stories to entertain me."

"I'm not making anything up."

"Mm-hmm." He sat back and crossed his arms, a rather bemused expression on his face. "Go on."

"After examining the other items, I went back to the sword. The two warehouse guys had a laugh trying to pull it out, so before I went back to my office, I thought I'd have a crack at it, too."

"Naturally."

"I grabbed the hilt and pulled. It slid out like the easiest thing in the world. Then the next thing I knew, I wasn't in the museum anymore. I was in a throne room. The same one that had been depicted in the tapestry, as a matter of fact."

"Nice detail."

She sighed at him. "Well, it was. Then some guards rushed me, I guess thinking I was an intruder, but when they saw the sword in my hand, they dropped to the ground and bowed."

He cocked his head to one side, still looking very unconvinced. "Sure. And then they crowned you queen?"

She shook her head. "No. I spent the night and part of the next day there, but I turned down the throne."

"Convenient. Why did you stay if you weren't going to accept the crown?"

"Because in the fae realm, your Aunt Violet is still alive and well."

His mouth opened, and his eyes widened. "Mom, that's not a very funny thing to joke about."

"I'm *not* joking. She's alive. When a fae dies in this world, they actually get transported back to their home realm. The fae live a lot longer than humans do. She owns a bakery. And a cute little cottage with a garden." Ro exhaled. "And she can't wait to see you."

"You ... want to take me there?"

"Yes."

A man at the counter smacked the order bell and called out, "Margarita pizza for JT." He put the pie on the counter on a silver tray.

JT pushed his chair back. "Be right back."

He returned with the pizza and set it in the middle of the table.

She helped herself to a slice. "So. You want to go?"

He shot her a dubious look as he grabbed a slice for himself. "Sure. Let's go right after dinner. Off to fairy land."

"It's fae, not fairy. That's apparently offensive."

He took a bite of his pizza and nodded. "Good to know."

She could tell by the way he was looking at her that he thought she was nuts. Well, he'd see soon enough how wrong he was.

CHAPTER THIRTY-FIVE

Anyka had to admit that the suite at the Centurion Hotel was very nice. Perhaps better than nice. It was, even by her standards, luxurious. The large suite included three bedrooms, a sitting room, a small kitchen, a dining room, an office area, a powder room, and three good-size full bathrooms attached to the bedrooms.

Her bedroom and bathroom were the largest and best, as befitted her station. Beatryce and Wyett each had one of the other bedrooms. Trog and the two guards they'd brought along would be sleeping in shifts on a cot in Wyett's room.

Trog was outside the suite's door. One of the guards was in the lobby, and the other was sleeping so that he could take the next shift.

Anyka stared at her bags and realized she should have also brought a housemaid. "Wyett."

He came in a few moments later. "Yes, Your Highness?"

"See to my bags, will you? And Beatryce's, too, when you're done."

"Yes, your ladyship." He went straight to work getting her unpacked.

She went through the suite to see how Beatryce was doing. She found her daughter unpacking her own bags. "You don't need to do that."

"Do what?" Beatryce tucked something into one of the drawers, leaving it open.

"Unpack your own bags. Wyett will do it."

Beatryce shook her head. "I'm perfectly capable. What are we going to do first?"

"Dinner. I'm famished. Aren't you?"

Beatryce added a few more things to the drawer. "I could eat. What is the food like here?"

"Not so different from what we eat, although so much of what passes for food in the mortal realm is processed chemical garbage. Be careful of it. Too much and you'll get sick." Anyka had learned that the hard way decades ago. She'd indulged heavily in what the mortals called candy and had spent almost a day and a half in bed. When she wasn't retching her guts out, that was.

Beatryce made a face. "If it makes a person sick, why do they eat it?"

"Because they are weak and lazy and favor convenience over their health." Just one of the ways the fae were superior to the mortal race. "Not all, of course. There are some who understand the value of making better choices, but they're in the minority."

"Are you changing for dinner? Should I?"

Anyka shook her head. "What we have on is fine. Although I will put on different jewelry and change out my purse and shoes." She was in simple blue trousers with a matching nipped-waist jacket and a gold patterned blouse underneath. Beatryce was in slim black pants with a long-sleeved green top with a wide neck that displayed her shoulders beautifully.

Anyka would have to watch the men around her daughter. Even though she now appeared human, her fae beauty was unmistakable.

"Okay. I'll be ready in a few minutes."

"Very good." She went back toward the sitting room. Wyett was coming out of her bedroom. "Beatryce has seen to her own bags. Find us an exceptional place for dinner this evening. Preferably in an hour's time."

He nodded. "I spoke to the concierge when we arrived. He suggested three places. I booked the most prestigious. Your reservations are in forty-five minutes. A car will be here in thirty."

She smiled. He was very good. "Well done, Wyett."

"Will you be taking more than one guard?"

"Just Trog. Make sure he knows. And order whatever you'd like for dinner from room service. For the guards as well."

"I will, ma'am. Thank you."

The restaurant was called L'Argent and was sleek and modern with lots of glass and steel and concrete. The space was softened by exotic greenery and the warm, flickering light of tall pillar candles, some of which sat on the floor and reached as high as Anyka's waist.

Beatryce seemed suitably impressed. "What an interesting space." She looked around as they were seated and given menus.

Anyka wondered how much it had cost Wyett to get

them a table here this evening. Not that it mattered. He'd done very well.

They ordered something called a tasting menu, seven courses of the chef's selections at an exorbitant price. None of the plates they were served had more than three bites of food on them. Most had one. The soup course was a flat-bottomed spoon filled with clear pink liquid and a single flower petal.

All nonsense as far as Anyka was concerned. But Beatryce practically vibrated with enjoyment.

Which meant Anyka's plan had to work or Beatryce would want to come back to the mortal realm.

She was still hungry, however, when they returned to the suite. She'd order something from room service. Something that actually qualified as food.

Trog opened the door for them, but Beatryce paused. "I'm not ready to go to bed yet. I want to see more of the city."

Anyka was about to say no, then decided she was in no mood to argue. "Fine. Take a guard with you and be back by midnight."

Beatryce looked slightly stunned that she hadn't needed to argue. "Thank you."

"You have money?"

Beatryce nodded. "I'll get Strom to go with me."

"Very good."

Beatryce raced inside.

Anyka put her hand on Trog's arm. "Follow her. Keep an eye on her."

Trog grunted his agreement.

"No one lays a hand on her, you understand? If they do, you kill them."

He nodded. "No touchy."

She patted his arm. It was like patting a tree trunk. "Good." She went in and found Wyett in the sitting room with the television on.

He stood as she entered.

"What did you have for dinner?"

"A steak with the vegetable of the day, broccoli, and a baked potato with butter and sour cream, and a slice of cheesecake."

"Was it good?"

"Excellent."

"Order me the same thing." She pursed her lips. "Dinner was good, but the portions were mouse-sized."

He smiled. "Wine?"

"Yes, that, too. Get a bottle."

He went straight to the phone. She went to change as Beatryce traipsed through. "See you later, Mother!"

"Have fun." Anyka's stomach rumbled, but her mind was on Summerton's almost queen. Tomorrow, if all went as planned, she would see the woman who could have been queen. The woman who had the power to pull *Merediem* from its granite prison.

The woman who had the power to make Anyka the ruler of both kingdoms.

CHAPTER THIRTY-SIX

"That was great pizza." JT pushed his empty paper plate away.

"Apparently," Ro said, looking at the empty pan. "You ate all of it."

He laughed. "You had three slices."

"I did, true. But I worked hard today."

He nodded. "You must have. I'm still impressed you made so much room for me." He pulled money out of his wallet and dropped a tip on the table. "Back to your place then? For the big trip?"

She grabbed her purse. "That's right."

They left the restaurant to walk back to her apartment.

"Maybe," JT said, "we should just go to the museum and see if I can pull the sword out of the stone, too. Being your son and all, it might be in the blood."

She snorted. "It might be, but the sword and stone are back in Summerton now. Uldamar, the First Professor of Magic, took it back there for safekeeping. And so I'm less likely to be forced into freeing the sword for the rival kingdom."

"Political intrigue is always a nice touch."

She slanted her eyes at him. "Go ahead. Make fun. You'll see."

"That my mom is losing it?" He was grinning like this was the biggest joke in the world.

He was in for a shock.

She practically jogged up the steps to her door. Once inside, she went straight to the bedroom to get the rings. She came out with them on the flat of her palm. "Ready to take a trip?"

He glanced at the rings. "I'm ready. What do those have to do with it?"

"These are portal rings. I don't know if that's what they're really called, but they're how the fae travel between realms. You just line up the gemstones on the inner bands according to where you want to go, making sure they're aligned with the little notches, and off you go."

He nodded, still clearly unconvinced. "Do we need to take anything on this trip? Water? A light jacket? Snacks?"

"Such a wise guy." She tucked Uldamar's ring into her pocket, then slipped Gabriel's onto her index finger. "I'm going to take us to a portal close to Aunt Violet's. She'll be in bed already, because she gets up so early to run the bakery, but we can at least look around the village a bit."

"I see. So she's alive and living in this other realm, but I won't get to see her. And no castle then, either."

"Is that what you want? To see the castle? Will that prove to you that I'm telling the truth?"

He nodded slowly. "Not saying I don't want to see Aunt Violet. I do. But if we can't see her, then the castle seems like the next best thing."

"Fine. The castle it is." She hoped they didn't get thrown out, since she technically had no right to be there anymore. She also really, really hoped this worked. This would be her first time crossing over on her own, and she did not want to mess up while trying to prove her point to JT. "Grab hold of my arm and don't let go."

He slipped his arm through hers.

She stuck her hand out and lined up all the bands.

A momentary darkness, a shift of time and space, and they were standing in the castle's portal. She grinned. "Welcome to Summerton."

Beside her, JT exhaled and put his hand to his stomach. "I shouldn't have eaten so much pizza."

"That feeling of nausea should pass in a few seconds."

"Good." He blew out another breath. "We are definitely somewhere else."

"Come on, I'll show you around." She walked him out into the hall and took a better look at him in the light of the sconces. She smiled. His ears were pointed now. And he was even more handsome than usual. The reality of his true fae self.

He caught her looking. "What?"

She pulled her hair back and turned her head. "We're fae."

"Holy …" He reached up to touch his ears. "Is this real?"

"Of course it's real. It's who we are. Who we've always been. But living in the mortal world has cloaked that side of us."

"You look … different. Besides the ears, I mean. You but *more* you. Younger. More alive somehow."

"So do you. These are our true selves without the mask of magic we live with in the mortal world."

"You say mortal world like we're not mortal."

"We're not, honey. We're fae. Always have been. And the fae live a lot longer than humans do. Uldamar, the wizard, is well over a century old."

JT put a hand to his forehead. "How is this real? How is it possible? This is crazy."

"This is the fae realm. And like I told you, it's very real."

He nodded. "I believe you now. I really do. How could I not?"

"You want to see more?"

"You better believe I do."

"Then let's go." As much as she wanted to take him upstairs to see the royal quarters, that would mean dealing with the two guards at the bottom of the steps. She was too unsure how that would go to risk it. The throne room was off limits for the same reason, although she wasn't sure there would be guards there at night.

Instead, she opted to take him down the hall and out the side entrance. From there, they should be able to access the rear gardens. Seeing luminous insects and glowing fish ought to give him a good idea of what this place had to offer.

Then two things happened very rapidly. The sound of someone running filled the hall. And that someone jumped on top of JT.

He fell back, crashing to the floor under Wiggy's assault.

"JT!" She kissed his face all over while kneeling on top of him.

"Mom," he wheezed out. "Help."

Ro grabbed Wiggy around the waist and hauled her up. "Wiggy, I know you love him, but you're crushing him."

JT blinked up at her. "Why are you calling that woman Wiggy? And why did she jump on me?"

Wiggy clapped her hands. "JT! You're here!"

Ro tried to smile. "Remember when I said Wiggy was staying with friends?"

He got to his feet. Wiggy wriggled out of Ro's grip to latch onto JT again, hugging him tight. JT looked at his mom over Wiggy's head. "And?"

"And those friends were here. That's Mrs. Wigglesworth. I brought her and Benny through the portal to stay with me during my visit, and apparently crossing over can change animals when they pass through. It's rare, but it happens. And it happened to Wiggy."

JT took Wiggy by the shoulders and stretched his arms out to make some space between them. "Edna? Is it really you?"

She nodded, all smiles. She held up her hands. "I have thumbs now."

"You sure do." He gave her another quick hug, which made her start purring. "It's good to see you. How do you like it here?"

"It's great," she said. "They have rodents."

"That does sound exciting."

She whipped around, eyes laser-focused on some unseen spot down the hall. "I hear one now. Gotta go."

She took off, leaving them behind.

JT's expression seemed to be a mix of uncertainty and amusement. "This place is nuts. Wiggy is a person."

Ro nodded. "She is. She seems pretty happy here. I didn't want to leave her, but I couldn't exactly bring her back to the apartment and keep her cooped up."

"No, totally." He glanced down the hall in the direction she'd gone. "Still, so weird. Right?"

"Right." Ro smiled. "You want to see more weird?"

"That's what I'm here for."

They made it outside without anyone else jumping on JT. She started around the corner to go through the side yard so they could find an entrance into the garden, maybe the same one she and Gabriel had used.

JT sighed. Not an unhappy sound but she stopped and looked back. His face was aimed at the sky, but his eyes were closed.

He opened them and smiled. "It smells really good here. And the stars are amazing."

"The air here is about as clean as air can be, I imagine."

"I bet it is. Where are you taking me?"

"The queen's garden."

"Lead on."

She did, and amazed herself by finding the wooden door in the hedge. She wasn't sure it was the same one Gabriel had taken her through—this place was a bit of a maze—but it looked similar. She opened it and walked in, holding it for JT to follow.

A faintly glowing green dragonfly with a wingspan of

about five inches flitted past them toward a bush covered in tiny, radiant berries.

JT stared, open-mouthed. "Oh, this is a whole new level of wild."

The berries reminded her of something else she wanted to tell him. "We're Radiant Fae, by the way. The Grym Fae live in the kingdom across the sea. Just wanted to mention that, since it popped into my head."

"Radiant Fae. Got it."

"Also, don't touch anything in here. There are flowers in here that could kill you."

His brows shot up. "Good to know."

"Come on. I'll show you." She led him down the path, pointing out the fire lilies. Their centers glowed like dying embers. "These are supposedly what killed the king and queen of Malveaux, which is the Grym Fae kingdom."

"And they're allowed to grow here?" He snorted. "That's a little in your face, don't you think?"

"I said if I were queen, I'd get rid of them."

"She did indeed say that."

Ro spun around to see Gabriel standing behind them. He was in breeches, boots, and a loose white shirt, a sword strapped to his side and a dagger in his boot. It was a very good look on him. "Professor Nightborne."

"Lady Meadowcroft. And guest." He nodded at JT. "I didn't expect you back quite so soon."

It was so nice to see him. "I had to prove a point to my son. JT, this is Professor Gabriel Nightborne. Gabriel, this is my son, James Thoreau Meadowcroft."

JT stuck his hand out. "Nice to meet you. Please, call me JT. Everybody does."

Gabriel shook his hand, giving JT a curious look. "My pleasure."

"Does everyone around here carry a sword?" JT looked as if he thought it was a great idea.

"I am the head of palace security. It's my job to be well armed and well prepared. Although, yes, most people carry some kind of blade on their person. They're useful for many things besides self-defense."

"Cool. And you're a Radiant Fae, too? I just learned that's what I am."

"No, I'm Grym Fae." Gabriel's brows drew together ever so slightly. He looked at JT, then at Ro, then back at JT. "Just like you."

CHAPTER THIRTY-SEVEN

"What do you mean he's Grym Fae? He can't be." Ro frowned. "He's my son. He's Radiant Fae."

Gabriel shook his head. "His ears say differently." Then he put his hands up in front of him and bowed his head slightly. "It's dark. Perhaps I'm wrong."

But Ro knew he wasn't. Gabriel wasn't the kind of man to say something like that unless it was true. She looked at JT's ears. Did they curve around the skull? Did they point back more than up? They kind of did on both accounts. "That means …"

She knew what it meant, but she didn't want to put it into words.

JT looked at her. "My father was Grym?"

Ro swallowed. "I guess he was. I had no idea. I didn't even know I was fae until two days ago." She glanced at Gabriel. "Does that happen a lot? Radiant and Grym, I mean."

"To be frank, no, it doesn't. The two kingdoms have lived rather segregated lives for well over a century."

JT ran a hand through his hair. "But you're Grym. And you're in charge of security here. So there can't be that much bad blood between the two."

Gabriel offered him a brief smile. "My family escaped Malveaux when I was a teenager, pledging full loyalty to the Summerton crown upon our arrival. We worked hard to integrate ourselves, but believe me, there are many who think my appointment to the high council a grave error in judgment."

Ro felt a little ill. She did not want this to be a problem for JT. She'd hoped Summerton would be a nice escape for him. She held onto her son's arm. "This isn't going to cause any issues with us visiting, is it? I swear, I didn't know."

Gabriel rested one hand lightly on the hilt of his sword. "I don't believe it will. Although your decision to refuse the crown now seems like a wise one." He smiled and changed the subject. "Why don't you let me show you around? You must say yes, otherwise I'll be forced to escort you out of the gardens, since they are on palace grounds, and you are, as discussed, not queen."

"That's fine. Thank you." She nodded, but she was still caught up in the revelation that JT's father had also been fae. And Grym, to boot. Her dalliance with Rhys had been a bigger mistake than she'd realized, although there was *nothing* she regretted about having her son.

JT didn't seem to be too bothered by the news of who he was. "Great, Mom. My first trip here and we find out I'm the enemy *and* we're trespassing."

She laughed without really meaning to. "The Grym aren't exactly the enemy." She looked at Gabriel. "Are they?"

He got them walking again. "Not the people, so much.

But there is a great deal of animosity between the kingdoms because of the history there. Murder has a way of doing that."

"I guess so." JT kept pace with Gabriel. "Who murdered who again?"

Gabriel took a breath as they approached the pond. "That, my boy, is a long story for another time." He gestured ahead of him. "Have you ever seen fish like that?"

"Fish?" JT caught sight of the pale, glowing shapes sliding past under the water's surface. "That is very cool."

Gabriel brought them to the bench he and Ro had sat on. The same bench where he'd kissed her. "Those are known as ghost arakoo. They're a kind of carp. They were a gift to the late king from the merpeople on the day of his coronation."

Ro looked at him. "Merpeople?"

Gabriel nodded.

"As in people with fish tails who live underwater," she said.

He nodded again. "They can shift into a more ordinary form with legs, but yes."

JT chuckled. "I love this place." He looked at Ro. "I'm sorry I doubted you."

She shrugged. "It's understandable. This is a lot to believe." She was glad she'd shown it to him, though. "And the next time we come, I promise we'll see Aunt Violet."

JT smiled. "That would be great."

"We should probably get back. I'm sure Gabriel doesn't want to babysit us all night."

"Right," JT said.

"It's no bother," Gabriel insisted.

He was such a good man. She got to her feet all the same. Tomorrow was a big day. "Do you want us to leave from a different portal than the one in the palace?"

"No," he said, standing. "I'll escort you back there."

He did just that, taking them in through a different way than they'd come out, maybe so JT could see a little more of the place. She wasn't sure. Either way, they stopped at the same windows where Ro had her first look at Rivervale.

"Those lights," Gabriel said, "are the village proper. Rivervale. That's where your aunt lives, down there."

JT stood there, taking it all in. "And that water, that's where the merpeople live?"

"The Whistling Sea," Gabriel answered. "Yes, that's part of their domain."

"Man, this place is really something." He shook his head, still looking out. "It's so quiet here."

Ro nodded. "I thought that too when I first got here."

Gabriel leaned against the stone wall. "My first trip into the mortal world and all I could think about was how the noise never stopped."

Ro touched JT's arm. "Come on. We'll be back."

He nodded but looked at Gabriel. "Thanks for showing me this."

"You're welcome. The portal's right this way."

He led them to it, then Ro and JT went to stand inside. She smiled at Gabriel. "Thank you for not throwing us out."

He made a courtly bow. "For the almost queen? Anything."

That made her feel warm inside. He was such a nice man, despite his fierce appearance. "Good night, Gabriel."

"Good night, Meadowcrofts."

She dialed in the sapphire band, and a moment later, they were standing in the subway station.

JT frowned. "Is this where we were supposed to end up?"

"Yep. Sheltered from the weather and always open. Subway stations are the return portals on this side."

"Makes sense."

They walked back to her apartment without saying much. She could tell he was deep in thought, processing everything he'd seen. She let him be until they were back inside. "So? What did you think?"

He let out a sigh. "That was the most interesting experience of my life. Not to mention finding out we aren't human. Thank you for taking me there. I can't wait to go back. And I really can't wait to see Auntie Vi."

"Same here. She's going to be so happy. Maybe next weekend after you get moved in, okay?"

"Yes, for sure." He grabbed his empty backpack and duffel, stuffing the duffel into the backpack. "You know, I don't even care about losing the promotion or Jeanine breaking up with me now. That all feels so insignificant knowing that I'm a part of this whole other world."

It did her heart good to hear him say that. "I'm so glad."

He hooked the backpack over his shoulder. "I'll be by tomorrow night again with more stuff. I figure if I make a trip every night after work, I'll have a lot less to deal with on Saturday."

"Sounds good. I'll see you then." She gave him a hug.

He hugged her back, hard. "Thanks again."

"You're very welcome, sweetheart."

He shook his head as he let go of her. "Grym Fae. Hey! Are my ears still pointed?"

"Yes, but no one, including yourself, can see them. See?" She pulled her hair back to show him her ear.

"Okay, cool. Because even in this city, that might raise some questions."

She laughed. "See you tomorrow night."

"Yep." He opened the door. "Have a great first day as curator tomorrow."

She smiled wider. "Thank you. I will."

She locked the door behind him, then headed to her bedroom to make sure her clothing was ready for tomorrow. She planned to be a few minutes early, just because.

Benny was lying on the bed, mostly upside down.

"Tomorrow's the big day, Benny boy." Her suit and blouse were ready to go. She knew what flats she was wearing, too. She'd accessorize with that chunky gold necklace she'd gotten on sale at Macy's and the gold hoops JT had given her. That was all she needed.

That and a good night's sleep. She was in bed twenty minutes later. Benny hadn't moved.

She read a little before drifting off, her thoughts filled

with excitement for tomorrow and gratitude that showing JT the fae realm had gone so well.

Life was good. And tomorrow, it was going to get even better.

CHAPTER THIRTY-EIGHT

Ro strolled up to the museum's employee entrance and handed Kwame his morning doughnut. "Chocolate glazed with rainbow sprinkles."

"Thank you." He took it as he scanned her badge and grinned at her. "Today's the day, Dr. Meadowcroft."

She nodded. "Yes, it is, my friend."

"You gonna be the boss of this whole place." He snorted. "Not that you aren't already."

She laughed. "Thanks, Kwame."

Her footsteps were light as she made her way up to her office. She drank the last of her mocha latte while answering a few emails and sending a couple of others. There was a fluttering feeling inside her that she couldn't shake. A mix of nerves and excitement.

At nine twenty-five, she took a quick look at herself in the mirror she kept in her desk drawer. Before leaving, she wanted to make sure her hair was in place, her makeup looked all right, and she hadn't somehow gotten something stuck in her teeth.

All good. She got up, buttoned her jacket, and left her office, closing the door behind her. Soon, it would just say Curator under her name. With a smile, she walked to the board of directors meeting room. It was down the hall from all the administrative offices and had a window that looked out onto Fifth Avenue.

A few of the directors were just walking in.

She smiled and exchanged greetings, slightly atremble with the anticipation of what was about to happen. All of her adult life, she'd worked toward this moment, and now it was finally here. She glanced down at the ring on her finger. The one Gabriel had given her. She'd worn it today because it made her happy.

And why not? It was like she was showing off her secret but without any fear of actually spilling it. Imagine if these people knew she'd turned down a throne to have this job.

She went into the meeting room and took a seat at the long conference table. There was coffee on the side table, but she didn't need more caffeine. As the directors filed in and took seats, a man she didn't recognize came in with them. She thought she knew all of the directors. Maybe he was filling in for someone? Although that wouldn't be standard operating procedure. He could be representing someone by proxy. That was probably it.

His short salt and pepper hair had receded into a widow's peak, but he wasn't unattractive. His round, wire-rimmed glasses, tweed jacket, and bowtie gave him a slight Indiana Jones vibe. He looked familiar, but she couldn't figure out why.

He saw her looking and gave her a nod, his smile quick. Then he went back to drinking his coffee.

Chairman Roland Peters tapped his gavel on the table to bring the group to order. "As you know, we are here today to appoint a new curator. We have discussed, in great detail, the need to keep the museum current and up to date and moving forward in a way that continues to bring revenue in while allowing us to maintain our ongoing projects and also delve into new ones."

Lots of nodding. She nodded, too. She'd done a lot of that already, so she knew he was talking about her.

"The new curator must be able to meet those needs. In addition, they must respect the reputation of this establishment while representing the MHA globally. Partnerships with other museums seems to be the path of the future. The means of survival for organizations like us. The new curator must be able to cultivate those relationships."

More nodding. A few soft words of agreement.

"To that end, we have voted. As chairman of the board of directors, it is my great honor to announce Dr. Alastair Horne as our new curator."

Ro's entire body went numb. There was no air in her lungs. A tinny sound filled her ears, and all she could see was the light glaring off Peters' eyeglasses. This couldn't be happening.

Alastair Horne. She stared at him, understanding now why he looked familiar. He was the author of *Ancient Monsters*, the best-selling thriller novel that everyone was comparing to Dan Brown and *The Da Vinci Code*.

"I trust you'll all make Dr. Horne feel welcome. Meeting adjourned." Peters tapped his gavel on the table again, the sharp crack of wood on wood bringing her around enough to force a smile and shake hands and pretend like what had happened was no big deal.

Passed over. *Passed. Over.* For a part-time anthropologist and genre fiction writer.

Pain throbbed behind her right eye. She wanted to scream and cry and turn the table over. Or maybe smash something. Like Peters' head with his own gavel. She wouldn't, of course, but the ludicrous fantasy brought her back to life. How could these idiots do this to her? How could they appoint a man who'd never even worked in this museum? What about all the years she'd put in? The hours of work? The weekends? The overtime? The blood, sweat, and tears?

For a moment, she thought she might hyperventilate. Then she realized she was on the verge of a breakdown. Her mouth watered with nausea. She swallowed against it and tried to breathe. She would not embarrass herself in front of these unappreciative, incompetent lunatics. She had to get out of this room. Maybe out of this building.

No one was moving. They were all standing around, too busy congratulating Dr. Horne. And congratulating themselves on their choice.

The woman in front of her moved, and Ro managed to take a few steps toward the door, then her path was blocked again. She stared at the man before her. At his round, wire-rimmed glasses and his stupid bow tie. He was no Indiana Jones. More like Benedict Arnold.

His hand shot out. "Looking forward to working with you, Dr. Meadowcroft. I've heard such great things about you."

She ignored his hand. A muscle in her jaw tightened. She could not work with this man. *For* this man. She would not. Her hands clenched into fists. Her thumbs wrapped over her fingers, and she felt Gabriel's ring on her right hand.

What would Gabriel do in this situation? What would a queen do? The answers to both questions gave her all kinds of ideas. She smiled for reasons that had nothing to do with the man in front of her. "Funny, this is the first I've heard of you at all."

She looked around the room. People were watching her to see how she was going to react. She could see in their eyes that they were worried. They should be. She met every gaze with her defiant stare. "This was quite the feat you pulled off. Leading me to believe I was getting the curator's job. Impressive. Really. I had no idea what a rancid load of garbage that was."

Peters frowned. "It wasn't a load of garbage. We just decided to go in a different direction. Surely, you understand—"

"I understand that you're the lead garbage man, Rollie. Now you need to understand that today is my last day. I am officially tendering my resignation."

Everyone in the room went deathly quiet.

Peters sputtered. "But we were counting on you to bring Dr. Horne up to speed."

"And I was counting on being curator. Looks like we both made a mistake." She started for the door, then stopped. "Also, how dumb do you have to be to hire someone who needs to be brought up to speed?"

She shot a look at Horne. "Good luck. You're going to need it."

She strode out, slamming the door behind her. She marched straight back to her office and gathered up the few things that mattered. A framed picture of Aunt Violet with a three-year-old JT on her lap. A book given to her by an old mentor. Her diplomas. A pen Aunt Violet had inscribed for Ro's fortieth birthday.

Everything that meant anything went into the cloth shopping bag she kept tucked in a drawer.

Then she logged out of her email, logged off of her computer, and powered it down completely. It was museum property, so it would be staying, but there was no way she was giving them any of her passwords.

She grabbed her purse, the shopping bag full of mementos, and headed for the elevator. There was one more thing she needed to do. She went down to Basement One.

The doors slid open, and she could see that the items from the Clipston bequeathment were all right where she'd left them, sitting in their crates.

Estevan was sweeping. Salifya, his back to her, was prepping a box for shipping. Both men had AirPods in and were jamming out to their tunes of choice. Estevan saw her first. He pulled out an earbud and gave her a nod. "Morning, Dr. Meadowcroft."

She smiled back. She was going to miss these guys. "Morning, Estevan. How are you?"

"Good, thank you. You?"

"I've been better."

Salifya realized something was going on behind him. He turned around, also taking out an AirPod. "*As-salamu alaykum*, Dr. Meadowcroft."

"*As-salamu alaykum*, Salifya." She needed the basement to herself. She pulled a twenty out of her purse. "Here. Coffee break's on me."

Estevan grinned and took the bill. "Thank you. But this is enough for us to bring you one back, too."

She shook her head. "It's enough for you each to get a coffee and a pastry from the cafeteria." She knew they didn't eat there much because their salaries didn't allow it. "Go on. Enjoy your break."

Salifya gave her a little bow, his hands in prayer pose at his chest. "Thank you."

"You're welcome." She watched them get on the elevator. "I've really liked working with you guys."

Estevan frowned as though he didn't quite understand why she'd said that. Then the doors closed.

She went over to the items from the Clipston bequeathment. She put the slippers and the jewelry into her shopping bag, which pretty much strained the limits for what it could hold. Then she hoisted the rolled tapestry onto her shoulder so that it balanced there, bending in the center a little.

The weight was about what she'd expected, but she knew she'd only be able to hold it for so long before her legs buckled. That much fabric and thread was heavy.

Next, she wrapped her arm around the celadon vase, gripping it as tightly and gently as it was possible to do. With her other hand, she grabbed hold of the wooden chest by its lid. Not the best way to lift an antique, but she had no other options. She wouldn't be coming back here.

With the items secured, she used her thumb to dial the inner bands of her ring, aligning the garnet and the nepheline so that they lined up with the notches.

A moment later, she disappeared.

Chapter Thirty-Nine

"Mother, you said we were going to go shopping. This is not a place to do that." Beatryce stared up at the stately building before them.

Anyka nodded. "We will shop, Beatryce, but first I thought it might be nice to take in a little culture. Despite the failings of the mortal realm, they are an interesting people. You need to know some of that to understand what drives them."

Bea nodded as they went up the steps and inside. "All right. I'm happy to learn. So long as it doesn't take all day."

Anyka laughed. "It won't. There will be plenty of time for shopping. And lunch. And more shopping." She had every intention of spoiling her daughter until the culmination of her plan later this evening. But before that spoiling began, Anyka needed to do some investigation for herself. To satisfy her own curiosity.

Wyett was with them. Trog was, too, in his private security outfit. He still stuck out, but he was given a wide berth. Anyka approved. Wyett bought tickets for all of them, then they went through into the large central lobby.

An enormous globe spun slowly in the center. People

all around it were taking pictures, mostly of themselves with the globe in the background.

"Wyett, take Princess Beatryce to the third floor. According to the sign, there's a gems and jewelry exhibition there I think she'll find interesting. I'll meet you shortly. Don't leave there until I find you. Trog, you stay with me."

Trog grunted. Wyett nodded and escorted Beatryce toward the bank of elevators behind the globe.

Anyka approached the information desk, a half circle of granite topped with more granite that sat against the far wall.

A short, dark woman with her hair in braids greeted Anyka. "Welcome to the MHA. How can I help you today?"

"I have a very old, priceless piece of jewelry I'm considering donating to the museum. I'd like to speak to the curator. Is that possible?"

The woman looked skeptical. Maybe these things happened all the time? Anyka had come prepared. Obviously. She reached into her handbag and took out the velvet pouch. She'd selected this piece from her vault because she thought it would give her the best chance. She'd last worn it on her wedding day, an heirloom passed down to her from her mother, who'd inherited it from her mother, and so on.

Anyka laid the pouch carefully on the counter and unwrapped it, revealing the necklace within.

The woman gasped.

Appropriate, Anyka thought, considering there was a queen's ransom before her.

The centerpiece of the necklace was a night phoenix, an enormous, legendary black bird that hadn't been seen in Malveaux since the kingdom fell under the curse.

The bird was carved from a single piece of gleaming black onyx. It had ruby eyes and rose up from flames made of rubies, fire opals, and yellow diamonds. The pendant was supported by flame-shaped links, each one crusted in more rubies and fire opals and outlined in yellow diamonds.

"As you can see," Anyka said, "it's an incredibly special piece. It's been in my family a very long time."

The woman nodded. "It's spectacular." She glanced up. "What did you say your name was?"

"Constance Rockefeller." That name had come from Wyett years ago. She'd wanted something that sounded like old money, and that's what he'd supplied her with. It was the same name that was on her credit card and license. The same name she'd registered at the hotel with, too.

The woman reached for the phone. "Let me make a call, Ms. Rockefeller, and see if I can get someone down here."

"I'll wait right here." Anyka folded the flaps of the pouch back over the necklace and returned it to her purse.

The woman stepped away from the counter, phone to her ear, and spoke to someone. She kept her eyes on Anyka the entire time. A brief explanation, a couple of nods, then a final yes, and the woman hung up. She came back to the counter. "The curator will be down to see you. There's a room you can wait in, if you like. It's more private."

"That would be fine." Anyka gave Trog a slight tip of the head so that he'd know to follow.

The woman took her down a hall just to the left of the information desk. She opened a door marked Private and stepped out of the way. "The curator won't be too long."

"Thank you." Anyka went in. The room had a small rectangular table with two chairs on each side. Museum posters decorated the walls. She took a seat.

Trog came in after her, walked the circumference of the room, then went to stand against the wall behind her.

She took the pouch out of her purse and placed it on the table but didn't open it. The reveal was much more dramatic when she took her time.

A minute or two later, the door opened. A man came in. He looked ... eager. "Constance Rockefeller?"

"Yes. Who are you?"

"Pleasure to meet you. Dr. Alastair Horne. I'm the curator at the MHA."

Anyka frowned. "You're the curator? I thought it was a woman."

"You must be thinking of our assistant curator, Dr. Meadowcroft."

Anyka nodded. Meadowcroft. That was it. "Yes. I'd like to see her."

"Ah, well, I'm sorry, but she's no longer with us."

Anyka blinked. "She ... died?"

He laughed. "No, no. Nothing like that. But today was her last day."

That didn't make sense. "Her last day?"

"Yes. But—"

"Was she fired, or was it her choice to leave?"

"I don't think that's germane to—"

"Trog."

Behind her, Trog took a step forward while a low growl spilled out of him like distant thunder.

Dr. Horne jerked back. "She left. Her choice. Look, if you have something to donate, I am perfectly capable of helping you." His gaze flicked to the velvet pouch. "I understand you have a piece of—"

Anyka slid the pouch into her purse, stood up, and walked out. Trog followed. She sighed in frustration. "That was pointless."

The gemstone and jewelry exhibit was on the third floor. She headed for the bank of elevators behind the globe. Why would the woman quit her job here? She'd turned down the throne. Had she changed her mind? Or had the beauty of the fae realm convinced her to move there? Maybe she wanted to be with her aunt?

Anyka definitely needed to know more about the aunt. She stopped in front of the elevators. There was no need to push a button to call one. Other people were already waiting. A few of them stared openly at Trog.

"Ma'am. Ma'am!" Dr. Horne had followed her to the elevators. "I'm sure we can work something out."

She was bored with him, but perhaps he could still be useful. "You can get Dr. Meadowcroft here?"

"I could try."

She narrowed her eyes. The elevator pinged,

announcing its arrival. "Try is not good enough. You have until dinnertime. I'm staying at the Centurion."

She turned and got on the elevator, already knowing the deadline she'd given him would not be met. Trog followed her in, ducking his head. He stood in front of her, shielding her. But no one else entered the car. Fine with her. Humans sometimes had a smell about them she found off-putting.

She leaned out to see Dr. Horne. "Dinnertime."

The doors slid shut.

CHAPTER FORTY

Ro looked around as she took a welcome breath of Summerton air, but there wasn't much to see. She was in a dark alcove, smaller than the one that held the palace portal. She shifted and let the tapestry slide off her shoulder to the ground.

She set the wooden chest down, then the bag and the vase. Her eyes adjusted a little more. There was a closed door a few feet from the portal. On the other side, there were stairs that led both down and up. Between them, a short hall that ended in a tapestry. Beside it was another door. There were a few sconces on the walls, but none of them were lit. The only light came from an arrow-slit window in the stairwell.

At least she was in the castle. That was a good start. She rolled her shoulders once to release the tightness from the weight she'd been holding.

This portal was supposed to take her close to Gabriel. Maybe his office was through that door. He must have an office, she thought. He was the head of palace security, after all.

She stepped out of the portal and went to the door. She knocked, but there was no answer. She tried the knob. It wasn't locked. She opened the door.

Before her was a cozy sitting room with a fireplace flanked by bookcases, the shelves stuffed full of books. The mantel held a pair of thick brass candlesticks and, above them, a portrait of a horse in battle gear. In front of the fire sat a big couch and an easy chair, well worn. The rug under them showed some age, too. The floors were dark polished wood. The walls were stone. Most of the colors in the space were shades of blue with some tan and brown added in.

It didn't feel so much like it had been decorated deliberately. More like it had been designed primarily for comfort and function.

In front of the windows on the right side was a desk with a chair and more bookshelves. The desk had a few papers on it, an inkwell and pen, an oil lamp, and a large bound book of maps. Any available wall space held either weapons or more maps, these framed.

There was another door on the opposite side of the room, directly across from the one she'd come through. A closet maybe? She had a feeling there'd also be weapons in it, if she looked.

Definitely Gabriel's office. It even smelled like him. Woodsy and masculine but underpinned with the scents of smoke and something sort of mechanical and oily. Not a bad scent. Made her think of the metal polish they used at the museum. Maybe that's what it was? Oil for the blades.

There was a ceramic mug on the desk with what looked like an inch or so of coffee in it. She touched the mug. Still slightly warm. She must have just missed him.

Maybe she could just leave the items she'd brought in this room and stick a note on them.

Then curiosity got the best of her. She opened the other door, intending just to have a peek at what kinds of weapons were in there.

But it wasn't a closet or an armory. Instead, she found a bedroom with a large bed, several wardrobes, a dresser, and a chair. More weapons decorated the walls. Beyond the bedroom was another sitting area with a second fireplace and doors that led to a balcony. She stood there a moment, feeling very much like she was intruding. This was his private space. She should go. But he intrigued her so much she lingered.

A soft sound came from deeper in and Gabriel appeared in the sitting room, hair damp, a towel wrapped around his hips. He wore nothing else. He walked toward the balcony, plainly unaware she was there.

She sucked in a breath.

He looked over. "Sparrow?"

She whipped around, but not before she'd noticed the scars on his body. One on his shoulder, another across his ribs, and three parallel stripes on his back near his shoulder blades. She was mortified. "I'm sorry. I didn't know this was your living quarters. I—I just came through the portal and was trying to find you because something happened and—"

"What happened? Are you in danger?"

"No, nothing like that." She could hear him doing something. She wasn't sure what. "I just, I need your help. Just for a little while."

"You can turn around."

She did so slowly, then realized he'd put pants on and was in the process of pulling a shirt over his head. "I'm really sorry. I didn't mean to intrude."

"It's fine. What can I help you with?" He tucked his shirt in as he spoke, acting like her seeing him half-naked was no big deal.

Maybe it wasn't. After all, the fae were into social bathing. She wasn't going to think about that right now. "I brought some things from the museum. The rest of the things that were donated along with the sword. I didn't think they belonged in the mortal world. To me, they clearly look fae."

He nodded. "Where are they?"

"Still in the portal. Can you keep an eye on them for me?"

"Of course." He tugged his boots on, then strapped his sword belt around his hips. He tucked a dagger into his boot before straightening. "You sure you're okay? You seem flustered."

"I'm fine. I've just never stolen anything from the museum before."

His mouth quirked up in a half-smile. "What did JT think of Summerton?"

She smiled. "He loved it. Thank you for being so kind to him."

"I like him. He's smart, good-looking, and a thinker."

She snorted. "You're not just saying that because he's part Grym, are you?"

Gabriel chuckled. "Are you accusing me of being biased?"

She shook her head, amused. "No, never."

He started for the door. "We'll bring your things into my office."

"Okay." She went out to the portal with him.

He hefted the tapestry like it was nothing, then picked up the vase.

"I'll get the bag and the chest," she said. She grabbed them and followed him back in.

He set the tapestry on the couch and the vase on his desk. He stared at it. "I'm no expert, but that looks old and valuable to me. Where did these come from again?"

"From a woman named Maybelle Brightwater Clipston."

He glanced at Ro. "She was one of *the* Brightwaters."

It wasn't a question, but she nodded anyway. "I guess."

"And she had the sword." He went back to staring at the vase. "Interesting."

"What are you thinking?"

"*Merediem* went missing not long after Uldamar embedded it in the stone. No one really knew what happened to it. Most assumed the disappearance was linked to the magic Uldamar had done. It kind of became part of the legend that finding the sword was the first step in being able to free it from the stone."

"Makes sense, I guess."

He shook his head. "I'm not so sure I believe that now. What I think happened was that the Brightwaters got ahold of the sword and sent it to their kin in the mortal world. They're a pretty powerful family when it comes to magic. They'd certainly be capable."

"But why would they do that? Wouldn't that make it harder for someone to become the next ruler of Summerton?"

"You just answered your own question. Ever since the Brightwater bridge became such a symbol of the rift between the two kingdoms, the Brightwaters have felt disgraced as a family. They moved out of Rivervale. Quite a few went to the mortal world. Those that remain here, or end up back here, stay far away in the country."

"So I've heard. But you think they were deliberately trying to keep another ruler off the throne? I still don't get why."

"Because they were mad about the bridge. It was supposed to be Lord Brightwater's great legacy, especially after he died during the construction of it. Instead, the bridge became a contentious object of strife. A dangerous passage now guarded heavily on both sides. I think hiding the sword was their way of getting back at Summerton for the hurt they felt. Or maybe for not brokering peace with Malveaux."

Ro crossed her arms. "Well, that didn't work out as planned, did it?"

Gabriel frowned. "I'd say it worked out very well. We still don't have a ruler."

Ro took a breath. "Yes, you do. I didn't just come back here to return these things. I came back because I've changed my mind about becoming queen."

CHAPTER FORTY-ONE

Gabriel stared at her for a long, hard moment. "You mean that?"

She nodded. "I do."

"What changed? If you don't mind me asking."

She didn't exactly want to tell him she'd been passed over for a promotion. That might make it seem like Summerton was her second choice. Which it was, technically. But not in a bad way. "I was lied to. In a pretty major way. And it opened my eyes to some things. I just realized that my life in the mortal world isn't fulfilling me."

"So you thought you'd give being queen a try?" He looked unconvinced.

She got it. "I'm not going to give it a try. I'm committing to it. I'm all in. Or whatever you say here when you mean that you're going to put a hundred percent into something. I make no promises about how good a ruler I'll be, but it won't be for lack of trying."

He smiled. "That sounds like a good attitude. My lady."

"Thank you. I need to get back to my apartment and get a few things. And Benny. I presume I need to tell the council I've changed my mind?"

"Or you could just go to the main square and pull the sword out of the stone."

"The main square?"

Gabriel nodded. "Uldamar moved it there. Citizens have been lined up ever since to give it a try."

A little ripple of nerves went through her. What if she couldn't do it again? Was that a possibility? "So there will be a crowd?"

He nodded. "Unless you'd rather wait until the middle of the night. There will still be the guards surrounding it, but most people will have gone to bed."

She thought about that.

He hooked his thumb through his belt. "May I make a suggestion?"

"Sure."

"Do it now. In front of the crowd. It will be undeniable that the throne is your right. No one will be able to claim otherwise if you have that many witnesses."

She frowned. "You think someone would try to argue I don't deserve it?"

He hesitated, like he was choosing his words. "Your son might be half Radiant, but he looks Grym."

She remembered what he'd said about her not being queen after seeing JT. "Is that going to be an issue?"

He nodded solemnly. "It will be. For some. You need to know that."

"It was an issue for some in my world when I had him because I wasn't married. I can deal with whatever comes. Besides, he won't be moving here."

"No?" Gabriel seemed surprised by that.

She shook her head. "No. I haven't told him about my

change of heart yet, but I'm sure he'll be okay with it. I'm going to give him a ring so he can visit."

She planned on letting him have the apartment, too, although she'd pay the rent as long as she was able. "Question. Does the queen get any kind of salary? I'd like to be able to keep my apartment in the city. You know, so I have a place to stay when I go back to visit."

Gabriel made a curious face. "I take it no one told you about the penthouse at the Oberon?"

The Oberon was a high-end apartment building, prewar, with huge apartments that had been maintained in the most luxurious way. "No. There's a penthouse?"

"Yes, and as queen, it's yours to use anytime you like."

"Good to know. But I'd still like to keep my apartment. JT will be living there for a while. So about the salary ..."

"Your needs will be met, I promise."

"All right. I guess we should go to the square so I can make this official. Then I'll head back, gather up a few things, and get settled in."

"One moment." He went back to his bedroom, returning with a leather vest on over his shirt and wearing a pointed cap with a single feather stuck in the band.

"Anyone ever tell you that you look like one of Robin Hood's merry men?"

"Who is this Robin Hood?"

"Never mind. He was probably Radiant Fae anyway." She laughed to herself.

Gabriel's only response was a slight bending of his brows. He led her out of his quarters, then closed the door behind her and locked it. They headed for the steps.

A young woman came out of the door down the hall. She was dressed in steely blue leather from head to toe, a sword at her hip and several daggers strapped in various places. "Hey, Dad. Where are you off to?"

Gabriel stopped. "Raphaela." He gestured toward Ro. "This is Lady Sparrow Meadowcroft. Lady Meadowcroft, this is my daughter. She's also my second-in-command." He looked at Raphaela again. "I'm taking Lady Meadowcroft to the town square. She's going to pull *Merediem* from the stone."

Ro looked at the beautiful young woman, completely taken aback by the fact that Gabriel had a daughter. She could see the resemblance. Did this mean he also had a wife? He'd kissed her. Twice.

She was all mixed up inside.

"You and half of Rivervale." Raphaela laughed. "Good luck with that."

"She won't need it," Gabriel said. "She's already done it twice."

Raphaela's expression went from simple amusement to shock. She went down on one knee. "I meant no disrespect."

"I know you didn't," Ro said. "Please, get up. I'm not queen yet."

Raphaela stood up. "I'm still sorry."

"Apology accepted. It's very nice to meet you."

Raphaela's contrite expression remained. "It's an honor to meet you, Lady Meadowcroft." She looked at her father. "I wish I could go with you, because I would love to see that in person, but I'm supposed to spar with Anders in about five minutes."

"Get him and come to the square."

She smiled. "Not a bad idea. See you there. Maybe." She raced down the steps, disappearing around the curve.

Ro looked at Gabriel. "You never mentioned you had a daughter. Any other children?"

He shook his head. "Just the one."

"Do you have a wife, too?"

His eyes narrowed. "Do you really think I would have kissed you if that was the case?"

She shrugged. "I don't know you well enough to answer that question. Although, no, you don't seem like the type."

"I'm not." He indicated the stairs.

She stayed where she was. "Why *did* you kiss me?"

He exhaled before answering. "Because I was attracted to you. And I wanted to see what it would be like to kiss the woman who could have been queen. I promise it won't happen again."

"That's disappointing."

He stared at her. "It's no longer appropriate."

She was pretty sure that was up to her. For his sake, she changed the subject and started down the stairs. "Raphaela is Grym, too?"

"She is. Just like her mother." He took a couple of breaths before saying more, the only sound their footsteps on the stones. "I married young. To another Grym. Her family had escaped Malveaux much like we had. Although her father didn't make it. He was killed by guards, probably because he was a council member and they thought he'd reveal secrets."

"How awful."

Gabriel nodded absently. "The marriage was not a good one. Lystra was unhappy. She thought we should go back to Malveaux. Her belief only increased after Raphaela was born. I refused. I saw no point in it, but she thought we'd be safer there."

"Were you being threatened here?"

They came out on the lower floor, and Gabriel led her toward some double doors.

"No. There were some people who wanted nothing to do with us. Some who didn't welcome any Grym, for sure. But there was no question life was better here than in Malveaux. When I continued to refuse, Lystra left us. Went to the mortal world." He held the door open for her. They'd come out at the same place where she and Aunt Violet had taken the carriage into town.

Gabriel lifted a hand to get the attention of one of the footmen nearby. "Carriage, please."

He nodded and ran off to get one.

"Is she still there?" Ro asked. "Still in the mortal world?"

"No. From what I know, she died there. When she crossed over, she ended up back in Malveaux. Where she wanted to be." He glanced at Ro. "I found out because she sent me a letter, begging me to send Raphaela to her."

"You refused, obviously."

"Raphaela did it herself. By then, she was an adult. I told her what her mother wanted. As expected, Raphaela wanted nothing to do with that. I wrote Lystra back and told her. The next thing I got from her was divorce papers."

Ro exhaled with relief.

The clip-clop of hooves announced the carriage before they saw it. This time, it was a simple cream and wood carriage led by a pair of chestnut-brown horses.

They were beautiful, and they reminded Ro of her childhood. She smiled. "I can ride, you know. I haven't in a while, but I don't imagine I've forgotten too much. Aunt Violet used to take me to the Catskills every summer for two weeks. It was our vacation, and honestly, I have no idea how she afforded it, but we did it. I took riding lessons while we were there."

He smiled. "That's good. You'll definitely have your own mount as queen. Would you prefer to ride now?"

She glanced down at her pinstripe suit. "Not in these clothes. And maybe not until I've had a little refresher course."

He nodded. "Perfectly understandable." He opened the carriage door for her before the footman could.

She got in. She'd expected him to sit beside her, but he didn't. He sat in front with the carriage driver. That disappointed her a little, but she understood it wasn't protocol. Or wouldn't be as soon as she held *Merediem* in her hands again.

She leaned forward. "Could we pick up my aunt first? I'd love for her to be there."

Gabriel turned around and nodded. "Anything you'd like."

"Thank you."

The ride into town seemed longer than the last time, but she'd had Violet to talk to then. Now Ro was alone with her thoughts. Mostly about what this new life would be like. And what JT would think of her decision.

She figured he'd be okay with it. Especially since he'd have the apartment to himself and be able to visit whenever he wanted.

As they rolled into town, Gabriel leaned back. "If you look down this next street, you'll be able to see the main square."

She turned, watching.

Her mouth came open. The crowd of people seemed to stretch as far as the eye could see.

CHAPTER FORTY-TWO

Violet took the footman's hand to help her into the carriage. She settled into her seat beside Ro, grabbing her hands and kissing her cheek. "I'm so glad you're back and even happier you decided to accept the crown."

Ro exhaled. "I'm still nervous about it."

"Of course you are. Only a simpleton wouldn't be. It's an incredible amount of responsibility. But you're going to be great. And you'll have the councils to rely on for help and advice."

"True." Although she wasn't sure what the council members would think about her changing her mind. Maybe they wouldn't care. Although some of them might worry that she was impulsive and unpredictable. "I'm going to do my best."

"You're not capable of anything else. That's how I raised you."

Ro smiled. Aunt Vi had definitely pushed her to put a hundred percent into her work, whatever it was. "Listen, I've been thinking. I know you love your cottage and your little garden and your bakery, but would you consider moving into the palace? I'm not asking you to give them up exactly. Maybe rent out the cottage and hire another employee or two? It would mean so much to me to have you close by."

And available for Ro to talk to. Aunt Violet always gave the best advice or had the right words. Ro also trusted her implicitly.

Vi looked surprised. "You want me to live in the palace with you?"

"More than you know." The carriage stopped near the square, just at the edge of the throng of people. Four guards surrounded the sword, one at each corner. "But you don't have to tell me now. You can think about it. I know it's a big decision."

"I don't need to think about it." Violet smiled. "If you want me there, I'll be there. I can work out what to do with the cottage and the bakery. You leave that to me."

Gabriel jumped down from the carriage and opened the door. He looked at Violet. "Madam Meadowcroft, it might be best if you watch from here. You'll have a better view, and there's less chance of you getting injured in the crowd. No telling what's going to happen when Lady Meadowcroft pulls that sword out."

Violet nodded. "Good thinking. I'm happy to stay right here." She patted Ro's knee. "You go get your destiny underway."

Ro smiled. "I will. Love you."

"Love you, too. Your Highness."

Ro took Gabriel's hand and got out. The sea of people before them was daunting. A few of them inspected the carriage and Ro, but Gabriel got more looks than she did.

"There's quite a line of people waiting to try their luck. I thought Uldamar would be here."

"Do you want me to get him?"

"Do you think it's necessary?"

"No."

"Then don't worry about it. I don't want to put this off any longer. How are we going to get to the sword? Do we need to get in line?"

Gabriel snorted. "Lines don't apply to the queen's head of security." He stared into the mob. "Follow me. Closely."

She nodded and stayed behind him as he started into the crowd. They parted at the sight of him and at the commanding tone of his voice. "Make way. Make way."

As he and Ro approached the sword, the two guards facing them saluted Gabriel. He saluted back. "Keep a close eye on the crowds. This is going to be a moment in history, men."

The two guards on the other side heard him and acknowledged him with a salute as well. With the guards' help, Gabriel moved the crowd a little farther away from the sword. They began to understand something unusual was going on. Quiet spread like a wave, the only sounds soft, speculative murmurs.

Ro's stomach did little flips. She'd spoken to auditoriums filled with academics. Given private tours to dignities and celebrities. Even participated in an auction where she'd outbid a very well-known billionaire in order to acquire an ancient spear for the museum.

None of that quite compared to this moment. There were so many eyes on her. So much expectation. She swallowed and stared out at all the people gathered. Her people. Her citizens. Her subjects.

It was a weighty thought.

"Any time you're ready, Lady Meadowcroft," Gabriel said.

She looked over at him. He gave her a nod. One that somehow managed to say he had every confidence in her. She glanced back at Aunt Violet, smiling proudly in the carriage.

Then she looked at *Merediem*, gleaming in the sun. She whispered softly, "Don't make a fool out of me."

She wiped her hands on her pants as she stepped up to the sword. The stone had been placed on a small platform, making it easier for the crowd to see each and every attempt.

She took hold of the hilt, just like she'd done before. She hesitated for a second. Then she pulled.

The song of metal against stone rang out with a sibilant hiss as the blade slipped free. Relief spread through her. Joyful, she lifted the sword over her head. The metal flared and flashed in the morning sun, showering the crowd with a prism of sparks.

Gabriel raised his fist, triumphant. "Citizens of Summerton, behold your new queen."

The crowd erupted in cheers and shouts, clapping and hugging each other. Ro saw a few women crying. She looked at her aunt, who was doing the same thing.

She brought the sword down to her side, overwhelmed by the reception but thrilled it seemed completely positive.

Then, almost as if they'd come to a collective realization, the crowd went silent and bowed.

It was the most humbling thing that had ever happened to Ro. Just like that, these people accepted her. They already trusted her to be their ruler. The moment filled her with awe and determination, more than she'd ever felt before.

She looked at Gabriel. He'd gone down on one knee, as had the guards. At the edge of the crowd, Ro spotted Raphaela. Ro made a little noise to get Gabriel's attention. In a whisper, she asked, "Should I say something?"

He lifted his head. "If you'd like."

She thought for a moment. Then lifted her voice to be heard. "Citizens of Summerton. Please rise." She continued as they got back to their feet. "Thank you for your show of faith and fealty. I give you my solemn promise that I take the role of queen very seriously and that I will endeavor to lead our kingdom with great fairness and a deep appreciation for Summerton's past, as well as an eye toward the future."

A man near the front pumped his fist into the air. "Long live the queen!"

The crowd took up the chant. Ro smiled and waved, unsure what else to do.

Raphaela threaded her way through the crowd to join her father. "You want some help getting her out of here?"

He nodded. "Since the sword no longer needs to be protected, we'll use the guards, too."

Ro realized the crowd was inching closer. "Am I in danger?"

"Not danger, exactly," Gabriel said. "But you're the new queen, even if the coronation hasn't taken place yet. The people are curious. And eager to know more. Some will want to petition you—"

Right on cue, a woman yelled, "Your Highness, when is West Oak Street going to be fixed?"

Then a man called out, "Do you plan on raising taxes?"

More questions and concerns started coming at her. Ro looked at Gabriel. "Time to go, I think."

"Indeed." He glanced back. "Men, flank position. Raphaela, take rear guard. Your Highness, stay behind me."

The guards took their places, two on each side of her. Then they began to move as a unit. Ro held *Merediem* tight to her side. She wasn't scared, but she had no answers for any of the questions that were being thrown at her.

Finally, she was back in the carriage. Gabriel took his spot with the driver, and Raphaela jumped onto the back. The guards held the crowd back.

"Go," Gabriel told the driver.

The carriage moved forward. Ro hated that so many people wanted something from her and she had nothing to give them. "Stop the carriage."

The driver did as she asked. She stood up and faced the crowd behind her. "People of Summerton. I know you have concerns. I know there are issues to be dealt with. Please, give me a little time to get settled into my new role, and I will make myself available to you."

She glanced at Aunt Violet. "How would I do that?"

Aunt Vi shrugged.

Gabriel spoke up. "There used to be one day a week where citizens could wait their turn to petition the king. It was announced in the paper."

"Okay." Ro looked out at the crowd again. "Very soon, I will arrange for a day and time when I will hear your concerns. An announcement with more information will be forthcoming."

She sat down. "Ready to go now."

Aunt Vi squeezed her hand. "That was very good."

"I'm glad you think so, because you're going to be with me on that day." Ro shook her head, the slight feeling of being overwhelmed creeping up on her already. "I want your input and your guidance. You've lived here long enough to be able to help me with that."

"Your Highness," Gabriel said as he turned to face her. "If I might make a suggestion?"

"Please."

"If I were you, I would require both councils be present for this day of petitions as well. Almost all of these issues fall under their jurisdiction. I don't want to assign blame, but some of these problems have arisen, because without a ruler, there's been no higher authority for them to report to, and they've become slack."

Ro nodded. "So there are council members who haven't been doing their jobs?"

"Not like they should have been."

She held her hand up. "You don't need to say anything else. But it looks like I have some housecleaning to do."

She'd done the same thing when she'd become

assistant curator at the museum. Apparently running a kingdom wasn't going to be that much different.

"I want a list of names, Gabriel. All those who haven't been pulling their weight."

"My lady, I am only in charge of palace security."

"I understand that, but how secure is Summerton if the council can't be depended on?"

Beside her, Violet chuckled. "That's my girl. Taking names and kicking butt."

Gabriel snorted. "Well said, my lady. I will bring you the list this evening."

She nodded and sat back. "That will give me a little time to get my things together in the mortal world and return."

And also to tell JT that everything had changed.

CHAPTER FORTY-THREE

As soon as she appeared in the subway station, Ro's cell phone vibrated with new notifications and incoming messages. She had a pretty good idea most of them were from members of the museum's board of directors, but the die had been cast.

Nothing could get her to go back now. She'd made her decision. She was Summerton's new queen. The coronation was set for tomorrow morning. Or at least Gabriel had promised he'd let the council know that's when she wanted it.

She ignored her phone and went straight home. Not home anymore, she thought. Just her mortal world apartment.

She stuck her key in the door and turned it, but it was already unlocked. She went in and found JT standing in the living room.

His brows went up. "Hey. What are you doing home?"

"Hey yourself. What are you doing here?"

He laughed. "I got impatient and put my notice in today, then realized I had a week and a half's worth of sick leave and vacation days to use up, so I figured I might as well move some more stuff." He crossed his arms. "Now you."

She sighed even as she smiled. "The board appointed someone else as curator."

His face fell. "And you're smiling about it?"

"It brought a lot of things into perspective for me. Namely how much of my time and my life I've given to that place. All to be passed over in favor of Dr. Alastair Horne."

JT looked confused. "Isn't he the guy who wrote *Ancient Monsters?*"

"Yep. That's the one."

"They're making that into a movie, you know. But that's no reason to appoint him curator. There's no way he knows more about antiquities than you do. No one does." JT looked mad, which she appreciated. "You want me to call Peters up and tell him what an idiot he is?"

Ro laughed. "I sort of did that already."

JT's eyes widened. "You did?"

She nodded and set her shopping bag down. "I just don't remember if it was before or after I quit."

"You quit? But you loved that job. You love that place."

"I did. I still do. But it's not where I belong anymore."

"What are you going to do?"

She took a moment. "I'm going to be queen of Summerton."

His mouth opened in surprise. "Are you really?"

"I just came from there. Look, it's all going to work out. You'll get this whole place to yourself, but I'll still pay the rent so you won't have to worry about that while you go to school. And I'll get you a ring of your own so you can visit whenever you want. Don't be upset. I just felt like this was what I needed to do."

"Upset?" He laughed. "I think it's awesome."

"You do?"

"Heck yes." He rubbed his chin. "Can I come with you?"

She hadn't expected that. "You mean … you want to move there, too?"

"Mom. The fae realm versus here? It's a no-brainer. And why can't I become a teacher there? They have schools, right? I could find something to do. And I'd get to be with you and Aunt Violet."

"I'm sure they have schools, but …" She thought about what he was proposing. "I'm not sure if you can hold down a regular job as a member of royalty."

"You're the queen, not me."

"No, but if your mother's the queen, I'm pretty sure that makes you a prince."

He tipped his head like he was thinking that through. "Prince JT." He made a face. "Might have to go by James. Prince JT sounds like a rap name."

"You seriously want to come with me? You realize what a huge change this will be? There's no television, no video games, no cell phones, no—"

"Mom. I'm okay with all of that. Although I may have to teach someone how to make pizza, because there are certain things I can't live without."

She laughed, almost teary-eyed that her son wanted to join her. "I have no idea if there's pizza, but that can easily be remedied." She hugged him. "I can't believe you want to come with me."

"I can't imagine not coming." He pulled back to smile at her. "How many times in life do you get a chance to really start over? Almost never. And certainly not with your family. And definitely not as royalty. I wouldn't miss this for the world."

"This is amazing. *You're* amazing." She kissed his cheek. "I guess we should work on packing then. We don't really need to take that much. Just the things that are most important and sentimental."

"What about clothes? Gabriel wasn't exactly dressed in jeans and a T-shirt."

She shook her head. "You can bring a few things, but yeah, it's a whole different look there. We'll get more appropriate wardrobes. It's important that we fit in and look the part."

He looked around. "I could pretty much be ready in about twenty minutes, but I'll have to come back at some point to clear the rest of my stuff out of Jeanine's."

Ro thought about that. "Is there much there you still want?"

He stared at the duffel bag sitting by the kitchen counter. "Not for what we're about to do. It's mostly suits, which I can't imagine wearing again, and my furniture. I was going to bring the mattress and bed frame here, though."

"This might seem drastic, but if it's nothing you really need, call a charity and donate all of it."

He nodded. "That is kind of drastic, but I like it. Solves

all sorts of issues. Not to mention, it'll probably drive Jeanine batty that she has no idea what I'm doing or why I'm doing it."

"Boy, did she screw up. I mean, you're about to be a prince." Ro laughed. "Big mistake. Huge."

"Yeah. Huge." He grinned and scrolled through his phone. "Hey, here's a veterans charity that looks good. I'm going to call them."

"Excellent. I'm going to round up all of the cat stuff I can." She went into the bedroom to find a bag. Benny was sleeping on her pillow, head turned upside down.

She sat on the bed next to him and scratched his tummy, which made him curl up more. "Hey, baby. We're moving today. Back to Summerton, where Wiggy is. You'll have more space to run around in. Maybe even some supervised garden visits. Once I have those fire lilies removed. And anything else that might be harmful to people or cats. What do you think?"

He stuck one paw out and kneaded the air.

She smiled. "I'll take that as you're good with the move."

She started gathering up his toys and other paraphernalia. She wanted to bring his cat tree, but that might require another trip, depending on how much they had.

When she had all of his things gathered, she went back out to the kitchen and added his cat food, both dry and canned, to the bag. What was he going to eat when that ran out? Maybe she'd have to do some shopping on her next trip back here.

JT was nodding into his phone. "Great. Thank you. I'll see you then."

He hung up and looked at her. "They're going to take it all. I have to meet them there Friday morning to let them in, and they'll handle the rest."

"You'd better supervise to make sure they don't take anything of Jeanine's."

He nodded. "I told them the situation, but yeah, I'll make sure." He laughed. "They said they'd give me an itemized list of everything for tax purposes. I don't suppose I'll need that, though."

"Nope. Although there are taxes in Summerton. One of the citizens asked me today if I planned on raising them. I don't even know what they are."

"Something to look into." He tucked his phone into his pocket and went into the small alcove that was to be his bedroom. "You know, the first couple of things you do as queen will really set a tone for your reign and what people will expect of you."

She wrapped Benny's favorite ceramic food dish in a hand towel and stuck it in his bag. "Are you trying to psych me up or freak me out?"

He grinned. "Neither. Just saying that first impressions mean a lot. I want you to be the most popular queen Summerton's ever had. Obviously."

"I can tell you that one of the first things I'm going to do is clear out some of the council members. There are two councils. High and low. From what I understand, they deal with everything from agriculture to finance to security."

"Like Gabriel."

"Right. And according to him, there are a number of council members who've been shirking their duties, since there's no crown to report to."

JT nodded. "I could see that. So you're going on a firing spree?"

"Yes, but I'll be hiring, too. Based on the recommendations of Aunt Violet and Gabriel, I guess. Possibly Uldamar, too. I haven't spoken to him about it yet, but I plan to when I get back." She sighed. "I feel like I'm learning to swim in the deep end of the pool."

"I bet. It's a lot to take on. But you don't have to do everything in the first week. Seriously, they've been without a ruler for how long?"

"A hundred and thirteen years."

"Yeah, so if it takes you a year to get things straightened out, they should be overjoyed." He made finger guns at her. "Don't let anyone intimidate you into making a decision you aren't a hundred percent happy with."

That was surprisingly good advice. "Thanks. I won't."

"Also, feel free to put me to work. Seriously, I want to. And I'm happy to do whatever you need me to."

She thought about that. JT had been involved in student government in high school and college. Maybe he'd be better at the politics side of things than she would.

"You're thinking about something. I can tell."

She leaned on the counter. "Just that you were pretty good at student government. I was wondering how that might translate into fae politics."

He shrugged. "I guess we'll soon find out."

CHAPTER FORTY-FOUR

There was no one waiting for them when they arrived at the castle's portal, but Ro hadn't expected there to be. She hadn't been able to tell anyone exactly when she'd be back, just that she would be. She let go of the handles of the carrier and the big suitcase she'd packed, then eased a few of the other bags to the ground.

She peeked in to see how Benny was doing. He looked unfazed.

JT dropped his bags, too, and smiled at her. "This is really happening, isn't it?"

She nodded. "It is. You haven't changed your mind, have you?"

He shook his head. "Not a chance."

"Let's leave everything here, and I'll show you the throne room. I remember where that is. And there should be two guards in there. We can ask one of them to get Gabriel for us." She didn't want to head up to the royal chambers until she had JT's quarters sorted out.

"Okay."

They started down the hall. No sign of Wiggy this time. Ro found the doors that led into the magnificent room where she'd first arrived. She pushed them open.

The two guards were in their places on either side of the room

She smiled. "Gerrard and Leo. Nice to see you again."

They bowed. Gerrard nodded at her. "Thank you, Your Highness. It was very good to hear that you claimed *Merediem* again."

"*Merediem*?" JT asked.

"That's the name of the royal sword."

"I have so much to learn," he muttered softly.

Both guards were giving JT some sharp looks.

Ro had a feeling she understood. "This is my son, James Thoreau Meadowcroft. I know you see him as Grym, but you need to understand that he has no knowledge of that world. He is as much Radiant Fae as I am, and he will be pledging himself to Summerton during my coronation." She'd just made that part up, but it seemed liked a very good idea.

They relaxed. Gerrard bowed his head. "My apologies, Your Highness."

"No need. You didn't know."

Gerrard smiled. "Summerton is gaining a queen and a prince. This is indeed a good day."

"Yes, it is." She nodded. "Could one of you let Professor Nightborne know I'm back? Might as well tell Professor Darkstone, too." She looked at JT. "That's Uldamar."

He nodded.

Leo stepped forward. "I'll do it, Your Highness."

"Thank you."

He took off.

She glanced at JT. "Quite a space, isn't it?"

He looked around. "It is. I can't wait to see you on that throne."

"Tomorrow morning. That's when the coronation is supposed to be."

"And it will be," Uldamar said as he walked into the room. He smiled broadly. "My dear Sparrow, forgive the informality of my use of your first name, but I am over-come with affection at your decision to become queen. I am so pleased that you changed your mind."

"Thank you, Uldamar. I hope you'll be equally as pleased that I brought my son with me. He's here to stay. This is James Thoreau Meadowcroft."

Uldamar looked at JT, and his brows arched sharply. "Your son?"

"Yes," she said. "He's half Grym. I'd like that not to be an issue, understood?"

"I do understand. However ..."

"Not everyone will feel that way, right?"

Uldamar nodded, his expression a little pained. "I'm sorry, but they won't."

JT held his hands out. "Hey, I didn't know I was any kind of fae until yesterday. And with my mom about to be queen, there's no way I'd do anything to cause problems for her."

Ro smiled at him. "He never has, except for a brief period of rebellion during his teenage years." She met Uldamar's gaze again. "As far as the citizens go, I have a solution. Tomorrow, during my coronation, James will pledge an oath swearing his loyalty to Summerton. That should do the trick, don't you think?"

Uldamar nodded, a happier light in his eyes. "Yes, I believe it will." He smiled at JT. "It's an honor to make your acquaintance."

"Thanks," JT said.

"I'm glad that's settled." It suddenly occurred to her that, as a whole, Summerton could stand to be more open about welcoming Grym Fae. If the Grym weren't happy in Malveaux and wanted to live in Summerton, what was so wrong with that?

As long as they were productive citizens and contributed, then Summerton and its citizens should welcome them.

Something to work on as part of her reign.

Gabriel walked into the room, Leo behind him. "You're back." His gaze skipped to JT. "And you brought your son. Hello again, JT."

"Hey, Gabriel. Good to see you." JT grinned. "I'm here to stay, too."

Gabriel nodded, clearly pleased. "Outstanding."

Uldamar's brows rose. "You are already acquainted with Lady Meadowcroft's son?"

"I am," Gabriel answered.

Uldamar blinked. "I wasn't aware he'd been here before."

"It was a quick visit, just to show him this place was real," Ro said, hoping that would suffice as an explanation. She changed the subject. "So, I know where my quarters are, but JT will need a place to sleep. Also, the portal is full of our baggage. Benny's there in his carrier, too."

Gerrard stepped forward. "I can help, Your Highness."

"Thank you. We should be able to manage then."

They all went back to the portal. Ro took Benny in his carrier, but before she could grab another bag, JT, Gabriel, and Gerrard gathered up the rest of them.

Uldamar picked up the last item, a potted African violet that Ro couldn't bear to part with. It was the last thing she'd given to Aunt Vi before she passed, and Ro planned on returning it to her, proud that she'd kept it alive all these years.

He held it in both hands, eyeing it suspiciously. "Your Grace, I'm not sure this plant is native to our land."

"I promise it won't leave that pot. And I don't think African violets are at all invasive. In fact, they're sort of notoriously hard to keep alive."

"I see."

Although she wasn't sure he did. "It won't be a problem finding a room for JT, will it?"

Uldamar looked at her again. "No, not at all. Right this way."

She followed him with JT, Gabriel, and Gerrard behind her. He led them to the stairs that went to the royal quarters. Apparently, they were dropping her stuff off first. That was fine. Benny could roam then.

She wondered if the litter box was still set up. Probably not. After all, they hadn't thought she was coming back.

Uldamar quickly introduced JT to the guards, then they all went up. At the top of the steps, Uldamar stopped by the door to Ro's quarters but didn't open it. He set the plant down on the table between her door and the large tapestry that covered the wall next to it, then he pulled the tapestry back, revealing another door.

He secured the tapestry in place behind an iron hook that Ro had never noticed before. "I believe these rooms will be suitable for Prince James."

JT grinned at the sound of his new title.

Ro shook her head. "I had no idea there was a door there."

Uldamar shrugged. "There was no reason to show it to you before." He opened the door and stepped aside.

JT tipped his chin. "Go ahead, Mom."

She went through into a sitting room much like the one at the entrance of her own quarters, although it wasn't quite as large. The colors were different, too. More muted teal and soft blue.

JT's smile had yet to fade as he walked in. "This is for me? This is epic."

The next set of doors led into a more casual sitting area with a balcony. There were two more doors. One had to be a bedroom.

They both were. One had a view of Rivervale and a balcony that stretched across the bedroom and the sitting room. The other had a view of the gardens. The large bathing and dressing areas were a shared space between the two rooms.

The dressing area was about as large as Ro's, but the pool in the bath was slightly smaller. Still very impressive.

Ro didn't need to ask which room JT wanted. He'd already put his bags on the first bed. He opened the balcony doors and stepped out. "Man, this is a great view."

Ro looked toward Malveaux. From this balcony, the sister kingdom was on full display.

"I have a feeling I know what that is," JT said.

"Malveaux," Ro confirmed.

"Home of the Grym Fae." He came to stand beside her. "Where my father was from."

She nodded.

"Kind of gloomy."

"The kingdom is under a curse, from what I understand."

He ran his hand through his hair. "No wonder people want to leave."

"I'd really love to sort things out between the two kingdoms. Figure out a way to have a better relationship with them. It would benefit us both. I think."

He looked at her. "Maybe. But what if their ruler wants nothing to do with that?"

She knew that was a possibility. "Then she doesn't. But the people shouldn't have to suffer because of it." What Ro could do to help, she wasn't sure. But there would be time to figure that out.

She leaned her head toward the door. "Come on. I'll show you my rooms, then we'll go see Aunt Violet. She's going to cry when she sees you."

He nodded, laughing softly. "I'd be a little disappointed if she didn't."

CHAPTER FORTY-FIVE

In the foyer of Ro's quarters, Uldamar again pulled back a tapestry on the wall to reveal a door that connected her apartment with JT's new living space. Then he went to the tapestry on the other side of the foyer and showed her *another* door.

"Okay," Ro said. "How many hidden doors are there?"

Uldamar smiled. "Just these two. This one leads to another royal apartment. I was informed your aunt might be moving into the palace?"

"That's right," Ro said.

"I believe this one might work very well for her. It's almost the same as Prince James's rooms but with only one bedroom."

"That would be perfect." Ro pressed her hands together in front of her, her fingertips touching her chin. "This is all perfect."

"I'm glad you approve," Uldamar said. "Now, I'm sure you'd like to get settled in. I'd be happy to send some help up to do your unpacking."

"I'm good," JT said. "I can unpack my own stuff."

"So can I," Ro said. "But there is the matter of the dressing room still being filled with the former king and queen's clothing. I'm going to need some of that space."

"There are several valets working on packing up the clothing right now. Although I believe there is more of the queen's clothing in the apartment your aunt will be moving into. She used it as a spare closet."

"She must have had a lot of clothing."

"She did," Uldamar answered. "Speaking of that, there are tailors and seamstresses ready to attend to both of you so that you might have wardrobes befitting your stations."

JT lifted his brows. "You had a tailor ready for me?"

"No, but I can assure you the royal tailor has nothing better to do than see to your needs. He will be here as soon as you're ready to begin."

JT nodded. "Send him up. No time like the present."

"I'll do that." Uldamar looked at Ro. "Would you like me to have the seamstress sent up as well?"

"Luena? Sure. She makes beautiful things."

"Very good. You will need a gown for your coronation."

"She had a few that were nearly ready to go for me for that dinner party. I'm sure one of them will work."

Gerrard, having delivered the bags he'd been carrying, stood by the door looking like he was awaiting her next command.

"Gerrard, thank you for your help. You can go back to your post."

He left with a nod.

Uldamar smiled. "I'll be on my way as well. The tailor and seamstress will be up shortly."

"Thank you." She spoke to JT. "We'll let them get whatever measurements they need, then we'll go see Aunt Violet."

"Sounds good. I'm going to unpack until they get here." He went back to his rooms through the sitting room door, leaving her alone with Gabriel.

"I should go, too," he said.

She wasn't quite ready for him to leave. "How's the list coming?"

"Good. Raphaela has been helping me with it. She spends more time with the royal guards, so she's a good source of information." He glanced toward JT's quarters. "At some point, you'll both need to come to the armory and be fitted for a few weapons."

"Weapons?" She hadn't been expecting that.

"Prince James will need a sword and at least two daggers. You'll need a pair of daggers as well."

She wasn't so sure about that. "I get that it's sort of standard gear, but I don't know how to use a sword or a dagger. Neither does JT."

Gabriel smiled. "Well, then, we'll have to teach you."

An hour later, JT and Ro were in a carriage, a large covered one with the royal crest on the side, headed into town to see Aunt Violet. Four matched silvery-lavender horses pulled it. The interior had purple upholstery and gold trim.

Gabriel rode up front again with the driver. They had a guard on the back this time. The three men were only visible through small windows.

JT hadn't stopped looking outside since they'd been

seated. "This place is beautiful. Really pristine, which makes sense, since they don't have the kind of pollution we have." He hesitated. "Had, I mean. This is home now."

He seemed to be reminding himself, but Ro hoped it wasn't because he was questioning his choices. He could always go back. He had to know that.

"The village is really lovely. Wait until you see it. Cobblestone streets and little shops. It's like something out of medieval England. Or at least what I think medieval England was like. Only a bit more progressed than that."

He looked at her, smiling. "And, thankfully, with indoor plumbing. I checked that out right away."

She laughed. "No showers, though. I plan to remedy that."

"Nice. But that bathing pool tub thing? You have to admit that's pretty cool."

"It is. I still want a shower. Just like you still want pizza."

"Yeah, I get that." He went back to looking out the window.

She went back to thinking about all she had to do. She hadn't really had a chance to speak to Gabriel about his list as much as she would have liked. Luena and the tailor, who turned out to be her father, Henry, had arrived not long after Uldamar left.

She and JT had been measured, JT much more thoroughly than Ro had, since Luena was already familiar with fitting her.

Then they'd changed into simple outfits that had been pieced together for them. JT was dressed very much like

Gabriel in a loose shirt and pants tucked into soft boots. She was in a gown of periwinkle blue with an embroidered silver belt and trim with silver slippers. They'd taken a peek at the apartment that was to be Violet's before getting straight into the carriage.

She wished Gabriel was riding inside with them, but she supposed that wasn't protocol. Most everything she wanted to do wasn't. The thought made her laugh.

"What?" JT asked.

She shook her head. "Just thinking about what's allowed and what's not. There's a lot of royal protocol that has to be followed, you know."

"Like what?"

"Like all sorts of things. What people can call you, how they treat you, what we can do and can't do. For example, I'd prefer Gabriel ride inside with us so I could speak to him, but I'm sure that's not allowed."

"But you're the queen. Or you will be, tomorrow. Can't you just do what you want?"

"Sure, I could, but if I don't maintain certain standards, I worry that the people won't take me seriously. Don't forget, we're crossovers from the mortal world. I'm sure they would have preferred a queen that was already living among them. One of them, I mean."

He nodded thoughtfully. "You worried that's going to be an issue? Being taken seriously?"

It had crossed her mind. "A little."

"So do something that will make the citizens see you as one of them. Like I was thinking I might grow my hair out so I can wear braids like the guards do."

"Not a bad idea, but what could I do?"

He shrugged. "I don't know. Maybe Aunt Violet will have an idea."

Ro smiled. "She probably will. I'm so glad I made you come along."

He snorted. "Is that how you're telling it now?"

She winked at him. "Yep."

He stayed glued to the windows until the carriage arrived outside of Violet's bakery.

"Here we are," Ro said.

JT reached for the door handle, but the guard on the back had already jumped down and opened it before JT could.

"Royal protocol," Ro whispered.

"Noted," JT said as he got out.

Violet rushed through the door, still in her apron. "My boy, my boy!"

JT opened his arms, and Violet fell into them, weeping the happiest tears Ro had ever seen. She welled up, too, and even JT wiped at his eyes.

Violet kissed his face, then held his cheeks in her hands, which required her to go up on her tiptoes. "You've gotten so big."

JT laughed. "Auntie Vi, I was this size when you left us."

"But you're a man now. Look at you." She stepped back, wiping at her eyes with the edge of her apron.

JT chuckled. "Come on, show me your bakery."

"Not mine for much longer," Violet said. "I'm selling it to Ginny and her husband. I'm going to rent them my cottage, too."

"That was fast."

Violet gave Ro a mischievous look. "Haven't changed your mind about me moving into the palace, have you?"

"Not in the least," Ro said. "In fact, JT and I had a look at your new apartment just before we came here."

JT nodded. "It's got a great view of the gardens."

Violet put her hands to her mouth and looked very much like she might cry again.

Ro quickly intervened. "Are your things packed?"

"Most of them. I can work on the rest tomorrow afternoon."

JT put his arm around her. "I can help you, Auntie Vi."

"That would be marvelous. Now let me show you my bakery before I turn the keys over."

About forty-five minutes later, JT had had the tour of the bakery and the cottage, they'd picked up Violet's bags and trunk, got them loaded onto the carriage, and were arriving back at the palace.

Gabriel was speaking to the valet at the door when Ro got out. He came over to her. "I've sent for some footmen to carry Madam Meadowcroft's things up to her quarters."

"Thank you."

JT offered Violet his arm. "Mom, do you mind if we go up?"

"Go ahead. I'll be there shortly."

Gabriel clasped his hands behind his back. "Is there anything else you need from me?"

She knew Aunt Violet would want to sit and talk to them for the rest of the evening. Probably even through dinner, a meal Ro assumed they might just have in their quarters. She also knew Gabriel had work to do. "No. Thank you for going with us into town."

"I am always available to you. Your security is my job, you know."

"I know. But you don't make it seem like it's your job, and I appreciate that."

A hint of a smile played on his lips. "Your son will need his own security detail. So will your aunt. Do you think he'd mind being guarded by a woman?"

"Not at all. He's a modern man. As for Violet, I'm not sure she'll go out all that much. Who are you thinking of for JT?"

"The best I have. Raphaela."

Ro nodded. "I'm sure he'd be fine with that. You don't think she'd mind?"

"Protecting the royal family is the highest honor. She'd be thrilled."

"Sounds good to me. Do you think we'll be able to meet before the ceremony tomorrow? To go over the list?"

"Maybe. I don't know. While I'm involved in the coronation to some degree, the man in charge is First Professor of Protocol, Everand Larksford."

Ro almost rolled her eyes. "More protocol."

Gabriel pursed his lips in what appeared to be a struggle not to laugh. "I understand he's eager to give you lessons."

Ro leaned in. "I hate you just a little bit right now."

Gabriel lost his composure, laughing out loud for a moment, then quickly covering it with a cough.

She laughed, too, unable to stop herself. "I do have another question for you before you go."

"Anything."

"Can you think of something I might do as queen that would endear the citizens to me? Make me seem less like an outsider and more like one of them?"

His eyes narrowed. "There is one thing that springs to mind. But it might be more than you want to do."

"What is it?"

"Restart the tradition of spending the summer at Willow Hall."

CHAPTER FORTY-SIX

Anyka was surprised Beatryce had any energy left after the day of shopping they'd had. They'd visited nearly every designer boutique along the high street, dropping bundles of money on clothing, shoes, purses, and jewelry. So much for only using the credit card in two or three stores.

Many of the purchases would never get worn because they were mortal fashions meant for the mortal world. Fae attire was far more sophisticated and timeless. Although the jewelry might be passable for certain occasions.

Now, at the end of their evening meal, Anyka knew that what happened next was pivotal. According to Wyett, everything was ready to go.

"Thanks for today, Mother. It's honestly the most fun I've had in ages."

Anyka smiled. "Spending money is always good for entertaining oneself."

Beatryce laughed. "I suppose it is. Especially because it's not something I get to do very often."

"You could go into Dearth and do the same thing, you know. The shopkeepers would be more than happy to see their princess patronizing their businesses. It would be good for them to be able to say Princess Beatryce shops here and all that."

Beatryce nodded, then shrugged. "I'm sure it would be, but I don't need to shop for anything."

"Did you *need* any of the things you bought today?"

She laughed. "I suppose I didn't. I see your point. I'll try to go into town at least once a week and visit a few shops."

"You wouldn't have to buy much. A pair of gloves here, a loaf of bread there. Just enough to make your presence known and allow yourself to be seen."

"It's a good idea. Maybe I could even get involved in village life somehow. Volunteer for something."

"Anything you do would be appreciated. The people love you. And I know they'd love to see more of you."

The server brought their check. Anyka finished the last of her wine before slipping her credit card onto the tray and waving him off.

She glanced out the windows. "That park looks lovely, don't you think?"

Beatryce glanced at it. "It does. I love how they have lights wrapped around the trees. We should go for a walk before we go back."

Anyka nodded. "Brilliant idea." Exactly the one she'd been hoping Beatryce would have.

They left the restaurant, trailed by Trog, and crossed the street to the park. Beatryce seemed lost in the trees and lighting, trying to take it all in.

As soon as the path took a turn, putting them deeper

into the wooded area, Anyka stopped. "I left the credit card at the restaurant."

"Mother."

"Don't worry. I'll send Trog." She gestured for him. "I've left my credit card. Go back to the restaurant and get it."

He nodded, grunting in understanding. "You stay?"

"No, we're going to walk. You'll catch up. We won't be far."

"Hmph." He turned and loped back toward the path's entrance.

Anyka took Beatryce's arm and strolled along with her, waiting ...

Footsteps behind them. Beatryce glanced over her shoulder. Her smile disappeared. She pulled her arm in tight, drawing her mother closer. "There's a man behind us. I think he's following us."

"Nonsense. This is a public park. Everyone's allowed to use it."

Beatryce took another look. "Maybe."

The footsteps picked up pace. Then a body was hurtling between them, splitting them apart. Anyka was knocked aside, but the man grabbed Beatryce, slapping his hand over her mouth. "Give me your money."

Behind his hand, Beatryce screamed, eyes wide in terror.

Metal flashed in the lights from the trees. He had a knife at her throat. His other hand was groping her body. She was sobbing and struggling to breathe as his assault continued.

That was *not* according to plan. Anyka slipped the dagger out of the sheath strapped to her thigh and charged, burying the blade deep in the man's side, under his ribs. She shoved the blade higher. "Unhand my daughter."

Gurgling noises came from his throat as his hands fell away from Beatryce. She was panting and crying and possibly about to faint, which might be better, Anyka thought.

The man collapsed into some bushes as Trog jogged up behind them. "Trouble?"

"Yes. Finish him if he's not already and hide the body." Anyka pulled the blade from the man's body, wiped it on his jacket, then sheathed the blade before putting her arm around Beatryce. "Are you all right, my darling? Are you hurt?"

She shook her head, still sobbing, face wet with tears. "I want to go h-home."

"Absolutely. As soon as we get back to the room."

"Now," Beatryce moaned. A single bead of blood dripped from the tiny cut on her throat left behind by the man's knife. "*Now.*"

Trog snapped the man's neck, then tossed him over the bushes and deeper into the thicket. He gave Anyka a nod.

She nodded back, then held Beatryce closer. "The princess and I are returning to Castle Hayze this moment. Let Wyett know to pack our things, will you?"

Trog grunted.

Anyka dialed the bands of her ring, then she and Beatryce left the mortal world behind.

Mission accomplished.

She'd dialed the portal for her chambers. As the familiar surroundings appeared before them, Anyka sighed as if it had been a mistake. "I'm sorry. I bought us back to my quarters out of habit. Come. I'll walk you back to the West Tower."

Beatryce shook her head. "I w-want to stay here tonight. Please."

"Of course. Anything you want. Why don't you take a nice hot bath and I'll order us some spiced cocoa and cakes? Would you like that?"

Beatryce nodded.

Anyka walked her toward the bath, pausing to pull the bell rope to summon a housemaid. Then she helped her daughter undress and enter the large, luxurious pool in Anyka's bathing room. The steam drifted up in little spirals as the water moved around Beatryce. She sank down onto one of the stone ledges, submersed to her neck. She pulled her feet up onto the ledge and hugged her knees.

Anyka crouched down. "What else can I get you? Anything. Just name it."

Beatryce stared into the steam, seeing nothing. Most likely reliving the moments in the park. She shook her head. "You warned me."

"No one could have known—"

"You said the mortal world was a dangerous place." She looked at her mother suddenly. "Why would that man come after me? He didn't know who I was. Or what I was worth."

"I don't know. I suppose he just saw you as an easy target." Anyka closed her eyes as though the memory was too much. She shook her head. "I hate to think what he would have done if he'd realized you were heir to a throne. If he'd understood exactly whose throat he was pressing his knife into."

Beatryce touched her neck, and a little sob ripped through her.

Anyka heard the housemaid arrive. "I'll be right back. You're safe now, I promise."

She went out to find the maid. "Spiced cocoa and a platter of cakes and sweets."

"Yes, my lady." The housemaid took off.

As she left, Wyett appeared at the open door.

"That was fast." She hadn't expected him yet.

"Because the packing isn't done. I came to see that you were both all right."

Galwyn cawed for attention from his perch.

Anyka held her hand out, and he flew to her, landing on her shoulder. He nuzzled his head into her hair. "We're fine. Beatryce needs some time, but she'll manage. And now with a better understanding of how I protect her."

Wyett frowned. "You killed that man. That wasn't part of the arrangement."

Anyka shrugged. "Neither was him touching my daughter in the ways he did. Compensate his family, but don't overdo it."

Wyett nodded. "As you wish."

"Oh and have all of Beatryce's purchases brought here.

I have a feeling she won't be returning to the West Tower just yet."

His gaze went toward the bathing room for a moment. "Then I take it the operation was successful?"

Anyka smiled. "Very."

CHAPTER FORTY-SEVEN

To Ro, it felt like she'd blinked, and the morning was gone. Lost to a whirlwind of activity that included breakfast, a mind-numbingly complicated explanation of royal protocol and the coronation's order of ceremony from Professor Larksford. She'd asked him if the royalty and any other important people from Malveaux had been invited, but he'd simply stared at her like she'd grown horns.

Ro found that disappointing and would have liked to discuss it further, but she was swept away to her salon to have her hair and makeup done by Helana and to be dressed by Luena.

While she was being coiffed and made up, she rehearsed what she planned to say in her address to the citizens of Summerton. According to Uldamar, a decree had been sent out magically to announce the coronation and there would be a crowd. She'd mapped out the general idea of her speech with JT and Violet last night, over dinner, which they'd had in Violet's new apartment. Roast game hen with buttery mashed potatoes and honey-glazed carrots. Dessert had been orange marmalade cake, and the whole meal had been delicious.

She hoped she remembered everything she wanted to

say, because she didn't want to speak from notes. She wanted the words to come from her heart so the people understood how deeply important all of this was to her. And if it went poorly, well, at least Ro would look good.

Luena had brought her a gown of royal purple trimmed in white and gold, promising Ro it would match the crown to be placed on her head later that day. She'd also provided Ro with purple velvet slippers.

Ro had seen the crown. It had been brought to her late last night for a fitting, to make sure it wouldn't topple off or slip down over her eyes. It was five inches tall at the front tapering to barely two at the back, lined in purple velvet. The center stone was a lavender diamond about the size of a baby's fist, surrounded by more diamonds and amethysts with a few pearls and sapphires thrown in for good measure.

Her best guess was that it weighed about three pounds. She had no idea what it was worth. Priceless, really.

Once Ro was dressed, hair and makeup done, she met with Diselle, the jeweler, in the sitting room.

"You look gorgeous, Your Highness."

"Thank you, Diselle." Ro went to look at the pieces laid out on the table. "What have you brought me?"

"First, your sash." Diselle fitted her with a thick ivory silk sash that went across her body. A brooch was already pinned to it. Diselle adjusted it. "This is the royal crest of Summerton. And here"—she indicated the leather loop at the end of the sash—"is where *Merediem* goes."

"Ah. Very good." The sword was currently sheathed

and resting in a mount over the bed. "Now tell me about what else you've brought."

"These are the pieces most worn for coronations over the years."

Ro nodded. She appreciated anything with a history. "I don't want to overdo it. That crown is quite a showstopper on its own."

Diselle nodded. "It is."

Ro pointed to the small diamond earrings. They dangled about an inch. "I'll wear those and the necklace that goes with it. I think that's plenty."

"May I make a suggestion? Perhaps a bracelet, too?" Diselle showed her a wide bracelet, almost a cuff but made of hinged panels instead of one solid piece. It was open-work, making it look light and airy, but the metal was encrusted with diamonds and amethysts.

"Very nice. I'll wear that, too, then." Ro held out her arm.

Diselle smiled as she secured the bracelet in place. "This piece belonged to Queen Celphinia. She was the late king's grandmother."

"And the earrings and necklace?"

"Queen Nora, another century back. They were gifts to her from the Kingdom of Malveaux in honor of her fiftieth year on the throne."

Ro studied the bracelet. "It's a shame the two king-doms have grown apart the way they have."

Diselle nodded. "I agree."

The adjoining door opened, and JT walked in. "What do you think?"

He was dressed in a dark purple frock coat and matching pants with a white shirt, ruffled down the front, and a cravat of purple and turquoise silk held in place with a fat diamond pin.

"You look like a prince."

"Hang on." From behind his back, he pulled a pointed cap with a long feather in it, very similar to the one Gabriel had worn yesterday. JT put it on his head and angled it to one side. "Now?"

"Even better. Have you seen yourself?"

"I have. But I was afraid I looked silly."

The women who'd gathered to help Ro get ready were all smiling. Ro looked around at them. "Ladies, what do you think of my son, the soon-to-be Prince James?"

"Very handsome," Luena said.

Helana nodded. "You do Summerton proud, my lord."

JT almost blushed. "Thank you."

Violet came in through the second adjoining door, saving him from any further attention. She was in a beautiful lavender gown with a dark blue sleeveless silk robe over it. She had on a little makeup, and her hair was beautifully coiffed in large curls.

"Auntie Vi," JT said. "You look like a million bucks."

She giggled. "Thank you, sweetheart. And you are going to make all the women faint with your handsomeness."

"Diselle," Ro said. "Is there a piece or two my aunt might borrow?"

"Of course," Diselle said. She looked through her case and pulled out a large, dove-gray pouch. She unfolded it to reveal a suite of pearls accented with diamonds. A long strand, a triple bracelet, dangling earrings, and a ring. "What do you think of these, Madam Meadowcroft?"

Violet inhaled a little breath. "They're beautiful." She looked at Ro. "Do you really think I should?"

"I absolutely do," Ro said. She waved a hand at Diselle. "Suit her up."

While that was happening, Gabriel and Uldamar arrived.

Uldamar greeted her with a bow. "It's time, your ladyship."

"I'll say." Gabriel nodded toward the far wall. "Have you seen the crowd?"

"No." Ro went to the windows and looked out. Below, the castle grounds teemed with people. They were everywhere and in every direction. Enough that yesterday's crowd in the square seemed like a small gathering. Guards on horseback, both men and beasts in all their royal finery, were positioned around to keep an eye on things.

But a little wave of worries hit her. She swallowed down the bitter taste it left on her tongue. "That's a lot of people."

Gabriel came to stand beside her. He was holding *Merediem* in its sheath. He attached it to her sash as he spoke softly, so that only she could hear him. "Those people are all thrilled that you are about to take the throne. They already love you, and after today, they will love you even more. Enough to die for you."

She shook her head. "That's a big ask."

"They've been over a century without a leader. They are very ready for this."

"I'm just not sure I am."

He smiled. "You might not feel as confident as you look, but you're going to do great. You already look every inch the queen. Which is to say you look regal and elegant and worthy of the fealty these people will pledge to you today."

She glanced at him. He gave a pretty good pep talk. "Thank you."

He was dressed in cream-colored leathers, a teal sash covered in ribbons and medals across his body. With his sword at his hip, and at least two other visible daggers on his person, he looked like Prince Charming, if Prince Charming had also been an assassin. "Are you ready, Your Highness?"

She wasn't. She might never be. But she'd figure it out. She nodded. "Take me to wherever I'm supposed to be."

CHAPTER FORTY-EIGHT

As it turned out, where she was supposed to be was a balcony off the second floor in the center of the castle, not the throne room as she'd imagined. The balcony was accessed from a grand sitting room that would host a formal reception after the coronation was done.

She vaguely remembered Larksford mentioning that. He was in the room, as were all of the other professors and council members. She took a quick look around, wondering which of them she'd be replacing after getting Gabriel's list.

Footmen stood around the walls, waiting for the slightest hint that anyone needed anything, but every single guest was looking at her.

Two footmen opened the balcony doors, and music began to play. The crowd cheered, understanding that something new was happening. Apparently there had been troop displays earlier.

She took a deep breath. No turning back now. But she didn't want to turn back. She wanted to go forward. She wanted to begin this new life. She glanced over her shoulder to make sure everyone else was ready.

JT stood behind her on the right, Violet on the left.

Behind them were Uldamar and Gabriel. He'd already told her he wouldn't be on the balcony with her but standing guard at the entrance.

Uldamar, as the eldest council member and the most powerful, would be the one to give her the oath of office and place the crown on her head.

She walked forward, stepping over the threshold and out onto the balcony to a rapturous applause. She waved, nearly tearing up due to how genuinely happy the people seemed to be.

JT and Violet took their places at the ends of the balcony, about ten paces away. Uldamar stepped forward, and a footman flanked him, carrying the polished wooden box that held the royal crown.

Uldamar held his hand up for quiet. "Citizens of Summerton. The day we have all waited for is upon us. *Merediem* has been freed! Today, we crown a new queen and welcome a new royal family into Castle Clarion!"

More applause and cheering and blowing of horns.

He turned slightly to face her. "Do you, Lady Sparrow Meadowcroft, before the citizens of this realm, the members of the councils, and your family, swear that you shall uphold the duties of the throne with sincere diligence and unwavering loyalty?"

"I do."

"Do you swear to defend Summerton with your life, if necessary?"

"I do."

"Do you accept this crown of your own free will,

understanding the duties and responsibilities that come with it?"

"I do."

He lifted the crown from the box and held it over her head. "By the power that lies within every citizen of this kingdom, I place this crown upon your head and declare you queen."

He set the crown on her, and the people bowed. He spread his arms wide. "All hail the new queen of Summerton, Her Majesty Sparrow Meadowcroft. Long live the queen!"

The crowd took up the chant, and the sound echoed through the valley until Ro held up her hand. She stepped all the way to the railing. "Citizens of Summerton, it is my honor to serve as your queen. Thank you for your gracious reception. I stand before you today, accompanied by my aunt and my son, ready to take on the challenges of the throne. I know there is much work to be done, and I look forward to that work."

She took a breath, surprised at how calm she felt. "I also know many of you desire an audience so that you might be heard. Petition days will begin very soon."

That got a strong cheer.

She smiled. "Also, it pleases me to announce that in one week's time, I will be reopening Willow Hall to spend the summer season there, along with those chosen by the lottery to join the royal court. It is time for us to take up tradition once more and live our lives as they were meant to be lived."

Another joyous cheer seemed to make the crowd before her vibrate.

"Lastly, I hope to foster unity between Summerton and Malveaux so that our two kingdoms might one day be considered sisters again instead of enemies."

That only got a smattering of applause, but she wasn't concerned.

"I trust you agree with me that peace is preferable to war. And that is what I want for Summerton. Peace."

The applause increased this time.

"Many of you already know my aunt, Madam Violet Meadowcroft, but as I mentioned, there is another member of my family with me today." She smiled and held her hand toward JT. "I would like to introduce you to my son, Prince James Thoreau Meadowcroft."

JT stepped forward to stand beside her. He waved, and those who weren't clapping waved back. He looked a little nervous as he addressed the crowd. "Thank you for welcoming us. It's my honor to be here. I pledge my loyalty and my fealty to Summerton and promise to support the crown and the people to the best of my abilities."

That bumped up the applause meter.

She glanced at Uldamar to make sure she hadn't forgotten anything.

He gave her a smile. "Well done, Your Highness."

"Thank you." With a long exhale, she stared out at the crowd again. She'd done it. She'd gotten through the ceremony, become queen, and said what she'd wanted to say. There were a lot of hills left to climb, but right now, it felt good to be standing on top of this one.

Uldamar raised his hands to the crowd again. "Citizens of Summerton, let the celebrations begin!"

Fireworks erupted from the top of the castle, sending brightly colored sparks into the blue sky. Music swelled again. Aunt Violet joined Ro and JT at the railing to wave to the crowd as Uldamar stepped back.

The people below started spreading out blankets and opening up picnic baskets. Ro exhaled and moved away from the balcony.

She looked at Gabriel, who was scanning the crowd. She knew there were guards posted all over the place. "Any signs of danger?"

"No, Your Highness. You did a remarkable job, if I may say so."

"Thank you. I think the idea of unity with Malveaux is going to take a little getting used to."

He shrugged. "It's well worth the effort. And you made friends today with the other announcements."

"That was my plan. Did the note go out?" She'd made a decision late last night that relations with Malveaux needed to be a priority.

"It did. Raphaela sent it the moment the crown touched your head."

"Good." Now to see if it worked. "You know, Queen Anyka wasn't invited to the coronation. No one from Malveaux was."

Gabriel slanted his eyes at Larksford. "That doesn't surprise me. I doubt she would have come, but the gesture would have been nice."

JT and Violet joined Ro before she could say anything else.

Violet put her hands to her cheeks. "My face hurts from smiling so much. I've never been so proud in all my life."

"You have good reason to be," Gabriel said.

Uldamar was standing by the door. He gestured toward the waiting council members. "Your Majesty."

She stepped back inside the grand sitting room and was immediately handed a narrow flute of lavender wine, effervescent with bubbles. JT and Violet were given flutes as well.

Professor Cloudtree, his wife at his side, lifted his glass. "May your reign be long and successful."

She raised her glass. "Thank you."

After that, a stream of footmen filtered in with trays of little bites of food, both sweet and savory, and the reception got underway.

She noticed immediately a new sense of deference from some of the council members. There were a few she still hadn't met, but most of them came up to her, waiting to be acknowledged before speaking.

One in particular stood before her now. She gave him her attention. "Hello."

He nodded. "Your Majesty. I'm Professor Martin Denwood, First Professor of Defense. Do you genuinely mean to approach Malveaux with some kind of peace accord?"

"I do." He didn't need to know she'd already taken a step in that direction. "And at the very least, I want it to be known that Summerton welcomes the citizens of Malveaux who wish to live here. I know that's not completely the case now. There are those who don't like Grym, but there's no reason for that."

His eyes narrowed in what seemed like consideration. "It hasn't gone unnoticed that your son carries Grym blood."

"He does. So do Professor Nightborne and his daughter, Raphaela. All are fine examples of why being Grym or even partially Grym shouldn't mean a thing."

"Except when that Grym means to do you harm." He shook his head. "I'm not against such progress. But I have a deep understanding of what's passed between our kingdoms. You face an uphill battle."

"I'm sure I do. But I've faced them before, and they've made me stronger. I trust I have your cooperation on this?"

He nodded and gave her a quick smile. "You do. Even with my doubts for success."

"Thank you."

Ro began to wonder if peace with Malveaux was too lofty a goal, but she wouldn't know until she attempted it. For all she knew, the queen of Malveaux might welcome such an accord with open arms.

CHAPTER FORTY-NINE

"Acoronation?" Anyka's coffee was growing cold as her anger was heating up. "You said she turned the throne down."

Wyett nodded. "That was the last I'd heard. Apparently, things changed while we were in the mortal world."

"*Apparently.*" No wonder Anyka hadn't found her at the museum. Or heard back from the curator. Not that she'd expected to.

"And she sent a missive, by messenger pigeon."

Anyka's lips parted in disbelief. *"She* messaged *me."*

"Yes, my lady."

"Read it."

He pulled the narrow tube of paper from his jacket pocket and unrolled it. "To Queen Anyka of Malveaux. My greatest hope for our kingdoms is peace. I am available to talk. I look forward to meeting you. Sincerely, Queen Sparrow of Summerton."

She got up abruptly from the table and strode out to her balcony. Mist shielded the view of Summerton. She waved it away with a touch of magic and leaned into her spyglass for a better view.

Even from this distance, the magically enhanced glass was able to pick up the crowds surrounding Castle Clarion. She had no reason to doubt Wyett's information. A coronation would absolutely draw those kinds of numbers.

With another wave of her hand, she pulled the mist back around Malveaux and returned inside. She was glad Beatryce had taken a few guards and gone into Dearth to buy pastries for her breakfast. Anyka paced across the room, then slowly turned and paced back. "I cannot ignore this. Some kind of response will be expected."

Wyett nodded. "Perhaps a gift?"

Anyka frowned. "I don't know. I could extend an invite? Bring her here?" Then Queen Sparrow could just mysteriously disappear. But that would be far too suspect to be considered coincidence.

Wyett arched his brows. "Do you really think the new Summerton queen will step foot on our shores?"

Anyka sighed. "No. She'd be a fool. Although for all we know, she is."

He shook his head. "I don't think they'd turn the crown over to a fool."

"They would have given the crown to me if I'd freed *Merediem*."

He acquiesced. "I suppose that's true. But all reports indicate she is an intelligent woman with strong family ties and a keen interest in all things Summerton."

"I need to know more."

"I'm working on it. You have my word."

Anyka let out a soft groan and tipped her head back. "I cannot remain silent until then. I must acknowledge her presence if only to let her know I am aware of her."

"Anything you send will be deemed suspicious. Food or

drink will be tossed out. A plant will be destroyed. A weapon could be seen as a thinly veiled threat."

She nodded, having already considered that. "It must be something too valuable to destroy. Something that will be seen as an item of such worth that it must be kept."

"Figuring out what that might be is the issue."

Anyka started pacing again, slower this time. "We know she worked at that museum, so she must value old things. Or at least respect them." She stopped walking. "What is in the archives that might be old and interesting enough to qualify?"

He adjusted his posture slightly. "I assume you want something that can be spelled in some way?"

"Of course. If I'm going to do this, it's going to benefit Malveaux. I need to use this opportunity to my advantage. The best way to discover your enemy's weaknesses is to make them a friend. She must believe this gift comes from my heart."

"Does it need to be impressive enough to be put on display? Like a sign of your intentions?"

She shook her head. "So long as she trusts those intentions, it doesn't need to be on display. I would prefer it be something the new queen deems useful enough to keep on hand. Preferably in the royal chambers."

Wyett nodded. "I understand. Useful. Old. Valuable. Able to hold magic."

"And beautiful. At least to the queen's eye."

"That's a stringent list of qualities."

Anyka sank into her chair. "I know. I was thinking

about a piece of jewelry, but what are the chances a sparkly trinket would be kept out or worn daily?"

"Slim, I think." He walked a little closer to where she was seated. "She might very well tuck it away in a vault and never look at it again, unless you were to visit."

She lifted her chin toward the chair across from her. "Sit. You're hovering."

"My apologies." He took the seat she'd indicated. "What were some of your mother's favorite things?"

Anyka thought back to her childhood. "She had a black diamond and ruby brooch that she wore almost every day. A gift from my father on one of her birthdays. But I'm not giving that away."

"I didn't mean to imply you should. Just that it might give us some ideas about what's useful and what's merely decorative."

She leaned her head back into the chair. Galwyn on his perch was eating dried strips of meat, holding them in one foot and tearing little pieces off with his beak. "Perhaps I should send her Galwyn."

Wyett snorted. "She has a cat, from what I've been told. Two, actually, but the crossing over transformed one."

Anyka blew Galwyn a kiss. "I'd never send my love, would I, Galwyn? No, I wouldn't. Because you are too dear to me."

"What about a book?" Wyett suggested. "A rare edition. Something she'd feel compelled to read."

Anyka sat up straighter. "That's good. Something thick and tedious that would sit on her nightstand for a long, long time."

"Or at least on a shelf somewhere nearby. The right book might even get displayed in her sitting room."

She nodded. "I like this very much."

He inhaled sharply. "My lady, what if you were to send two gifts?"

"Wouldn't that seem like I was trying too hard?"

He shook his head. "One from you, one ostensibly from Princess Beatryce?"

"I'm listening."

"The book from you. And something a little more ... trivial from the princess. Something pretty and feminine and altogether benign. At least for appearance's sake."

"Yes." Anyka warmed to the idea instantly, understanding what he was aiming for. "Something still useful that might be kept around but something that won't be suspected as anything but the gift that a young woman like Bea might send."

"Exactly."

She stared at Wyett, utterly impressed by him. "You may have earned yourself some gold. How quickly can you get these gifts to Summerton?"

He smiled. "Thank you, my lady. I have a man who can deliver them by this evening if that's what you desire."

"I do." She jumped up from her chair so quickly that Galwyn flapped his wings. She went to her vanity, studying all the objects laid out there. Thinking about what she used the most.

Wyett followed at a respectful distance. "Do you know what the second item might be?"

Her hand went to the last birthday gift Beatryce had given her. She picked it up, turning it over and admiring it. "I believe I have. Fetch Chyles immediately. I believe he can duplicate Beatryce's hand. Then fetch Nazyr. It's time for that old spellcaster to earn his keep."

CHAPTER FIFTY

The sun was down by the time the official Queen's Supper was over and Ro was allowed to return to her chambers and stop being queen. At least in the sense that she was no longer meeting new council members or having to discuss her position on things. Or sign things.

She flexed her hand, surprised it didn't ache more from all the declarations she'd scrawled her name on. Actually, only three separate declarations, one proclaiming the kingdom of Summerton was now under the rule of the House of Meadowcroft, another confirming by oath that she was the one who'd freed *Merediem*, and then a second oath that was basically a repeat of the swearing-in ceremony Uldamar had performed in front of everyone.

But there had been thirty copies of each one. A few copies would be archived, some put on public display, but the bulk were to be distributed to the council members for their own libraries.

Hers wasn't the only hand that probably ached. JT had acted as the Queen's Witness for half of the declarations, Violet for the other half. Gabriel and Uldamar had been the Kingdom's Witnesses.

A knock sounded from the door that adjoined JT's quarters. "Mom?"

"Come in."

He walked into the sitting room, tugging his cravat loose. His hat was already off. He slumped down onto one of the couches and put his feet up on the table. Probably not royal protocol. "Man, that was a day, huh?"

She nodded. "You can say that again."

"Aunt Violet might be going right to bed."

Ro let out a little laugh. "Smart woman."

"Are you going to bed, too?"

"Eventually, but I have a meeting with Gabriel first. Which is fine, because I'm a little too wired to sleep at the moment anyway. Tired. But wired. Weird, right?"

He shook his head. "No, I get it. I feel the same way. I could use a beer. They must have beer, right?"

"Probably. Pull the bell cord."

He didn't move off the couch. "I hate to make someone run up here to take my order, then have to go back down, get it, and come back up."

"It does seem like a lot to ask, but that is what the staff is for. To take care of things like that."

He shrugged. "I've been prince for less than twelve hours. I don't feel like I've earned that level of care yet."

Ro got up. "Well, I have. Especially after signing all of those declarations. Plus, I want some wine. I'll see if they have beer if you go check on Aunt Vi and see if she wants to join us for a drink."

He pushed to his feet. "Will do."

As he knocked on Violet's door, Ro pulled the cord to

summon a member of staff. While JT talked to Violet, Ro went to change into something less royal. All of the king and queen's clothes were gone from the dressing room now, replaced by a few pieces Luena had already made and some of Ro's mortal world clothing.

The drawers held more of that, too. From one drawer she took out a set of pajamas, pants and a button-up top. Those would be fine, even for a meeting with Gabriel. She put on one of Luena's contributions over her nightwear, a gorgeous, lightweight ivory velvet robe with a satin cord tie. She put her feet in the matching slippers.

She looked at herself in the mirror. With her hair and makeup done, she still looked pretty regal.

The door chime sounded, but JT answered it before she did. Gabriel and a housemaid stood waiting.

"Gabriel, come in. Do you want something to drink? I was just about to order some wine and beer, if such a thing exists here."

He smiled. "It does, I assure you."

JT pointed at Gabriel. "What's a good sturdy ale? Something with a little body to it?"

"Do you mind a darker beer?"

"Not at all."

"Try the roasted wheat stout."

"Sounds good. You want one?"

"Thank you, Your Highness. Since I am off duty, I will." He glanced at Ro. "Another guard is already stationed in the foyer outside your door."

"Good to know."

JT looked at Ro. "What kind of wine?"

"Red." Aunt Vi had taken a seat on the couch. She looked tired, but then this was well past her bedtime. "Violet, are you joining us in a drink?"

She held up a finger. "Only for one small glass, and I'd rather it be sherry."

Ro nodded at JT. "You got that?"

"Got it." He repeated it all to the housemaid.

Gabriel had changed out of his dress uniform and was back in a loose white shirt with a fitted vest and dark pants with soft knee boots. His sword and dagger were ever-present. As always, he made everything look good.

She went back to her chair. "Have a seat, Gabriel. Thank you for doing this for me."

"Gladly, Your Highness."

JT shut the door and sat across from Ro on one of the other couches. He shook his head. "I am never going to get used to the Your Highness bit. That's just weird."

Ro laughed. "I agree." She smiled at Gabriel. "When it's just us, you can drop that business."

Amusement danced in his eyes. "As you wish, my lady."

Violet laughed. "He's a pot-stirrer."

"Yes," Ro said. "I think he is." She looked from Violet to JT. "Gabriel and I have some names to go over. If you guys don't want to stay, you don't have to, but Violet, I'd appreciate your opinion. And JT, it would behoove you to hear this information."

Violet yawned. "I should have ordered coffee. I'll do my best."

JT patted the arm of the couch. "I'm not going

anywhere. I ordered some food besides the beer. I spent most of dinner talking to the people around me. It was hard to eat much."

"Same here," Ro said. "I hope they bring a lot."

Gabriel snorted. "They will. The kitchen is still trying to impress you."

"Good," Ro said. "It won't go to waste. You have your list?"

"I do." Gabriel reached into his vest and pulled out a few folded papers.

He'd only made it through the job and background of five council members when the chimes announced there was someone at the door again.

"I got it," JT said. He opened the door and let in the housemaid with a tray of drinks and three footmen. Two had covered trays from the kitchen. The third had a wooden crate about the size of a large shoe box.

"What's that?" Ro asked.

He bowed. "A package for you, Your Highness. From the kingdom of Malveaux."

That was unexpected. All around the room, eyes widened and brows went up. Ro pointed to the table. "Just set it there. Thank you."

"Hold on." Gabriel got to his feet. "Why wasn't this brought to me first?"

The footman took a step back, clearly startled. "You're here, Professor."

"But you brought it with every intention of giving it to the queen."

"I—I was told to bring it to her." The footman paled. "I was clearly mistaken. My apologies."

Gabriel shook his head. "This staff has gone too long without a ruler to serve. They've gotten careless." He sighed, his gaze in Ro's direction. "I will see that doesn't happen again."

"Thank you." She was sure there was nothing to be alarmed about, but she didn't want to undermine Gabriel's authority, either.

Gabriel turned back to the footman and pointed to the table. "Put it down. I'll inspect it now."

The footman did as he asked and scurried out of the room.

The housemaid and other footmen laid out the food, which looked like a tray of sandwiches and pickled things, plus a tray of cookies, fruit tarts, and brownies. Drinks were served, then they were alone again.

Ro picked up her wine, her eyes on Gabriel, who was studying the package. "Do you think this means someone in Malveaux got my note?"

He nodded. "Seems that way."

Violet almost choked on her sherry. "You sent a note to Malveaux?"

"To the queen," Ro said. "I know that probably seems like a bold move, but look what a hundred years of *not* talking has done. If I'm going to make changes, I have to start somewhere."

JT looked at her. "Way to get things going, Mom."

"Thanks."

He leaned forward. "What do you think is in there?"

Gabriel shook his head. "Nothing good."

She made a face at him. "Don't be so pessimistic."

"I'm not being pessimistic. I'm being realistic. Queen Anyka definitely wants to reunite the two kingdoms but only so she can rule them both. Whatever's in that package will ultimately serve her needs, not yours."

Ro thought he was being a little overly dramatic, but she had to give a little. He knew the history of this place far better than she. "And what do you think, Aunt Violet?"

She put her now empty glass of sherry on the table. "I have no idea. Open it and find out."

Ro scooched forward in her seat, but Gabriel held up his hand. "Please, let me. If there's anything dangerous in it, let me take the brunt."

He was so adamant that she sat back. "Okay. Go ahead."

He pulled the dagger from his boot and used it to pry the crate open. He carefully lifted the top. The box was stuffed with straw. He pulled it apart, revealing a package, this one wrapped in dark blue silk and tied with silver ribbon. An envelope was tucked under the ribbon. He pulled it out, sniffed it, then handed it to Ro. "Doesn't smell of any poisons I recognize."

"Well, that's reassuring." She took the note and opened it. The handwriting was a beautiful, clear script with a feminine touch. She read the words out loud.

"To the new Queen of Summerton, I am delighted that you have reached out. Our kingdoms have been separated for far too long. Perhaps that is something we can remedy.

Please accept these gifts as a token of my intentions toward that end. Queen Anyka of Malveaux."

Gabriel snorted. "Her intentions indeed."

"Oh, hush. That wasn't so bad. Maybe not super warm and fuzzy, but you can't expect that for a first contact." Ro unwrapped the package, although she already knew it was a book. She read off the title on the hefty volume. "*The History of Malveaux.*"

She weighed it in her hands as she looked at how thick it was. "Apparently it's a very long and detailed history."

JT laughed. "Hey, that's right up your alley."

"I do like history."

Gabriel dug further into the crate. "She said gifts. That implies there's something else."

He found it a moment later, also wrapped in dark blue silk with a silver ribbon. This item was wide and flat on one end, narrow on the other. It, too, had a note. He handed both to her.

She took out the note and read it. "Dearest Queen Sparrow, I am so pleased that you've arrived, as I'm sure the people of Summerton are. I hope that we might become acquainted soon, just as I hope this small gift finds a useful place among your things. All the best, Princess Beatryce."

Ro unwrapped the present. "That's lovely." It was a hand mirror, carved of shiny black stone with a pattern of vines, leaves, and berries, which were garnets set into the stone.

She held it up so everyone could see.

"The princess is a better gift-giver than her mother,"

Violet said. "I'm sure the book is … interesting, but the mirror is gorgeous and probably a whole lot more expensive."

"I look forward to reading the book and finding out everything I can about Malveaux. How better to broker peace with them?" Ro got to her feet, the gifts in her hands.

"Where are you going?" Gabriel asked.

"To put the book on my nightstand and the mirror in my dressing room."

His eyes narrowed. "You think that's wise?"

"You obviously think it's not."

"They could be … more than they seem. We should let Uldamar inspect them."

Ro sat back down, slightly skeptical. "For what? Secret magic spells?"

"Yes," Gabriel said. "Exactly."

Ro huffed out a breath. She didn't want to believe that the kingdom she was trying to make peace with might be so underhanded. "Fine. Go get him. Let's see what he says. But I already know what my next step is going to be."

"What?" Gabriel asked.

She smiled. "I'm going to invite them to join us at Willow Hall."

Want to be up to date on new books, audiobooks, and other fun stuff from me? Sign-up for my newsletter on my website, www.kristenpainter.com. No spam, just news (sales, freebies, releases, you know all that jazz.)

If you loved the book and want to see the series grow, tell a friends about the book and take time to leave a review!

ALSO BY KRISTEN PAINTER

PARANORMAL WOMEN'S FICTION

First Fangs Club Series:

Sucks To Be Me

Suck It Up Buttercup

Sucker Punch

The Suck Stops Here

Embrace The Suck

COZY MYSTERY:

Jayne Frost Series:

Miss Frost Solves A Cold Case: A Nocturne Falls Mystery

Miss Frost Ices The Imp: A Nocturne Falls Mystery

Miss Frost Saves The Sandman: A Nocturne Falls Mystery

Miss Frost Cracks A Caper: A Nocturne Falls Mystery

When Birdie Babysat Spider: A Jayne Frost Short

Miss Frost Braves The Blizzard: A Nocturne Falls Mystery

Miss Frost Says I Do: A Nocturne Falls Mystery

Lost in Las Vegas: A Frost And Crowe Mystery

HappilyEverlasting Series:

Witchful Thinking

PARANORMAL ROMANCE

Sin City Collectors Series

Queen Of Hearts

Dead Man's Hand

Double or Nothing

Standalone Paranormal Romance:

Dark Kiss of the Reaper

Heart of Fire

Recipe for Magic

Miss Bramble and the Leviathan

All Fired Up

URBAN FANTASY

The House of Comarré series:

Forbidden Blood

Blood Rights

Flesh and Blood

Bad Blood

Out For Blood

Last Blood

The Crescent City series:

House of the Rising Sun

City of Eternal Night

Garden of Dreams and Desires

Nothing is completed without an amazing team.

Many thanks to:

Cover design: Cover design and composite cover art by Janet Holmes using images from Shutterstock.com & Depositphotos.com.
Interior Formating: Gem Promotions
Editor: Chris Kridler
Copyedits/proofs: Raina James

About the Author

USA Today Best Selling Author Kristen Painter is a little obsessed with cats, books, chocolate, and shoes. It's a healthy mix. She loves to entertain her readers with interesting twists and unforgettable characters. She currently writes the best-selling paranormal romance series, Nocturne Falls, and award-winning urban fantasy. The former college English teacher can often be found all over social media where she loves to interact with readers.

For more information go to www.kristenpainter.com

For More Paranormal Women's Fiction Visit:
www.paranormalwomensfiction.net